ILLUSIVE

— BOOK 6 IN THE STORM MC SERIES —

NINA LEVINE

Editing by Karen Louise Rohde Faergemann at The Word Wench Editing Services
http://wordwenchediting.wordpress.com
Cover Design ©2015 by Romantic Book Affair Designs

Dedication

To the people we once were.

It's okay to leave the pain and hurt behind and step into our new skin.

The past is part of us, part of our story, but it doesn't have to be who we are today, and it doesn't mean our story won't get better.

"Butterflies can't see their wings. They can't see how beautiful they are, but everyone else can. People are like that." ~ Anonymous

To Jodie,

This book is yours.

Sophia would not be as awesome as she is if I didn't know you.

You are the bomb.

I've never written a character based on someone I know, and I didn't realise I was until I was half way through.

Except for the steps, that is . . . the steps are me because my girls have to have something of me in them.

Thank you for being my friend.

#SophiaIsShortForJodie
#IWouldDoAOneNightStandForGriff
#EatTheFuckingChips
#RegroupingForGriff

Chapter One
Griff

I settled back into the barstool and raised my beer to my lips, chugging the drink until there wasn't any left in the bottle. Jerking my chin at the bartender, I indicated for him to get me another. I'd been here for two hours – he knew my drink and had it to me fast because he also knew I'd tip him for that, and in a city that didn't do tips, and in a job that didn't pay well, he was out to make every last cent he could. I knew that because this bar happened to be my local and I frequented it daily at the moment.

Christmas fucking time.

The time of happy families and presents and love and time together...

Time.

People had no fucking clue how little time they had left on this Earth, and they pissed that time away on mindless pursuits and petty arguments that, when all was said and done, didn't mean a damn thing.

I knocked back more of my drink, letting old memories take over my thoughts.

My mother smiling as she served our traditional roast meal for lunch on Christmas day, my father settled in his armchair with his beer as he watched the cricket on Boxing Day, and my younger brother, Simon, playing with his Lego. He fucking loved that Lego, even as he got older.

Yeah, Christmas at the McAllister's was all about the food, the cricket and the goddamn Lego.

Fuck.

I lifted my drink to my lips and finished it.

Why the fuck do you do this to yourself every fucking year?

My hand squeezed the bottle as I placed it back on the counter. Staring at it, I thought about that question. This was the only time of the year I allowed these thoughts to come. They were out of bounds for the other fifty-one weeks.

10

Why?

Fuck knew, but what I *did* know was that as much as I had tried to move past what had happened to them, the murders of your family weren't something you ever got the fuck over.

And when those murders had taken place the day after Boxing Day, the memories of cricket and Lego and food didn't surface quite as easily as the memories of blood and horror that a murder scene never let you forget.

Yeah, the gift that keeps on fucking giving.

I'd thought this year might be different. Madison and her Christmas party had almost dragged me away from my yearly ritual of trying to wipe the memories out with alcohol every day leading up to the anniversary, but in the end, nothing ever pulled me from it.

Storm might be my family now, but sometimes, even family isn't enough in life.

Sometimes, all you have is you and the choices you've made, and the bed you choose to lie in.

And I'd made my bed years ago.

"You want another one?" the bartender asked, pulling me from my thoughts.

I nodded. "Yeah, it's gonna be a long night. Keep 'em coming."

"Sure thing."

11

A pang of guilt hit me that I'd missed the Christmas party, but I quickly pushed it aside. I didn't attend many of the club get-togethers so it wasn't like they were used to seeing me at one. For some reason, though, this time felt different.

The bartender saved me pursuing that line of thought when he placed another bottle of beer in front of me. "Thanks," I said, and promptly swallowed a quarter of the bottle. And then a set of long legs caught my attention, and my gaze followed them up to a firm ass covered in denim shorts that – *fuck me* – would make a man give up a day doing that one thing he did that no one ever got to interfere with. I lazily drank more of my beer as I watched the woman exit the bar. Couldn't even tell you what she wore on the top half because my eyes never left that ass and those legs.

The things I could do to that ass.

As the door swung closed behind her, my gaze zeroed in on something she'd dropped. I moved off my barstool, walked to the door, and picked it up. A piece of paper with an address scribbled in female handwriting – she'd likely need this, so I exited the bar in search of her. The muggy night air rushed at me, and I welcomed the warmth. Looking around the crowded car park, I eyed her to my left.

"You dropped this on your way out," I said, holding the paper out as I approached, trying like hell to keep my eyes on her face, rather than on her body.

"Thanks," she said as she took it from me, her eyes widening, and her body shrinking away from me. After quickly running her gaze over the paper, she looked back up at me and added, "I need this so I really appreciate you taking the time to bring it out to me." Her voice wavered slightly, but she forced her words out.

"No worries."

As much as she seemed like she wanted to get as far away from me as she could, her eyes narrowed on me and she asked, "Do we know each other? You seem familiar."

"Sweetheart, trust me, I'd know if we'd ever met, and we never have." I finally gave up the internal battle to keep my eyes on her face, and dropped them to her body. Bad fucking move. This woman was made of lethal curves and hollows that I wanted to dedicate some serious time and attention to. The shorts and tight black v-neck she wore revealed them all.

A neck I could wrap my hands around.

Wrists I could decorate with rope.

An ass I could paint red with my palm.

13

My gaze shifted back up along her neck to her face, and my hand curled into a ball as I imagined gripping her long, blonde hair from behind and pulling her head back so I could sink my teeth into her neck.

Marks on her skin, put there by me – the vision came out of nowhere and hit me fair in the gut.

Fuck.

"I don't know, you seem so familiar," she said with a shrug, grabbing my attention again. And then she smiled, and *god-fucking-damn* if it wasn't the sexiest smile I'd ever seen. "And you're too good-looking for me to be getting mixed up with someone else." Her voice held no more uncertainty of me, and her body relaxed.

Time to get out of here; this woman might be turning me on, but everything about her screamed pure, and I was far from the kind of man who should be trusted with pure. Taking a step away from her, I spoke a little harder than I meant. "No, I can assure you we've never met." I jerked my chin at her. "Have a good night," I added before turning and striding back to the bar.

Once inside and settled back on my stool, I finished my beer and ordered another. And attempted to put the blonde out of my mind. She was not the type of woman I pursued so it should have been an easy task.

It was far from fucking easy.

She'd stirred my deepest primal desires. From her easy smile to her trusting nature to the sense I'd gotten from her that she was untainted – it was like waving a red flag at a bull, and I was the bull, ready to take and bend and break.

Just as I was envisioning a long night being taunted by not only the ghosts of my past, but also the blonde, my phone rang, distracting me. And fuck, the number flashing on caller ID stunned the hell out of me.

"Danny," I answered, wondering what the hell my cousin was doing calling me out of the blue after two years of no contact.

"Michael," he greeted me, his voice clear of emotion.

"To what do I owe the pleasure?" I asked as I took a swig of my drink.

"I'm giving you a heads up...the Bond case is finally going to trial and you may be called as a witness. I couldn't find a way around it."

"Fuck," I muttered as I ran through scenarios in my mind of how this could play out. Any way I spun it, not good.

"Yeah, I thought you'd want to know, especially since it seems as though the media is all over this." He paused for a moment. "Michael, if they call you, your name and identity will be splashed all over the media in Australia. There will be no way for you to avoid it."

I threw the rest of my beer down my throat and slammed the bottle down on the bar. "I fucking realise that, Danny," I snapped.

"Don't take this shit out on me. I told you to get out of that club years ago. You had what you needed from them so I never could work out why you chose to stay. The boys and I can try to protect you from them if this all comes out, but there's only so much our badge can do for you. Storm has a long reach, and if they want you dead over this, I've no doubt they'll go to every length to make that happen."

I drew in a slow, steady breath, trying to keep my anger in check. "I *am* fucking Storm, Danny. I know how far our reach goes and I sure as fuck know how we deal with shit like this, so don't try and tell me what I already know. I never wanted anything to do with that Bond case all those years ago, and I damn sure don't want a thing to do with it now. You need to find a way to make it go away, and you also need to make sure nothing else comes back to haunt me. I'm done with that part of my life, and mark my fucking words, if you *don't* fix this, you won't like the ramifications."

Before he could respond, I ended the call. Then I paid my bill and stalked out of the bar. Staying here drinking was not a good idea in this frame of mind. Taking my frustrations out on a punching bag, however, *was* a fucking good idea.

Chapter Two
Griff

I walked into the clubhouse early the next morning with a pounding head and aching muscles that I'd thrashed last night during a brutal training session. I'd pushed myself to the brink with exercise, needing to feel the burn – needing to forget everything else for a few hours.

Not many members had arrived by the time I got there, but I found Scott in the office going through paperwork. He glanced up at me. "You look like shit."

Dropping into the chair across from him, I rolled my shoulders in an attempt to unkink some of the knots there and grimaced. "That about sums it up. How was the party?"

"Madison outdid herself. You missed a good night, brother, and by the looks of it, you possibly would have had a better time at the party."

"Highly likely," I mused, "but *I* wouldn't have been good for the party; not in the mood I'm in at the moment."

His brows pulled together. "You got something going on that you need help with?"

Guilt flashed through me. Jesus, where the hell was all this guilt coming from? Not an emotion I was used to, I shoved it away. "No, I've got this. A week, two at the most, and I'll be done with it." I shifted in my chair to try and find a more comfortable position. "Where are we at today?"

He leant back in his chair and scrubbed his face. I'd been watching Scott for weeks now and the stress the club had been under was written all over him. Dark circles sat under his eyes, his clothes hung a little looser on him from the weight he'd lost, worry lines creased his face, and he'd taken to not shaving which was something he'd never done in all the time I'd known him. "Ricky wants to meet today. Just you and me."

"Why? We've already met with him and come to an agreement." After Marcus's death, we'd agreed

19

not to deal drugs in Ricky's territory and he'd appeared happy with that arrangement. Of course, while we intended not to deal drugs, we'd been working towards ridding the world of that scum; we just needed a little more time to get the club ready for any blowback. Trust in Scott still sat low for a lot of members so he was building that back up, but it was a slow process. It felt like we were walking a tightrope of keeping Ricky at bay while repairing club ties. We were aware of Ricky's playbook, and figured it was only a matter of time before he came for us.

"I've got no fucking idea, but I'm guessing we're gonna need to reassess where we're at after it because I'm damn sure he wouldn't be meeting just to have a catch up. The meet is at ten this morning so can you round up J and Nash for this afternoon to go over it all? I've got shit to deal with all morning and then I've gotta head over to Indigo and go through some things with Cody at about one so make it for after that. If it needs urgent attention, we'll drop everything, so have them ready for that outcome too."

I stood. "Will do." As I turned to leave the office, something struck me. Looking back at him, I said, "You don't seem as on edge as you have been. What's different?"

He blew out a long breath. "I finally got Harlow to talk to me."

"Thank Christ for that," I murmured. "She okay?"

"Yeah, she will be. She just needs some time, but at least now I'm not wandering the fuck around bashing my head against the wall, getting nowhere, you know?"

I nodded. "I know, and it's good news, man."

Stepping out of the office, I closed the door behind me and headed into the kitchen to grab a coffee.

Wilder stood at the counter with his back to me as I entered the room. Twisting to face me, he jerked his chin. "Morning, VP."

I'd hated being called that when I'd taken the title from Scott through deceit, but now that I'd earned it, I didn't mind so much. "Morning." I took in his disheveled appearance. "Did you have a late night?"

He grinned. "Yeah. Madison sure knows how to throw a party."

"That your first one since you were patched?" We'd patched Wilder a couple of weeks ago.

He nodded as he drank some of his coffee.

"What time did she kick your sorry ass out?"

His grin grew and he chuckled. "She didn't; it was J who threw us out at about three this morning. Pretty sure the poor fucker's balls had turned blue and needed taking care of."

"I'm pretty sure you're right," Nash contributed as he joined us. "It's a beautiful thing to watch - Madison stringing him out like that."

Stirring sugar into my coffee, I couldn't stop the smile forming on my lips. "He's nothing if not predictable when it comes to that woman."

Nash grinned at me and nodded. "Very true, brother," he said, acknowledging me in a way he hadn't for weeks. Both Nash and J had been pissed off they weren't clued in on the plan for me to take the Vice Presidency role from Scott, and had been vocal in that. I'd sensed a thawing in their attitudes toward me last week and it looked like we were making progress. Finally. That was a damn good thing – we needed everyone on board to make Storm strong again, and not to have the full support of our Sergeant-at-Arms and Road Captain hadn't made this an easy task.

Grabbing my coffee, I said to Nash, "You got a minute?"

"I'll grab a coffee and meet you in the bar," he said.

I nodded and then turned my gaze to Wilder. "I need you to do a security check on all of our businesses today. Make sure all the surveillance is working perfectly, ensure all the buildings are locked down tight, and also make sure the managers are reminded that shit could go down at any time. You good with that?"

"Yep, I'm on it." I liked the way Wilder never argued with a directive and the way he carried that directive out perfectly. He was also a stickler for attention to detail and I respected the hell out of that trait.

I left them and found a table in the corner of the bar. My mind drifted to my family while I waited for Nash. However, instead of my thoughts centering on my parents and brother, today they focused on my cousin. I'd half expected him to show up at my place last night, but he hadn't. In fact, I hadn't heard from him since our phone call. I hoped that meant he would take care of what I'd told him to, because I really didn't want to have to carry out my threat against him if he didn't. I would, though, and I wouldn't hesitate. I refused to allow anyone to jeopardise my life or my membership of Storm.

Nash pulled up a seat across from me. "What's up, Griff? And where the hell were you last night?"

23

I watched him for a moment while I drank some coffee. "I had something to take care of, but I heard I missed a good time."

His lips pressed into a thin line and he tapped the table with his finger. Leaning forward, he said, "You must get a lot of fuckin' sex, man. We hardly ever see you at club get-togethers." Leaning back in his chair, he smirked. "Can't say I blame you, though. A man's gotta take pussy when it's offered."

I hadn't been sure where he was going with that at first, and my gut had tightened, but I relaxed when I realised he thought it was all about sex. I played along. "First rule in a man's life is to never knock back pussy, Nash."

He chuckled. "Brother, it's the *only* rule in a man's life. That is, until he finds a woman to settle down with, and then there are two rules in life - never knock back pussy, and keep your woman happy so she never stops offering that pussy."

Memories appeared out of nowhere and sliced through my heart with their clarity. *Legs wrapped around me while I took care of her pussy, her smile when she came, her laughter when I scooped her up in my arms and carried her to our bed.*

Fuck.

24

Four years and I still couldn't get what she'd done to me out of my mind.

I cut to the chase with Nash, more to change the subject than anything. "Scott and I are meeting with Ricky this morning. Not sure what his agenda is, but we figure we'll need to regroup after the meet so keep yourself free after two this afternoon. If it's more urgent, and we need to go over it sooner, I'll let you know." Without waiting for him to reply, I pushed my chair back and stood. "Can you line J up for this, too?" I added, and at his agreement, I left him and headed back into the kitchen.

After rinsing out my mug, I rested against the kitchen counter and dropped my face into my hands, and attempted to catch my breath.

This didn't get easier each year; if anything, it was getting harder.

***

Ricky had organised to meet us at an old abandoned house in West End. Scott had been in contact with Blade who'd insisted on sending some of his guys along, too. They waited down the end of the street, only to be called upon if shit went down with Ricky.

We found Ricky out in the back. He'd brought his second-in-charge with him, and they faced us, their faces expressionless. "Boys," Ricky said with a jerk of his chin.

"Ricky," Scott replied.

He took a step in our direction and came closer. My fingers twitched, wanting to pull out my gun. I trusted this motherfucker less than I trusted my ex-girlfriend, and I didn't trust her at all.

Ricky's eyes dropped to my hands and he smirked as he looked back up at me. "Easy, Griff, no need to get excited. I just want to talk."

I scowled and demanded, "Well, spit it out so we can all get on with our day."

Ricky raised his brows and looked at Scott. "Your boy here is an impatient asshole."

"So am I, Ricky. We've got shit to do today so let's not draw this out. What are you after?" Scott said, his eyes flashing his annoyance.

"I heard a rumour you boys would be receiving a shipment of coke this week, and that concerned me. I mean, we do have that agreement in place so I'm left wondering why you'd go back on our deal? Unless of course - "

Scott cut him off, his nostrils flaring, and the vein in his neck pulsing. "I don't know who your source is for this, but you need to get yourself a new one. Storm is out of drugs; I don't know how I can tell you that in another way that you will understand. There will be no shipment this week or any other week."

Ricky's lips curled in a sneer, and his shoulders tensed as if he were getting ready for battle. My hand moved closer to my gun. "My source is fucking reliable, Scott, which means I'm now in a quandary."

"I tell you what, get more information from your source – time and place, for instance – and you be there and intercept the delivery. It won't be us there. And another thing, I've been nothing but honest with you in all our dealings, and I want the peace we have to continue; I'm hardly going to do something reckless to fuck that up. Think about that."

The two of them continued their face-off in silence for a few more moments until Ricky took a step away from Scott. "I'll go back to my source, and if necessary, I'll be at that drop-off. And *I'll* tell you what – whoever is at that delivery won't be as lucky as you two today; they won't walk away breathing."

Scott glared at him. "We done?"

Ricky nodded his head once, and Scott turned and indicated for me to leave with him. I gave Ricky one last scowl before following Scott out.

When we were back at our bikes, he said, "I don't know what the fuck he's talking about, but I have a bad fucking feeling there's something to it. What do you think?"

My gut roared its agreement. "I think this is something we need to look into. Now."

He reached for his helmet. "You start digging. I'm gonna grab Wilder and make some house calls and see if anyone knows anything."

"I've sent him out to make sure Indigo and all the restaurants are secure."

"Is J free?"

"Yeah."

"Okay, I'll take him while you do your thing. Call me if you find out anything, and I'll do the same," he said before taking off.

Jesus. This was a bad way to start the week.

***

Scott's and my efforts were futile. We discovered nothing, and after making a plan for tomorrow with J and Nash, I had to leave them and head out to take care of something.

A little over half an hour later, just after five-thirty, I pulled up outside a house I'd been visiting for every one of my thirty-six years; a house I'd continue to visit until I was no longer needed.

"Michael," my aunt called from the front verandah, "did you remember the milk?"

I jogged the short distance to the verandah and took the stairs a few at a time. Bending, I placed a kiss on her cheek, and smiled. "Yeah, I got it. I'm gonna put it in the fridge and then I'll be back."

The lines on her face crinkled into a smile and she nodded as she motioned with her hand for me to move along.

A couple of minutes later, I returned and surveyed the front yard. "I'm gonna mow today; get you ready for Christmas," I said. I mightn't celebrate this holiday, but Aunt Josie did. She'd always been better at finding ways to move past her sister's murder than I'd been.

Her hand found mine as I stood next to her, and she squeezed it. "You're a good man, Michael, thank you."

I squeezed her hand back and let it go. "Don't tell anyone, Josie, they wouldn't believe you," I said. This was our standard conversation each week.

As I started taking the steps down, she asked, "When are you going to find yourself a girl?"

Her question caused my steps to falter; this was not our standard conversation.

When I didn't reply, she said, "I want to see you happy before I die, young man, and I'm not getting any younger."

I spun around to face her. Frowning, I asked, "Are you trying to tell me something?" My heart began beating a little faster in my chest. Josie was the only blood family I had left. Well, the only one I cared about. I wasn't ready to lose her.

She nodded. "Yes, I'm trying to tell you to get your head out of your ass and start looking for a woman." Relief sparked through me that she hadn't been trying to tell me anything else.

The way she spoke so seriously and the way her mouth wrapped itself around language she never used, made me throw my head back and laugh. Aunt Josie had been raised a lady and I'd never seen her be anything but that, so she'd caught me off guard - enough to loosen my lips. "I found one once, Josie. It didn't work out and I'm in no hurry to do it again."

Her lips pursed and she shook her head. "So whenever things don't go your way in life, you just pack it in and give up? That's not the McAllister way."

Jesus, she was being feisty today. "No, but when I'm screwed over like I was, I'm gonna do everything in my power to make sure that doesn't happen again. *That's* the McAllister way."

She tsked. "I think you need to revisit that and find a new way. The old way clearly isn't working for you."

If it had been anyone else telling me how to live my life, I would have told them where to go, but Aunt Josie held a piece of my heart so I always listened to what she had to say. I couldn't figure out what had gotten into her today, though, because this was not typical Josie talk.

"I'll take that under advisement," I finally agreed, and the smile she gave me, and the nod of her head told me I'd given her the words she wanted. "And now I'm gonna go mow. Is that okay with you?"

"No need to get smart," she murmured, and I fought the grin forming on my lips. She waved me away. "Go. I'll have a cold drink ready for when you're finished."

I left her and found the mower in her back shed. Five minutes later, I started on her back yard, and disappeared into my thoughts, trying to figure out the riddle of the cocaine Ricky had mentioned. We'd contacted our suppliers and reached out to

31

other contacts, but none of them confirmed anything for us. Either Ricky's source was wrong or we were being lied to. My gut feeling was the latter, and Scott had the same instinct. Tomorrow, we'd work more on getting to the bottom of it.

When I finished the back yard, I took a five-minute break before heading out to the front. The humidity was cruel today and my shirt clung to me, so I ripped it off and dumped it at the bottom of the front stairs. I kicked myself for not changing into shorts, but the front yard was a lot smaller and I'd be done soon, so I persevered.

Ricky invaded my thoughts again, but at least that was a good distraction from thoughts of my family.

Anything was better than that.

Chapter Three
Sophia

I spotted him the minute I turned my car onto my street.

The guy from last night.

And I realised why I'd recognised him – he visited Josie across the street at least weekly, if not more often. I'd been living here for nearly two months now and I'd seen him working on her roof, her stairs and her yard. If she hadn't told me she had no children, I would have assumed he was her son.

I'd never paid too much attention to him except to note he was tall, built and dangerous. The only reason I'd picked up on the dangerous part was due to the time I'd come home late one night and found him threatening a lowlife for attempting to steal my neighbour's car. Threatening wasn't perhaps the right word; more like, he was beating the guy up. I took no issue with his actions – if a person was willing to commit a crime, he should also be willing to suffer the consequences.

Today he had the mower out and I had to concentrate hard to keep my eyes on the road. This man and that body could singlehandedly cause traffic to halt. I did sneak a look before I pulled into my driveway, and caught an eyeful of his arms flexing as he pushed the mower.

What a way to start my night, especially after the craptastic day I'd had. Hot arm visions would help get me through the night.

I parked my car in the garage and then walked the short distance to the mailbox. My eyes were still glued to him. He, on the other hand, hadn't noticed me. I considered crossing the street to introduce myself, but my sister, Magan, called so I grabbed my mail and headed inside while talking to her.

"How was your day?" Magan asked as I juggled my bag, the mail and unlocking the front door.

"Let's just say, some days I hate graphic design. And some days, I hate my clients. I'm going to pour myself a glass of wine and sit in the bath for hours tonight."

She groaned. "I swear you seem more like thirty-nine than twenty-nine, Sophia. Why don't you go out with your friends and get smashed or something?"

"You're only saying that because you're seventeen. When you're my age, I bet you grow tired of going out drinking every night." I dumped everything in my arms on my kitchen counter and headed straight for the fridge. The wine called me.

"You're telling me that when you were younger you used to go out every night?" she said, her voice full of disbelief.

Laughing, I said, "Some weeks, yes. And contrary to what you may think, I *do* go out with my friends a lot. But I need a night to myself tonight. I had too many conversations today and just need some silence."

Silence filled our conversation for a moment before she said softly, "I wish I'd known you back then. I can imagine that you would have been really cool to hang out with."

Sadness washed over me at her words. Magan and I had only discovered each other existed six months ago; we'd missed out on so much together. "I wish we'd known each other, too. But we've got the rest of our lives and we're going to spend so much time together that you'll get sick of me soon enough."

"I don't think I could ever get sick of you." The jagged tone of her voice made my heart break for her because I knew the same heartache and disappointment she did. Our mother had a lot to answer for.

Trying to change the spirit of the conversation, I asked, "So, how's your job hunting going?" She'd been struggling with writing her resume and I'd tried to help her with it because God knew, her foster mum didn't care enough to help.

"Ugh."

I frowned as I took a sip of the wine I'd just poured. "Magan, you *are* doing that resume, right?"

"Yes," she said, but my sister always failed when she lied, and I heard the hesitation in her voice.

"Magan?" My voice was firm; she needed someone in her corner, pushing her, and I'd been more than happy to assume that role over the last couple of months. Surprisingly, she'd allowed me to take it on. I figured that had to do with her need to feel someone in her life cared enough to be thinking of her.

"Sophia," she answered me in the way she often did when I quizzed her like this. And then, when I didn't speak again, she sighed, and said, "Fine, I'm doing the damn resume. Are you happy now?"

I smiled to myself. "Yes."

She made a noise as if she was pushing herself up off her bed. "I'm going now... to work on my resume. I'll catch you later."

"Okay, babe. Make sure you call me if you get stuck. I've written some good resumes in my lifetime." I took my glass of wine and padded into my bedroom.

"I bet. You know, I looked at your school reports; you did well in everything. You're like the older sister no one could ever compete with."

"Well, the one thing I can tell you is that it doesn't always matter how well you do in school. Life happens and plans go out the window, so just do your best and don't stress too much, okay?"

"You're going to make an amazing mother one day," she said. And then – "I'm really going now. Bye."

I dropped my phone on my bed and smiled to myself again. Having Magan in my life made my days better, and I loved talking to her. The day she'd shown up outside my office and told me I had a sister would always be etched in my memory.

37

One of the best days in my life.

Taking a sip of wine, I searched through my wardrobe for something to change into while I cooked dinner. Settling on a pair of denim shorts and a red tank top I loved, I quickly changed and headed back into the kitchen. As I opened the freezer to grab the steak, a knock on my front door pulled me away.

Less than a minute later, I stood in my doorway, looking at the man from across the road. Unfortunately, he'd thrown a t-shirt on, but it did little to hide the muscles underneath. Upon closer inspection, I realised he'd had a shower. His towel-dried hair caused visions of him in the shower to flash through my mind.

Damn, it had obviously been too long between men for me. I was drooling over this guy like I was a teenager.

"Shit," he said when I opened the door, recognition dawning on his face. Those beautiful green eyes of his failed to hide his surprise at seeing me.

"Not the usual way someone greets me when I answer my door to them," I said with a smile. Goddamn, he was even more gorgeous in the daylight and up close.

His brows pulled together. "How long have you lived here?"

"About six weeks," I replied, wondering where this conversation was leading, but enjoying the sound of his voice and more than happy to continue listening to it. He had one of those deep voices I loved, the kind of voice I imagined would sound commanding and hot as hell when he was bossing his woman around during sex.

Jesus.

Get a grip, woman.

"Figures," he muttered. It looked like he was connecting dots in his mind.

"What figures?"

"I hadn't realised Bev had moved out but I've been distracted with work for the last two months, so that'd be why," he answered, and he seemed distracted while he put all that together.

"So, handsome, what can I do for you?" Not that I wanted to hurry this along or anything.

He stared at me for a beat, seemingly surprised at something I'd said, but quickly recovered, and said, "Have you met Josie from across the road, yet?"

I nodded. "Sure have. She's a gorgeous lady and has been really welcoming to me."

He took a moment before explaining further, his voice holding hesitation. "She asked me to come across and see if you have any gravy powder. She's out."

I fought the grin trying to force itself across my face. He seemed as if he was uncomfortable to be asking me for gravy. "Sure, I'll check if I've got some." I turned around and called over my shoulder, "Come in."

The sound of my front door clicking shut and then his boots on my tiles told me he'd followed me in. A shiver ran through me at the thought that this gorgeous man was in my house.

I searched through my pantry for the gravy but came up empty-handed. Turning to face him, I frowned. "Sorry, I'm out."

He stood leaning against the counter, one foot crossed in front of the other, and I took a moment to study him while I had him up close. His tanned skin made me think he spent a lot of time out in the sun, and I figured he spent a lot of time working out if his muscles were anything to go by. The way his hair hung a little long and the lack of a wedding band led me to think he wasn't married and perhaps single. Men with partners tended to – in my experience – have haircuts more often. Personally, I loved his hair. I also loved the masculinity he exuded. He was the kind of man who only had to be in your presence to make himself known – he didn't need to say anything, you just knew he was in charge. This man owned his maleness, and yet, I sensed a vulnerability to him as well.

Pushing off the counter, he said, "All good. I'll head out and buy her some." His gaze swept over my kitchen before coming back to me. "I like the changes you've made in here. It needed some updating."

The first thing I'd done when I moved in was rip the kitchen out and put a new one in. I loved to cook and spent hours in my kitchen so that was a no-brainer. The outdated pale blue tiles had to go, and I replaced them with fresh, white tiles and white paint. I'd added splashes of colour with prints on the walls and red appliances. And the plants I always had in my home finished the room off.

I smiled. "Thank you. Next up is the bathroom." I couldn't wait to get started on that room; I had grand plans.

He started walking down the hallway to the front door. Pausing, he asked, "You doing the work by yourself?"

"Yeah. My weekends and nights tend to be filled with renovations these days."

A look crossed his face, like I'd impressed him, but not knowing him, I couldn't be sure. In the end, all he said was, "Good. There's some guys out there who will rip you off, so best to steer clear of them." And then he walked the rest of the distance to the front door.

I followed him, and held the door as I watched him walk down my path. Realising I didn't know his name, I called out, "I didn't catch your name, handsome."

His step faltered, and he came to a stop before slowly looking back at me. He took a moment to speak, as if he was unsure about sharing his name with me. Odd. "Griff."

Smiling, I leant against the doorframe, and folded my arms across my chest. "Nice to meet you, Griff. I'm Sophia."

He gave me a nod and turned away from me again.

As he took another step, I called out again, "And Griff?"

Stopping again, he turned his whole body this time to look at me. His lips pressed together and his eyes narrowed on me while he rubbed the back of his neck. "Yeah?" he said, his voice all kinds of gravel, the kind of gravel that made me thank God for men.

"Tell Josie, anytime she needs something, just call out, okay?"

Blowing out a breath, he nodded again. "Will do."

And then he was gone, and I couldn't help but hope like hell that I ran into him again. Soon.

Chapter Four
Griff

Fuck, it's too early in the morning for this.

I reached for my phone on the bedside table, fumbling when I couldn't grasp it. Frustration punched through me and I squinted my eyes open to see where the phone was. Locating it, I snatched it up and eyed the time. Just after five in the morning. Then I saw the name on the caller ID, and that jolted me out of bed.

Scott.

Fuck.

"What's up, brother?" I asked as I stretched. Jesus, the workout I'd given myself last night had left me in a world of hurt.

"There's been a fire at Trilogy. Can you meet me there?"

One of Storm's restaurants.

"Yeah. Any idea how bad?" I asked as I began pulling clothes on.

"Not sure yet," he answered, and I heard Harlow's voice in the background. Scott said something to her and then came back to me. "See you soon," he said before ending the call.

I finished throwing on clothes and headed out to my bike. The minute I stepped foot outside, the humidity stuck to me. Fuck, this summer was brutal – not even six in the morning and already a scorcher.

As I sped off towards Trilogy, I thought the only good thing about leaving for work this early was the lack of traffic. My home in Bulimba wasn't far from where Trilogy was in The Valley, but peak hour traffic more than doubled the time to get there some mornings. The lack of traffic today meant I pulled up outside the restaurant just over fifteen minutes later.

Surveying the damage from the fire, I estimated the restaurant was as good as fucked. I found Scott talking to one of the firies. When they'd finished their conversation and we were alone, Scott confided, "Looks like arson. They found empty fuel containers, and while they won't voice their suspicions, I know we sure as fuck don't keep fuel containers on the premises."

"Fuck," I muttered, my brain scrambling to figure out who would set fire to the restaurant and what their motive would be.

A vein pulsed in his neck as he scrubbed a hand over his face. Taking a deep breath, he said, "You and I have got some visiting to do today, brother. Nash and J can keep digging for the info on Ricky's deal, but I want us to figure this fire out."

I nodded. "Agreed."

"Wilder can take the lead on dealing with the staff and insurance."

"I'll go over it with him, make sure he's up to speed," I said, wanting to take some of the load off Scott.

"Thanks," he said as he kicked some debris on the ground in front of us. Looking at me, exhaustion clear in his eyes, he muttered, "When do you think all the shit will let up? Because I'm getting fuckin' tired of it landing in our laps. It feels like just when we sort out one issue, another one flares up."

It was a question I'd asked myself often lately. "No idea, man. But I hope it's soon because every time we get dragged into shit, it's taking us away from the one thing we really need to be putting time into. And that concerns the fuck outta me."

"You're talking about the club, yeah?"

Nodding, I said, "Yeah. There's still a divide between the boys and us. Marcus made damn sure of that before he died, and as much as I hate to admit it, we're really fucking struggling here to come back from that." The motherfucker had spread so many lies about Scott and turned most of the club against him. My unwavering support of Scott after Marcus's death had caused them to doubt me as well.

"Trust can't be bought; the only way we're gonna get it back is with time. And you're right, that's going against us at the moment." He paused and stared at me as if a million thoughts were running through his mind, and I figured they probably were. "We need to put some time into rebuilding those relationships. I can't do anything tonight but let's organise drinks for tomorrow night at the clubhouse if you're free."

"I'm free. I'll make it happen."

He checked his watch. "I've got stuff to do with Harlow, but let's meet at nine and get this shit sorted."

"I'll clue Nash, J and Wilder in."

He nodded and turned his gaze to what was left of the restaurant. "Whoever did this will pay, Griff. I've let shit slide lately, but I'm done." He looked at me through hard eyes. "Storm's not going to roll over and be fuckin' walked over, and if they thought we would now that Marcus isn't here, they seriously underestimated us."

I couldn't have agreed with him more.

***

Three hours later, I'd organised everyone who needed organising, and was working through paperwork in the office when Scott walked in with a scowl on his face.

"King and Kick just pulled up," he informed me.

I sat back in the chair, dropped the pen I held, and let out a low whistle. Our relationship with the Sydney chapter of Storm had been strained since Marcus's death, and for King, their President, to turn up said things weren't looking up.

I followed him out to the bar area where King was deep in conversation with Kick and Nash. He

48

glanced in our direction as we entered the room, and gave Scott a nod before turning back to Nash.

Kick left their conversation and made his way to us. His hand reached out for Scott's and he shook it before doing the same with me. "Scott, Griff," he greeted us, his voice somber and his expression void of any emotion.

Before we could speak, King joined us. "Boys," he boomed in greeting, his eyes flicking between us. King always had an unpredictable air to him, and tension ran through me as I waited to hear why he'd made the trip to Brisbane.

"What gives?" Scott asked, cutting to the chase.

King's face broke out in a grin, and he turned to Kick. "That's what I fucking love about Scott Cole – that no-bullshit, tell-me-how-the-fuck-it-is attitude." Turning back to Scott, he said, "I thought it time I paid your club a visit to put to rest this shit about your father."

Scott's body remained taut. "As far as I'm concerned, there's no shit to put to rest, King."

King's eyes widened a little. "I've heard differently. It would seem some of your boys believe we had something to do with Marcus's death. And as much as I don't make it my business to ever answer unfounded accusations, I feel it in me to ensure *you* know I had nothing to do with it."

I'd never known King to go out of his way like this. And it seemed Scott hadn't, either. He remained silent for a beat, and then said, "I appreciate that, brother, but I never doubted you in the first place."

King assessed him closely before finally nodding once and saying, "Good, I'm glad we have an understanding." He turned and looked around the room. "Anyone else got doubts over this?" His deep voice cut through the silence, and all eyes were on him. We had about ten members in here today, some of whom I knew to have their suspicions about King's involvement in Marcus's death. However, none of them came forward which seemed to piss King off.

He jerked his head for Scott and I to follow him outside. When we had some privacy, he said, "I call bullshit, boys." Pointing his finger at the clubhouse, he added, "Someone in there has been talking, and I don't fucking like what I'm hearing."

I should have known the conversation with him a few minutes ago had gone too smoothly. King wasn't a man to let shit go, and he'd been breathing down our necks for a few weeks about this.

"Are you saying that you and I have a problem?" Scott demanded.

King's eyes flashed a warning. "No...not yet. But what I *am* saying is that you and I are going to spend some time together and figure out which one of your boys I *do* have a problem with."

Scott's jaw clenched and he cursed under his breath. "I appreciate you wanting to get to the bottom of this, but we're in the middle of something at the moment and my attention needs to be on that. For today at least."

King's brows raised and I caught a flicker of interest in his eyes. "Kick and I can help you with that, and then we can all work on this. I'm not going home until I have what I came for."

"And I take it you came for more than just a name?" Scott asked, his gaze shifting between King and Kick.

"You would be correct," King confirmed.

Fuck.

As if we didn't have enough problems to worry about. It looked like we were about to be down a member or two.

***

"What have you heard, Jimmy?" Scott asked with the kind of patience he wasn't known for. We stood in Jimmy's living room, and *my* patience was waning due to the stench in his house. A mixture of cat piss and rubbish that should have been taken out days ago made my stomach roll.

Jimmy was one of the locals who had a finger in everything. If it involved drugs, guns or pussy, Jimmy was bound to either be involved or know something about it. Storm had an easy relationship with him, and he often fed us information when we came calling, but today he'd clammed up. Scott had been questioning him for a good ten minutes and had come up with nothing. I was surprised his patience was still at a high.

Jimmy's beady eyes flicked from Scott to King who stood in the background. He'd remained silent but King's presence could never be misconstrued – he radiated a don't-fuck-with-me energy. Everyone who came in contact with him knew it, and didn't dare question it. I figured it was the reason the Sydney chapter remained a strong force in not only their city, but throughout the country.

"I've told you what I know - nothing," Jimmy replied, but his voice sounded off. Not quite the Jimmy we knew.

Scott stared at him with distaste, but before he said another word, King pushed past him. Grabbing Jimmy's wrist, he dragged him to the table in the kitchen and shoved him down onto a chair.

Grabbing a handful of his shaggy hair, he yanked his head back, and snarled, "You're a lying piece of shit, Jimmy. And you're wasting our time. Either you open your mouth and let the words Scott wants to hear fall the fuck out, or I shove my gun down there and we all stop wasting our time here. Your choice, motherfucker."

The fear on Jimmy's face matched the fury on King's face. The seconds ticked by, and if panic were a sound, the silence in the room would have been drowned out by Jimmy. He squirmed under King's hold, and muttered, "Dude - "

King's nostrils flared. "Don't fucking dude me, asshole," he roared, tightening his hold on Jimmy's hair.

Jimmy blinked in quick succession as he stared up at King. His breaths came hard and fast, and I figured he'd reassessed his predicament. "Shit," he finally muttered.

King didn't relent. "Keep talking," he ordered.

"I swear, all I know is what Slug told me...that there'd be a hit on the restaurant last night, but I swear I don't know by who or why." His words tumbled out, fast and uncensored, but they didn't shed much light on the fire.

King glanced up at Scott. "You know this Slug?" he asked, maintaining his firm hold on Jimmy.

53

Scott nodded. "Yeah."

King gave Jimmy's hair one last yank before letting go and smacking the back of his head. The force caused Jimmy's head to snap forward, and he yelped in pain.

"Next time, don't fuck with us," King muttered.

Scott eyed Jimmy. "Any idea of Slug's whereabouts today?"

Jimmy's eyes darted to King quickly and then back to Scott. His fear breathed on its own, and it seemed he wasn't keen on messing with King again today. "Yeah, he's working down at The Eclipse Bar today."

King grinned and I saw a trace of the crazy in his eyes that he was known for. "So much easier when you just give us what we want," he said as he slapped Jimmy on the back.

Scott was already on his way out the front door. "Griff, we might need back-up for this." He voiced what I'd been thinking.

Shit was really about to go down.

***

An hour later, after calling in Nash, J and Wilder, the seven of us entered The Eclipse Bar. It was a dive of a bar in The Valley. I'd been here before and my memories consisted of stale alcohol, worn carpet, peeling paint and two-bit hookers looking for a john to get them through to their next hit. My memories were accurate.

It was still early in the day so there weren't a lot of customers around yet. We split up and searched the bar, but Slug was nowhere to be found.

King scowled. "If Jimmy has fed us the wrong information, I'll personally make sure he never takes another fucking breath."

"Right there with you, brother," I muttered.

"You boys want a drink?" The skinny, forty-plus, redheaded waitress who was aiming for sexy with her skimpy outfit, but who didn't quite pull it off, sidled up to Scott as she asked her question.

Scott looked her up and down, his lack of interest in her clear, and said, "Slug in?"

"Now, sugar, that's no way to greet a beautiful woman." She pouted and placed her hand on his chest, moving closer to him. "How about you grab a seat while I get you a drink." She winked at him. "And I'll bring you my number, too."

He took hold of her hand and removed it from his chest as if it was a piece of garbage. "I've already got the only number I ever want," he snapped.

She shrugged. "Doesn't matter to me. You can have two numbers; she doesn't need to know what you get up to on the side."

Scott leant in close to her. "I obviously haven't made myself clear enough. My woman's number is burned into my memory, as is the way her lips feel around my dick, and let me tell you, there's not another set of lips that'll ever get that close to my dick again. And as far as her not needing to know what I get up to on the side? I've never been interested in sides; I'm a mains kinda man."

Surprise crossed her face. "Never known a man to say no to a bit on the side," she muttered.

Jesus, do I have to listen to this shit?

I stepped forward so I could speak. "Did Slug come into work today? Yes or no? That's all we're interested in."

Her eyes widened. "You guys got out of bed on the wrong side today."

Staring at her, I repeated my question. "Yes or no?"

"No," she muttered. At fucking last.

"We're gonna need an address," King asserted, his tone full of impatience. He was obviously as done with this conversation as I was.

"I don't know where that asshole lives," she said, straightening her shoulders as if she was preparing for a battle.

King glared at her, but before he said anything further, Wilder piped up. Holding up his phone, he announced, "I've got his address."

"Thank fuck," J said as he slapped Wilder on the back.

A minute later, we exited the bar. As we crossed the street to where we'd parked our bikes, my gaze narrowed on three guys down the road. I recognised two of them, but not the third. Jerking my chin in his direction, I asked Scott, "You know who that is?"

Scott squinted through the sun. "No idea; never seen him in my life. But if he's consorting with those two, we need to make it our business to know who he is."

"Yeah, my thoughts exactly."

While we were watching him, another guy joined the group. "No idea who he is, either," Scott muttered. Turning to Wilder, he called him over. "I want info on who those guys are. After we deal with Slug, you take off and look into that for me."

"Done," Wilder agreed before heading to his bike.

"Jesus, this town is beginning to crawl with scum," I said, convinced those two were deserving of that label simply because of who they were laughing and joking with.

Scott nodded. "Sure feels like it, brother."

King sat on his bike looking at Scott expectantly. "Let's go fuck some shit up, Cole," he said. "I've had about enough of pussy-footing around; it's time to get down to business."

And there was the King we knew. God help Slug when we found him.

***

"Jesus fuck," Nash said, looking at the bloody scene in front of us.

We stood in Slug's living room, all seven of us silent as we took in his dead body. Or more to the point, his body parts that were strewn across the room.

King whistled and turned to face Scott and me. "I don't know what the fuck's going down, but going by this, it's something you need to figure out fast. I'm gonna put a call into Hyde and get him to start asking questions; see if we know anyone who knows anything."

"Thanks, man," I said. Between his VP and our guys, surely someone had to know something.

Anger clouded Scott's face as he took one last look at the death scene. Then he directed his attention to us, a look of determination on his face now. "Wilder, you check into those guys like we discussed. J, you and Nash follow up on that drug deal Ricky's talking about. Griff, you and I are gonna spend today visiting every fucking person Slug knew and see what we can find out." Eyeing King, he said, "And you and Kick can either ride along with us or you can question my boys." He paused for a moment while a darker look shadowed his face. "And if you figure out who's been spreading that shit about your club, I want time with them before you do whatever the fuck you've got planned."

King's lips quirked into a grin. "I like the way you think, Cole."

I was with King there. We'd been treading carefully with the club for too many weeks now; it was way past time to deal with misplacements of loyalty.

Chapter Five
Sophia

I sat in my car outside the diner I ate dinner at occasionally, and pulled the rearview mirror down so I could take a good look at my face. After a long day at work, I'd gone to the gym and spent an hour there trying to work some of the stress out of my body. I'd showered afterwards and changed into shorts and a shirt with the intention of going home, but on the way, I'd had a craving for a hamburger.

Looking in the mirror, I decided that tonight perhaps wasn't the night to eat out. My hair hung half dry after I'd washed it, and my face held no trace of makeup. Some days I had no problem going out without my hair or makeup done, but I wasn't sure today was one of those days. Not only were my hormones all over the place, but I'd had a run in with one of my work colleagues today, and she'd made me feel little. I fucking hated giving people that power in my life, but some days I struggled not to. And today, I hadn't won the battle.

Fuck it.

I opened the car door and stepped out. Locking the car, I began walking towards the diner. My tummy growled, eager for a hamburger because, *goddamn*, they were the bomb at this diner.

Pushing through the front door, I entered and looked for an empty table. As I scanned the room, my heart fell into my stomach when I saw the guy at the back smile at me.

Worst luck today.

I should have just gone home.

My ex-boyfriend, Tommy, sat at one end of the diner smiling at me as if he'd never stuck his dick in any other woman's vagina before coming home and whispering sweet nothings about growing old with me.

He stood and walked my way, and in my haste to avoid him, I swiftly turned and headed in the other direction.

Shit, there are no empty tables.

The universe is conspiring against me today.

And then I spotted him.

Griff.

He sat by himself at a table near the back and was engrossed with something on his phone so he didn't see me coming. His head snapped up, though, when I slid into the booth with him, and announced loudly, "Sorry I'm late, handsome. I got caught up at work."

His eyes widened right before he frowned. I didn't give him time to speak before leaning across the table and pressing a kiss to his cheek. My hand moved to his cheek once I'd kissed him, and I let it linger there, hoping like hell my ex was taking this all in.

Easing back into my seat, I realised Tommy now stood next to Griff's table with a look of disbelief on his face. "Sophia," he said before turning his attention to Griff. "And you are?" His voice held that possessive tone he'd liked to bring out whenever we'd gone out and another man had even so much as looked at me.

What did I ever see in him?

Griff didn't even skip a beat. "None of your fucking business," he replied, his eyes hard as he watched Tommy.

Tommy scowled at him and then turned to me. "You've stooped so low as to date a biker now?"

Huh? A biker?

Griff stood. Towering over Tommy, he spoke in a low, harsh voice. "If I were you, I'd turn the fuck around and walk away before you say something I might take offence to." His rigid body stayed rooted to the spot while he glared at Tommy, waiting for him to make his next move.

I held my breath, wondering if perhaps I had made a bad decision to sit with Griff and act like we were together. My intention had not been to cause a problem; I'd simply wanted Tommy to leave me alone and I figured if he thought I had a new boyfriend, he would.

Tommy held Griff's glare for a few moments, and then he muttered something under his breath before stalking away from us. Griff watched him go and then sat again. He rested both arms on the table, either side of his plate, raised his brows at me, and said, "Care to tell me what that was all about?"

Oh, man.

That voice.

It's like liquid sex.

He could bring me to orgasm just by speaking to me. I was sure of it.

"Sophia?"

Shit. I blinked and got my head back in the conversation. "Sorry about that." I sighed, and leant my elbows on the table. And then proceeded to make a fool of myself. "I've had one of those days at work – you know, the ones where everything goes to shit – and then I went to the gym, and usually that helps, but tonight it didn't. I've got all these knots inside and the gym should have unkinked them, and I don't know why it didn't. Anyway, I decided on the way home that a hamburger would help, but then I got here and realised I look like shit with no makeup and crappy hair, but I thought 'fuck it' and came in anyway. But then I saw my ex, and shit, it's bad enough to see your ex, but to see him when you look like you're not coping with the breakup – and don't get me wrong, I *am* coping – but, it's not the right time to run into an ex, you know?" I took a deep breath and waited for him to acknowledge that. When he gave me a nod, I continued, "So, I saw you, and thought if I just sat with you, he'd back off and leave me alone. Story of my life that he didn't." I removed my elbows from the table and sat back in my chair. He sat staring at me like I was a freak, and – *oh, my God* – he was probably right. *Why did I just let all that shit spill out of my mouth?*

I sat in my mortification, waiting for him to say something. Anything. But he didn't. He sat back in his chair, and watched me for a minute. It was the longest minute of my day, and I'd had some long minutes today. Finally, he said, "You don't look like shit."

Cocking my head, I asked, "Out of everything I just said, *that's* what you focus on?"

He shrugged. "Seemed like the most important thing to mention at this point." Leaning forward, he added, "That, and the fact your ex is a dick. And that you can do so much better than him."

My belly fluttered, and I relaxed a little. "Yeah, I can," I said softly.

"What did you do at the gym?"

"Huh?" I wasn't sure what he meant.

Gesturing with his hand, he explained, "You said you couldn't unkink your knots at the gym. What exercise did you do?"

"Oh, that...I did a Body Combat class."

"A what?"

"It's one of those classes with karate and kickboxing type moves. It's supposed to be awesome to burn calories."

He scowled as he ran his gaze over my body. "I don't think that's anything you need to worry about."

65

A thrill ran through me at his words, even if I did disagree with him. I opened my mouth to speak when the waitress approached. "Can I get you something to eat?" she asked me.

I smiled at her and nodded. "Yes, please. I'm starving. Can I please get one of your beef burgers with salad, and cheese, but hold the tomato, and add avocado. And can I have it without the barbeque sauce but add honey mustard, please?"

She scribbled all that down, and asked, "A drink? And do you want chips, too?"

"Oh, honey, I really do want chips with that, but hell, I know you'll know exactly what I'm saying when I say to you that even though today is the kind of day I *need* chips, I am so far from needing them that I'll have to say no. And, yes, can I please have some water?"

She nodded at me, and said, "I hear you. Boy, do I hear you." Looking at Griff, she muttered, "Our men have no idea how easy they have it."

I laughed.

He didn't.

I wonder if he's always this serious?

"You want anything else?" she asked him as she collected his empty plate.

He shook his head. "No, thanks."

A man with manners. I liked that.

"I'll have this out to you soon," she said to me, and then she was gone. And I was left with Griff who was watching me with a look I couldn't pick.

Deciding I needed a moment, I excused myself. "I'll be back; just gotta use the ladies," I said, and didn't give him a chance to say anything before heading in the direction of the bathroom. I hoped he'd still be at the table when I returned.

Five minutes later, as I was washing my hands, I stared at my reflection in the mirror. Goodness, I needed some lipstick. But I had the issue of food. I hated eating when I had a full set of lips on. But, damn, I had a gorgeous man sitting across from me. And what woman wants to sit in front of a hot guy looking washed out?

I rested my hands on the sink and took a deep breath. He'd already seen me without the lipstick so really, what was the point of even worrying about this? Besides, after Tommy had trashed my heart, I'd promised myself I'd never date a man again who was more concerned about my appearance than my feelings.

Time to respect myself.

Griff might be drop dead gorgeous, and I might be interested in him, but if he preferred a woman who always had colour on her lips, he wasn't the man for me.

I grabbed my bag and exited the bathroom. When I found him still sitting at the table, my heart did a little dance of happiness.

He was on his phone as I approached, and I didn't miss the way his eyes swept over my body, lingering on my legs, and – *good God* – that felt good. I sat across from him just as he ended his call.

"Do you always wear the shortest shorts known to mankind?" he asked, placing his phone on the table.

"What? You don't like them?" I asked with a teasing smile. The way he'd eyed my legs led me to believe he *did* like them, but a little flirting never hurt anyone.

Heat flashed in his eyes and he shifted forward in his seat. "Sweetheart, there isn't a man alive who wouldn't like those shorts on you."

His words hit my core, and I squeezed my legs together. Words failed me – not something I was used to. Thankfully, the waitress saved me when she brought some water to the table.

I poured myself a drink and took a gulp. Griff had flustered me, and I needed a moment. Hell, it felt like I needed a lot of moments when I was around him.

"You should try boxing," he said, confusing me.

"What for?" I asked, taking another gulp of water.

"To unkink your knots. It'll help."

I placed my glass on the table. "I've seen the punching bags at the gym; maybe I'll give it a go tomorrow."

He stood, and disappointment spread through me. "Make sure you get a trainer to teach you proper technique," he said as he grabbed his phone. "And next time, eat the chips, sweetheart. Life's too fucking short not to eat the chips."

I watched as he walked out of the diner, and when I saw him head to a motorcycle, I realised what Tommy had meant earlier. *He's a biker.* It was written clearly on his vest – Storm Motorcycle Club. He hadn't been wearing that vest the other times I'd spoken to him, and I'd been so busy making a fool of myself while he sat in front of me tonight that I had failed to take it in.

Well, shit. I'd never known a biker before. Didn't bother me, though, especially because I'd seen the way Griff cared for his aunt. In my books, the way a person treated their family said more about them than any judgement handed down by society. I'd known people that society deemed upstanding citizens, but their behavior towards family behind closed doors painted a vastly different picture.

Society's opinion meant very little to me and could kiss my ass.

Chapter Six
Griff

"Drinks are off tonight," Scott said as I drank the remainder of my coffee. We were in the clubhouse kitchen going over our plans for the day.

"Yeah?"

Nodding, he confirmed, "Yeah. King's ripped through the club and pissed a lot of the guys off so there have been a lot of cancellations for tonight. I figure there's no point doing it with just a few of us. We'll have to wait until we weed the assholes out. Maybe then we'll have half a chance to start rebuilding, without anyone working against us."

I rubbed the back of my neck and shoulders, trying to work the knots out that only seemed to get worse every day. "Makes sense."

Scott's brow furrowed. "You look even worse than you did the other day. You okay?"

I rinsed my mug and placed it in the dish rack. "I will be. Just got some stuff going on this week."

"Not that we can really afford it, but do you need some time?"

I shook my head. "No, I'm good."

He watched me thoughtfully for a moment before nodding. "Let me know if that changes." He waited for my response and at my nod, he continued. "Will you be okay without me for a few hours later today? Harlow's got an appointment with her doctor and I want to take her. She's happy to go on her own but it's important to me to be there if possible."

"You go, brother. I'll keep things ticking over here."

"Thanks." His shoulders relaxed a little and I wondered at the reason for his level of stress over her. Last I'd heard, they were doing better.

"Everything good with her?"

"I suggested she talk with her doctor about her depression. I mean, fuck, I don't know if how she is would be classified as depression, but she's not

72

right. And I don't think it can hurt to talk to someone about it and find out what her options are for treatment."

"She took that okay?"

"Yeah, she's let me back in so that makes shit easier." He scrubbed his face before changing the subject. "You hear anything from Wilder about those two guys?"

"Not yet, but he said he'd be here soon with some information when I texted him this morning."

His eyes revealed his concern when he said, "We've gotta get to the bottom of everything, Griff. I've got a bad fuckin' feeling about some of this. And I think Ricky's tied up with it all."

I agreed with everything he'd said.

And on top of all that, I had a bad feeling swirling in my gut about the shit from my past. I needed to deal with that, too, and fast.

***

"So, you're telling me we've got nothing to worry about where those two are concerned?" Scott asked Wilder after he'd filled us in on what he'd found out about the two guys we'd seen outside the Eclipse Bar yesterday.

73

Wilder nodded. "Seems to be that way. From what I've heard, their gig is robberies here and there, but nothing that impacts us. Arrived in town a couple of weeks ago but aren't connected to anyone of concern."

"Thank Christ. We don't need anyone else to worry about at the moment," Scott said.

"No luck with the restaurant fire?" Wilder asked.

"Not a damn thing. Brisbane's not fuckin' talking. And Hyde hasn't been able to uncover anything either," Scott replied.

Wilder frowned. "Can I do some digging today? Or do you need me on other things?"

"You got an idea who it might be?" Scott asked.

"No, but I know someone who might know something."

"Who?" Scott urged.

Wilder fidgeted which was unusual; I'd never seen him fidget before. "I can't say, sorry man."

Scott's shoulders tensed. "Wilder, you're a patched member of this club now. Your loyalty is expected to be one hundred percent with us, and that means if you know something, we expect you to share that with us. Regardless of who it affects." He paused for a moment, his eyes boring into Wilder's. When he spoke again, his voice was harder than

74

usual. "The *only* people you should be worried about now are members of your club. Are you reading me?"

Wilder stood across from him, his body now also tense, as if he was preparing for a fight. "I read you, Scott, but I'm gonna need some time, because if this person does know something, the blowback on her won't be pretty, and I refuse to put her in that situation without preparing her for it. I will give you her name, but not yet."

After contemplating that, Scott asked, "How much time are we talking here?"

"A day."

Scott nodded. "You have a day, but within twenty-four hours I want that name and that information." It stunned me that Scott gave him that, and it showed me the respect he had for Wilder.

"You'll have it," he agreed.

As he walked away from us, Scott called out, "And Wilder?" Wilder turned back to look at us, and Scott continued, "This is the first and last time we have a conversation like that."

Wilder gave a nod of understanding and then left us.

My phone rang at that moment, distracting me because of the name on the caller ID. "Josie. Everything okay?"

"Michael, I've hurt myself. Can you come now, please?" Her voice was off, and alarm coursed through me.

"I'm on my way," I replied.

***

I jogged up Josie's front stairs, worried as fuck for her. She never begged me to come and help her. I half expected to find her passed out when I walked through her front door.

Her front door that was open right now. That was odd.

Fuck.

"Josie," I called out as I entered and strode down her hallway.

"We're in here."

I halted. I'd know that voice anywhere. Sweet as fucking sin, and more dangerous than half the danger I'd ever come up against in my life. That voice could make a man do things he never dreamt he'd ever do.

When I didn't reply, Sophia stepped from the kitchen into the hallway and smiled at me. That

76

smile shot straight to my dick, and I sucked in a breath at the force of it. She wore goddamn shorts again. Jesus fucking Christ, those shorts would be the death of me.

"Hey, handsome," she greeted me as her gaze travelled over my body.

"Shit," I muttered, and started walking again. Our eyes met as I moved closer to her, and as much as I was irritated she was here – *teasing me with that body made for pleasure* - I couldn't deny the warmth in her eyes. And I sure as fuck couldn't deny how good it made me feel.

When I reached her, I slowed. "What are you doing here?" I asked, knowing the words came out all wrong, but unable to put them a better way.

Hurt flashed in her eyes. "That's not a nice way to greet someone, Griff," she said softly, and she was right. But I was an asshole who had no desire to make a woman want me, so nice wasn't anything I strived for anymore.

I watched her for a few more minutes, and then turned my gaze to the kitchen, looking for Josie. Time to do what I came here for and then get the hell out.

Josie sat at her kitchen table with her leg resting on a chair, an ice pack on her ankle. A huge smile plastered across her face. "Michael," she welcomed me.

I narrowed my eyes on her as I moved closer to her. "I thought something had happened to you, Josie."

She gestured at her ankle. "It did. I hurt my ankle."

"How?" I demanded, struggling to believe her.

Sophia had joined us in the kitchen and stood near Josie, watching me with disapproval. I did my best to ignore her, but – *goddamn* – I found myself not wanting her reproach.

Josie now waved her hand in front of her. "Oh, you know, I tripped down the stairs."

I raised my brows. "And then you just happened to walk back up those stairs to phone me?"

"When I got here, she was in a fair bit of pain," Sophia said, her tone full of the same disapproval as her gaze.

My eyes snapped to hers. "And you just happened to come over at the same time that she hurt herself?"

She placed her hands on her hips and stood taller, causing her breasts to jiggle. Her fucking perfect handful that she'd stretched a sexy pink tank over today. My eyes dropped momentarily to take all that in before shifting back to her face.

Displeasure now filled her features. "She called me and asked for my help if you must know," she retorted.

Fuck, I knew it.

I clenched my jaw as I turned my attention to Josie. "Whatever ideas and plans you've got going on in your head need to end now, Josie. I love you, but I don't take kindly to people interfering in my life, regardless of good intentions." I fought to keep my voice even, but my reaction had been extreme, and I struggled to maintain my cool. Fuck knew why, and I didn't have the time to analyse it; all I knew in that moment was my need for Josie to know not to meddle in my life.

Disappointment marred her face. "Michael, please - "

Fuck, now I'd upset both of them. I raked my fingers through my hair and blew out a long breath. Looking at Sophia, I asked, "You got this?"

Her eyes widened. "Yes, but you're not really going to leave, are you? She's hurt and wanted you here."

"No, she wanted both of us here, and not for her ankle, sweetheart. If you've got this, I've gotta get back to work."

I waited for her reply, and after glaring at me for a good few moments, she said, "I've got this." Her tone made it clear how pissed off with me she was, but I ignored that.

"I'll drop by and see you later," I said to Josie, and ignoring that she was upset with me, too, I turned and stalked out of the house.

I was almost to my bike when Sophia called out angrily, "You're seriously going to go?"

Spinning around, I stalked to where she stood. "Josie is a matchmaker, Sophia, and she's trying to get us together. It's what she does, and *that's* what today has been about. She knows I'm not interested so she's trying her hand at getting me to change my mind. I don't usually lose my cool like that, but I've got too much stuff going on at work today to have been called away, so yeah, I lost my shit. I'll come back and apologise to her later when I've calmed down." I took a breath and then added, "Don't let the old lady charm fool you; she may be putting on a good show of looking upset, but she's not. You can bet your ass she's sitting in there right now plotting her next move."

Staring at me, she looked like she'd had the wind knocked out of her, which made no sense to me because, although I'd been firm, I hadn't been an ass. She took a minute, and then said, "Okay, I've got you. Message understood, loud and clear. But one question – why does she call you Michael?"

You can run but you can never escape your past.

"It's my name. Griff's a nickname – one I prefer to be called so please call me that."

When she raised her hands in a defensive type gesture, I realised I'd probably been more forceful than I'd meant to be. "By the looks of it, we probably won't cross each other's path too often for me to fuck that up, but I'll do my best to get it right," she snapped, and then turned and stalked back inside Josie's house.

I watched her go, feeling something I hadn't felt for fuck knew how long.

Regret.

And that confused me.

And for some reason, it also hurt.

Chapter Seven
Sophia

As my hand flew over the page, adding lines here and shading there, my drawing came to life. I'd been sitting in my art room listening to Kelly Clarkson on repeat for the last hour, doodling with no plan to sketch anything, when my hand began moving of its own accord. My sketches often took shape that way.

When I realised who I was sketching, my hand stilled, and I sucked in a breath. I dropped the sketchpad onto the desk.

Damn.

I stood and stretched. It'd been another long day at work, with a break in the middle to go and help Josie. *A break to go and hear Griff tell me he was far from interested in me.* A shitty day all round, really. Who had I been kidding even thinking a man as good-looking as Griff would be interested in me? Better to hear straight from his lips now how uninterested he was than to kid myself and keep flirting with him, hoping he might feel the same way.

I padded into the kitchen in search of wine. Opening the fridge, I came to the sad realisation I was out. Bugger. I pulled the diet coke out instead, and then reached up into the cupboard where I stored my bourbon. A few moments later, I lifted a glass of bourbon and coke to my lips and enjoyed the taste of it going down.

Walking to the kitchen table, I placed the glass down and walked back to my art room to grab my sketchpad. Turned out I did want to finish that sketch.

Two hours later, after a few more glasses of bourbon, I'd finished my sketch, painted my toenails bright red, baked some shortbread, surfed Facebook for a while and now sat on my couch with a mask on my face.

Christmas Eve.

Not only had today been long, shitty and disappointing, it was also Christmas Eve – a day I always struggled with. A person could have all the friends under the sun, but when they didn't have a family to call their own, there were some days that just sucked. Birthdays and Christmas tended to be the worst. I'd called Magan earlier, hoping she might have wanted to come over, but her phone had gone straight to message bank, and she hadn't called me back.

I sat on the couch and finished another glass of bourbon before deciding it was time to take my mask off. As I stood to head into the bathroom, a knock on the front door surprised me. A spark of hope flared in my heart – perhaps Magan had decided to come over. After all, it was just after ten; who else would knock on my door at that time of night?

When I peered through the front window to make sure I did in fact know the person, my heart skipped a beat when I saw Griff standing on the other side of the door. And then I remembered his words from today and I pushed that feeling deep down. *She knows I'm not interested so she's trying her hand at getting me to change my mind.* Yeah, he'd made himself clear. However, I figured he visited his aunt often enough that we'd see each other around, and just because he wasn't interested in me didn't mean we couldn't be friendly to each other.

I opened the door and greeted him with a smile. "This is late. Everything okay?"

He stared at me for a moment, as if I'd surprised him, before saying, "Yeah, everything's okay. Can I come in for a moment?"

Stepping aside, I waved him in. "Sure."

I closed the door and followed him into my kitchen. The bourbon buzzed through my body, causing my tongue to loosen. "If you've come to tell me again how uninterested in me you are, you don't need to; I understood it the first time."

His brows pulled together as he frowned at me. He didn't say anything, just stared at me like I was a freak with three heads. And suddenly, I remembered I had a facemask on.

"Shit," I muttered. "Can you give me a moment? I'll just take my mask off and then I'll be back." Without waiting for his reply, I scurried into the bathroom and quickly removed the mask.

When I returned to the kitchen, he stood at the table with my sketchpad in his hands. Mortification flooded me as I realised what he was looking at. The sketch of him I'd done earlier.

Can this day get any worse?

Choosing to ignore the sketch, I walked past him into my kitchen and grabbed the bourbon and diet coke, and poured myself another drink. Double strength, because at this point, I needed it. Stat.

I was so engrossed in my drink and shoving my embarrassment aside that I didn't hear him move next to me. The first I knew he was there was when he placed his hand over mine that was holding the bottle. His touch sent jolts of electricity through me, and my legs wobbled a little as I tried to keep my balance.

Oh, God.

This man.

"How do you figure I'm not interested in you?" he asked, his voice all deep and gravelly, just the way I loved it.

I stilled. My breathing slowed as anticipation flowed through me. I looked up at him. "You said as much today at Josie's."

"No, I didn't."

Had he suffered some kind of memory loss this afternoon?

"Yeah, you did, Griff."

His gaze remained steady on mine. "When?"

"You said Josie knew you weren't interested in me and that she was trying to get you to change your mind."

86

He took a deep breath and his chest rose and fell with a hard thud. His hand slid off mine to take hold of the bottle, and he reached for an empty glass out of my dish rack. A few moments later, he'd poured himself a bourbon, neat. As he took a long gulp, his gaze found mine again, and I caught heat there.

"I am as far from uninterested in you as a man can get, Sophia."

"Oh." He'd caught me off guard with such an honest, straight-to-the-point statement, and words failed me. Excitement snaked through me, though, and I let that sink in. This gorgeous man standing in front of me, in my house, was interested in me.

"But, I don't date," he said, and in four words, obliterated everything he'd just given me. A man who didn't date meant one thing – he only wanted sex.

I lifted my glass to my lips and drank some before saying, "Is that what you came here to tell me? Because I'm not really sure what to do with that, handsome. I'm as far from the kind of girl who settles for one-night-stands as a woman can get."

"Yeah, I figured that. And no, that's not what I came here to say. I actually wanted to apologise to you for acting like a prick today. I was in the middle of a shit of a day, and Josie knows how to push my buttons. I love her, but goddamn, she can push me to places that make me act like an asshole, and I'm sorry for that."

"I can appreciate that. And I can totally understand how a bad day affects you because I've been having a few of those lately, too." I paused before saying, "Apology accepted."

He seemed surprised, and didn't say anything more before finishing his drink.

"Do you always use your words so economically?" I asked, a little frustrated because I was the kind of woman who liked conversation.

He finished off his drink and then gave me his eyes. God, those eyes were full of secrets and depth and hurt. I was sure of it. Something about Griff screamed damage. Perhaps it was the way he watched you – as if he was always assessing a threat – or maybe it was the way he held himself back – not only his words, but he also held his body as if he didn't want to get too close; didn't want to get burned. "I've never met a woman like you. You're like this odd combination of all woman – in the way you seem to suffer from female insecurities that, in my opinion, aren't warranted, and in the way you have this sexy-as-fuck way you move and talk – but then you've got this other side where you speak with honesty in a way a lot of women I've known don't," he finally said, taking my breath away with his own honesty.

I smiled. "So that would be a "no" in answer to my previous question."

The corners of his mouth lifted as if he was going to smile, but he didn't. Instead, he simply said, "Correct. Sometimes I have a lot to say, but not often. Mostly, I find people aren't interested so much in what other people have to say; they're more interested in the sound of their own voice, and only want to hear yours if you're agreeing with what they're saying."

I grinned. "For the record, handsome, I like the sound of your voice more than the sound of my own, so feel free to talk as much as you want around me. I'm all ears."

He stared at me. "Fuck."

I cocked my head to the side. "I'll take that as a good 'fuck' rather than a bad one, shall I?"

He raked his fingers through his hair and grimaced. "I'm not sure yet, sweetheart."

Sweetheart.

I could get used to him calling me that.

He's already told you he doesn't date.

"Why don't you date?" The words were out before I could censor them. Damn alcohol.

89

He didn't skip a beat. "Why don't you do one-night stands?"

"Shit, you sure know how to turn a question back on a woman," I noted. "But seriously, the commonly accepted thing for people to do is date, so what's caused you to stop?"

"Is it the commonly accepted thing to do, or is that just what they sell you in the movies and TV?"

I frowned. "I'm pretty sure it's the accepted thing."

He shrugged. "In my world, nothing is commonly accepted except for the belief in each to his own. I don't do things just because society tells me to. The world's too fucked up to even begin to know what's best for me. I say, figure out what shit works for you, then do that, and fuck what anyone else has to say about it."

For a man of few words, he was giving me a lot tonight. And I never wanted him to stop speaking because I loved everything coming out of his mouth. Griff was the kind of man who, even if I didn't agree with something he said, I could appreciate the thought and time he'd put into it. And I could respect the hell out of a man like that.

"I take it you're not going to share with me why you don't date, then?" I asked, still wanting to know his reason.

He reached for the bourbon and poured us both a drink - his neat, mine with diet coke. As he slid my glass to me, he said, "I'm more interested to know why you don't like one-night stands." He threw back half his drink and waited for me to speak.

I passed him the bottle of bourbon while I picked up my glass and the coke. "I need to sit for this conversation," I said, and turned to walk into the living room.

I settled myself at one end of the couch and watched as he joined me, taking a seat at the other end. Keeping himself as far from me as he could. "Do you have family, Griff? I mean, I know you have your aunt, but do you have a family who love you and care for you and make you feel special?"

He blinked rapidly and sucked in a deep breath. When he put his drink to his mouth and downed what he had left, I figured I'd hit a nerve. "Not anymore," he said, his voice hard, his body just as rigid.

Shit, I hadn't expected that, but I figured he wasn't the kind of man who would want me to dwell on his admission, so I carried on. "You did once, though?"

"Yes."

I drank some of my drink, swallowing the alcohol and the shitty memories that reared their ugly heads. "I never have. Well, not unless you count the few years I had with my parents when I was younger, but I don't count those years because I was too young to remember them, let alone for them to mean anything. All I had was the foster care system from the age of nine, and let me tell you, there wasn't any love or care or being made to feel special in that system."

"Yeah, so I've heard," he murmured.

"I want to feel loved and special. I don't want to ever know the feeling of being discarded ever again, like I did over and over with the families who were happy to have me for the money they made off the government, but quick to discard me when I no longer suited their life anymore. You hear stories of kids who are abused in the system. I never experienced abuse, but neglect and lack of love fucks you up, too. So, after a couple of one-night-stands when I was younger, I decided they weren't for me. I'd rather have no sex than casual sex that means nothing, and makes me feel like shit all over again when the guy leaves without a second glance." Shit, this was dredging up feelings I usually did my best to avoid; feelings I buried so deep I didn't even know where to look for them anymore.

He sat watching me, and I knew he was processing every word I'd said by the thoughtful look on his face. Ghosts of the past filled the room, lingering like a nightmare you wanted to forget, but couldn't. And I sensed they weren't only my ghosts. I sensed that Griff carried ghosts the way most people carried happy memories.

"I had love once...well, at least I thought I did. Fuck, I thought I had something special, but that's the thing about love – how do you know when the other person feels the same way? How do you know they're not playing you, and hedging bets between you and someone else? *That* makes you feel like shit. I won't go there again," he said, and I watched him sitting in his pain, and my heart hurt for whatever he'd gone through. I wanted to slap the woman who'd done that to him, because she'd taken a man who was open to love, and made him close his heart to the possibilities of everything love had to offer.

"We're not all like that," I said softly.

"Neither are the men who know how to treat a woman right for one night only," he replied, watching me closely, and I felt like we were at a checkmate. Both clinging to what we needed, neither willing to bend.

Not sure where to take the conversation now, I sat in silence, and then Griff stood abruptly. He looked down at me with an expression I couldn't pick, but if I were to try, I'd say he seemed torn over something. "It's late. I'll let you get to bed," he said before leaving me to take his glass into the kitchen.

I followed him, wanting every moment I could have to watch him. Even the way he moved was a turn-on. His body moved with a sense of authority and power, and I'd always found men who had that take-charge attitude hot.

Leaning against the kitchen counter, I waited while he rinsed his glass and placed it next to the sink. When he faced me again, the desire I saw in his eyes made my core clench.

He closed the distance between us and stepped into my personal space. Although his body remained rigid in the way I was grasping was Griff's way, and although he kept his emotions tucked away and his face bare of them, his desire rang out loud and clear.

He wants me.

But he's denying himself.

In that moment, I felt everything he was feeling.

Want and denial seemed to be something we had in common.

He surprised the hell out of me when he reached out, cupped my cheek, and traced his thumb over my lips. His touch was so gentle and yet so firm in

94

the one stroke. He shifted his gaze from my lips to my eyes. "Beautiful," he murmured, and my heart beat faster at that word. "Don't doubt yourself, sweetheart," he added before letting my cheek go and striding down my hallway without another word.

I wanted to go after him and take back everything I'd said about one-night-stands. And I wanted to let him take over my body for this one night, regardless of the fact he'd get up and walk out when he was finished. And, damn, I wanted to try and make him change his mind about dating.

But I didn't.

I stood rooted to the spot and watched him walk through my front door.

I let him leave, and I let our want and denial swirl in the air like a memory of a moment that you wanted to be so much more than a moment.

Chapter Eight
Griff

I hit the bar half an hour after leaving Sophia's house. The bartender jerked his chin in greeting and placed a drink in front of me a moment later. I sucked the alcohol down, and hissed at the burn, but, fuck, I needed it.

Sophia was stuck in my mind, parts of our conversation on repeat.

We're not all like that.

Fuck, I believed everything that came out of that woman's mouth, but my mind got stuck on this, unable to believe it, but at the same time, unable to move past it. And yet, even if I accepted it to be true from her, she was not a woman I should even consider tainting with my needs. Sophia was all lightness, while all I had running through my veins these days was dark.

"Hi, gorgeous," a voice came from beside me. I turned and found a hot brunette smiling at me. "Wanna buy me a drink?"

I assessed her. Sexy with curves in all the right places, and the look of a woman who did this kind of thing often, she would be perfect to take my mind off everything. I *wanted* to want to buy her a drink. Hell, I wanted a lot of fucking things – and it had been so fucking long for me that I *needed* them at this point – but I couldn't bring myself to say yes. Shaking my head, I said, "Sorry, babe, I'm tapped out tonight."

She shrugged. "How about I buy you a drink then?" Her gaze travelled over my body, lust flashing in her eyes. And Jesus, that should have gotten me hard, but here I sat, soft as a fucking eighty year old.

"Another time, maybe," I said with regret. I wasn't sure if my regret stemmed from not wanting her or from wanting someone else who I'd never allow myself to have.

Surprise flickered on her face, but she got the message and left me alone. Thank Christ my phone rang at that point, because I didn't want to sit with my thoughts of Sophia any longer.

"Danny," I greeted my cousin. "You're finally returning my call." I'd left a message for him hours ago. "Was beginning to think I'd have to pay you a visit."

"Don't be an asshole, Michael. I was working and didn't have time for a family catch-up call," he said, sounding as impressed to be having this phone call as I was.

"This isn't a family catch-up. This is a have-you-sorted-that-shit-out-yet kinda call."

He blew out a harsh breath. "Fuck, it's not as easy as phoning someone and getting you taken off a roster."

I threw more alcohol down. "You need to make it as easy as that or I will. And, Danny, you don't want me to get involved in this. You thought I didn't have much of a conscience back then...I have even less of one now."

He made a noise and I practically heard his scowl through the phone. "I remember the kid you used to be. What the hell happened to you to turn you into this thug?"

"You know what the fuck happened to me," I snarled. *Fuck.* "And now I have nothing to lose, except my freedom, so I'll do whatever it takes to protect that."

"Jesus." He stopped talking for a moment, before saying, "We lost our main witness. Without you, the case isn't as solid."

I wanted to give a fuck. I truly did. Mostly because as much as we'd cut ties four years ago, he'd had my back when we were younger. But also because the asshole on trial deserved to be punished. However, I had nothing in me. I'd lost the ability to care about anyone or anything but Storm and Josie somewhere along the line.

In the end, I suggested, "Find a way to cut him loose. I'll take care of him once he's back on the streets."

"Do you think you're some kind of God? You wouldn't even get past his first line of defence, Michael. Bond's got men watching his back, and taking care of any threat that comes up. Why the fuck do you think we don't have a star witness anymore?"

I slammed my glass down on the bar. "You wanna see just what I'm capable of, Danny? Give me a day and I'll show you. And then maybe you'll stop underestimating me, and start taking what I'm

99

saying seriously. I'm not going down for the shit in my past I can't erase."

"Do you want to know what *I* take seriously? My job. So stop fucking talking before I have to do my job and fucking investigate you."

"Have at it, you won't be able to pin anything on me. My work is clean as fuck."

"Jesus!" He swore under his breath. "This conversation is over. Bond is going to trial and you're going to have to testify. Get your shit together and get ready for it." He ended the call, and I placed my phone down on the bar as calmly as I felt.

Time to get to work.

***

Josie: Come to lunch at mine today. It's Christmas Day and I want to see my nephew.

Me: I'm busy.

Josie: Make yourself unbusy.

Me: Is this another attempt to set me up with Sophia? She and I have spoken and nothing will happen there.

Josie: No, I'm gathering all my orphans together like I do every Christmas. It's been ten years this year, Michael. You need to come this year. I don't want you alone today.

I swore as I dropped my phone on my bed. I should never have taught her how to send a text. Unwrapping the towel from around my waist, I used it to dry my hair. I had plans today – plans that didn't include Josie and her good intentions. However, I knew she'd never let me hear the end of it if I didn't go to her lunch. And having to see her give me that Josie look of reproach for the next few months wasn't something I wanted to experience.

Me: I might be late.
Josie: I'll save you a plate.

I got dressed, shoved my phone in my pocket, grabbed my keys and headed out to take care of business.

And then it'd be happy families with Josie.

And a waiting game for Danny to realise I meant business.

***

I sat down the street from the familiar building of years ago. I'd lost count of how many hours I'd spent outside this building during that investigation.

Bond's mansion.

Supposedly an impenetrable fortress.

I knew better and had confirmed it during the hours I'd spent last night hacking into their surveillance and computer systems. Not much had changed in the last four years, and that was a major error on their behalf because it would make what I was about to do that much easier. Knowledge is king, and I had all the knowledge I needed to make this happen.

Leaving my bike, I pulled my leather gloves and ski mask on and walked around the block to the back gate where I knew they had one guy stationed. As I rounded the corner, I took him in. Not as big as he'd appeared on the surveillance footage which went in my favour.

He had his back to me as I approached. When I made it to where he stood, I tapped him on the shoulder, and when he turned to face me, I pointed my gun in his face and reached for his two-way.

"What the fuck?" he sneered. "You *do* realise you're about to have at least three guys on you, right?"

"How long do you give them?" I asked, not wanting to drag this out but unable to resist playing with him a little.

"Less than a minute. Probably less than thirty seconds."

"So they should be here by now, then?"

"Any minute, asshole," he spat out, his nostrils flaring, and his face full of contempt.

I pressed my gun hard against his forehead. "I'll give you a head's up, *asshole* – we'd grow old waiting for them."

Understanding dawned on his face – he finally realised I'd fixed the surveillance so it didn't show anything I was about to do. "Who the fuck are you?"

Yeah, that's the question I'd be asking, too. I put my hand out while I kept my gun firm against his forehead. Ignoring his question, I said, "Give me the keys to the gate and the code." Bond's house had codes all the way through it, but I'd discovered the front gate code changed every hour as an added precaution.

"Fuck you."

I raised my brows. "Really? You'd rather die here and leave a beautiful family behind that I might be inclined to pay a visit to than give me the goddamn keys?"

103

His eyes widened. "You're bullshitting me. You know nothing about me or my family."

"Oh, you'd be surprised what I know, Justin. Like the fact your wife attends pilates every Tuesday morning and your daughter goes to swimming lessons every Thursday afternoon after school but only after your wife makes her weekly stop at Baskin Robbins for ice cream."

He stared at me for a moment, taking all that in. "Motherfucker."

"Yeah, the world's a bitch now that we have all this technology, but the kicker is when someone actually knows how to access that information and use it to their advantage. I'm all your nightmares come to life, so hand the fucking keys over and give me the goddamn code." Time was ticking, and I needed to hurry this along.

He gave me the keys and told me the code.

"Good doing business with you," I muttered as I eyed the fear on his face. "Take a breath, asshole, I'm not gonna shoot you. It's Christmas, and you've got a family to get home to later. But if you get any ideas to do anything crazy, just recall how much I know about your wife and kids."

Before he had a chance to say anything, I punched him hard in the face. He dropped to the ground, and I finished the job with a few more

104

punches. I needed him unconscious long enough for me to get in and get out, which I'd calculated had to be ten minutes at the most.

I moved fast, entering through the back gate, and making my way quickly and quietly along the path to the entrance at the back of the building. The map of the house was burned in my memory, and I needed to get to a room on the other side of the house to where I was. I knew through the research I'd conducted last night that most of the housekeeping staff had been given today off due it to being Christmas Day so that made my goal a little easier. But I had, at most, four guys to get through before I reached my target, so I remained alert and focused, ready to deal with them as they came my way.

The rugs on the floor helped silence the sounds of my boots as I tracked through the rooms. Each room had a locked door on it, and thanks to my research, I had the codes for each door, so I keyed them in as I went. Thank God for a photographic memory. I was halfway to my destination when I came across the first guard. He was sitting in front of a television watching it when he caught sight of me. Surprise crossed his face, and he tried to stand, but I was too quick for him. I moved directly in front of him, and punched him on the cheek with such force it caused him to fall onto the couch. Before he was able to get his bearings and attempt to come back at me, I continued punching him until he was unconscious.

Once I was sure he was out cold, I kept moving through the house. I was almost at my destination when another guard stepped into the hallway in front of me. Surprised, he whipped his gun out fast and aimed it at me. He pulled the trigger, but I ducked just in time to avoid the bullet. As I ducked, I aimed my gun at his foot and shot him there.

"Fuck!" he roared as he collapsed in pain, blood going everywhere. Looking up at me, he demanded, "Who are you?"

I crouched next to him, grabbed his gun from him, and answered, "All your bad dreams rolled into one." And then I punched him. He didn't go down without a fight, though, and attempted to roll away from me.

Watching him, I said, "It's kinda hard to walk when you've been shot in the foot. You could probably limp but you wouldn't be going anywhere fast. And you'd be pissing me off, and then you wouldn't be seeing your son anytime soon if I lost my patience, and decided to shoot you rather than simply knock you unconscious and let you live." I shrugged. "Your choice."

"Leave my family out of this," he snarled.

"Can't do that, seems as though they're all I've got to barter with. And damn, man, that wife of yours? She's a cracker. You wouldn't want to leave her behind." I needed to push him hard so he made the right choice here.

His eyes narrowed on me, assessing, deciding. "You fucking would, too, wouldn't you?"

I could only hazard a guess at what he meant, but it didn't really matter what he meant. All that mattered was the fear I heard in his voice, and that fear was the key to me reaching my goal today. "I would," I agreed.

"What do you want?"

"Ah, now that's a more useful topic of conversation," I said as I advanced towards him. Without hesitation, I pulled my fist back and knocked him out cold in three punches.

I straightened and checked the time on my watch. Still on track.

As I headed down the last part of the hallway before I reached my destination, I prepared myself for what I might walk in on. My target today was Bond's brother, a pig of a man known for his predilection for young boys. I had to remind myself why I was here – to get in, make the kill, and then get out. As much as his preference sickened me, and

I'd prefer to bring him a world of pain today rather than simply end his life, it wasn't part of my plan.

I keyed in the code to his room and entered. He was still asleep. Thank fuck. I moved to his side of the bed and removed his gun from the bedside table. After placing it in his chest of drawers, I made sure there were no other weapons in his reach. When I was convinced there were none, I tapped my gun on his head. "Wake up, motherfucker."

He was a deep sleeper and only stirred slightly, so I moved my mouth closer to his ear, tapped his head harder and said louder than before, "Wake up, Richard. The devil's calling today."

His eyes blinked open and he scrambled to a sitting position. Staring at me, he snapped, "What the fuck?"

The element of surprise was a wonderful tool, and I had my hand wrapped around his throat before he even formed a thought to defend himself. Shoving him hard against the headboard of his bed, I placed my gun to his forehead, and said, "I've got a message from all the boys whose lives you've fucked up. Your dick won't get to ruin anyone else's life." I moved my gun, aimed it at his dick and fired.

He screamed in pain – a glorious fucking sound as far as I was concerned – and yelled some obscenity at me. I hardly heard him. Death had come calling and the thirst for blood had overtaken me.

The thirst for vengeance.

A chance to right so many wrongs.

As the adrenalin flowed through my body, and the need for violence overtook me, I fought not to go there – fought not to let the hunger for revenge consume me. I'd never suffered at the hands of a paedophile but I had an extreme level of hate towards anyone who subjected children to that.

I've got ten minutes.

I need to get out of here.

I took a few steps back, pointed the gun at his chest and without any further thought or conversation, pulled the trigger. The way his eyes widened with fear and the knowledge he was about to die would stay with me, and I had no issues with that. A small price to pay for ridding the world of another piece of scum.

As I backed away further, I aimed the gun at his head and fired again. Then, satisfied he'd taken his last breath, I tucked my gun into my jeans, shrugged the backpack off my back and quickly ripped my shirt off. I had another one on underneath it – one that was clean of blood. As I shoved the blood-splattered shirt in my backpack, I began to make my way out of the house. I'd planned to run into more guards, however none bothered me, and I decided Christmas Day was a good day for this type of work.

Ten minutes later, I was on my way home.

And Danny had his proof I meant every word I'd said.

I never made promises I didn't intend to keep.

Chapter Nine
Sophia

I sat at Josie's table feeling overwhelmed. In all of my twenty-nine years, I'd never experienced a Christmas Day lunch like the one she'd just given me. And it wasn't just about the food. Josie had given me the whole package – amazing food, good company, a beautifully decorated table, thoughtful gifts, and friendship and care on a day that was supposed to be all about those things.

She'd treasured me.

Tears pricked my eyes, and I blinked rapidly in an attempt to stop them from falling. When I stopped blinking, I looked up to find Josie watching me closely. She smiled at me and nodded.

She knows what she's given me.

I returned her smile before standing and saying, "I'll be back in a moment."

She nodded. "Take your time, dear."

Looking around the table at the five other guests, I found them nodding at me, too, with similar expressions on their faces as Josie had on hers. They understood, but of course they did. We were all orphans in one way or another.

I headed outside to sit on Josie's verandah, and as I pushed through her front door, Griff came up the front stairs.

He slowed when he saw me and narrowed his eyes. "Are you okay?" he asked, and I heard the concern in his voice.

I wiped my face; I hadn't been able to stop the tears once I'd left the table, and they flowed down my face now. Nodding, I assured him, "Yes, I just had a moment, but I'll be okay in a minute or so."

He took another few steps up and a moment later he stood next to me. Good God, he smelt good today – sandalwood and something else, and whatever it was, I wanted to buy it by the dozen. I took in his towel-dried hair, the scruff on his face, his dark grey t-shirt and jeans that hugged his muscles, and aviators, and I felt weak in the knees. The fact he stood so close to me didn't help, but it did take my mind off how overwhelmed I'd felt right before he arrived.

"Josie's something else, isn't she?" he said in the gentlest voice I'd ever heard from his lips.

"Yeah, she really is. You're lucky to have her in your life."

"I'll give you some space," he said, and took a step towards the door.

"You don't have to."

He paused, mid-stride. "Yeah, I do." His eyes were trained on mine, and the way he looked at me gave me shivers.

He made no sense to me so I simply nodded and let him go.

I found a chair and sat, letting my thoughts consume me again. Josie had phoned me a couple of days ago and invited me to Christmas lunch. I'd hoped Magan would come with me, but she'd told me she was spending the day with her boyfriend. I'd worked out she spent a lot of time with him, and I only hoped he was a good guy. When I was her age, I'd had terrible taste in guys, and had accepted less than I deserved. Hell, even in my twenties, I still had trouble picking good guys. I was working on that, and had gone on a lot of first dates that didn't eventuate into anything more.

Even though Magan hadn't come today, I'd had a wonderful day with Josie and her friends. They ranged in age from early twenties to possibly late sixties. If I had to hazard a guess, I'd put Josie at about sixty-five.

"Sophia." I turned to find Josie watching me from the door. "I'm making tea and coffee, dear. Would you like a drink?"

I stood and smoothed my dress. "I'll help you make them."

Smiling, she nodded. "Thank you."

I followed her into the kitchen and we worked together to make the drinks. When we carried them to the dining table, my gaze met Griff's briefly. He sat eating the lunch Josie had put aside for him, and as I gave everyone their drinks, I felt his eyes on me, but when I looked back at him, his attention was on his food.

"Sophia, sit," Josie said, motioning for me to take the seat next to Griff instead of returning to the kitchen to help her.

"No, I'll help you clean up."

She tsked me, and Griff chuckled. My head snapped around to look at him. I'd never seen him smile, let alone laugh. He raised his brows. "There's no point arguing with Josie," he explained. "No one wins against her."

Fixed to the spot, I stared at him like an idiot. He'd surprised the shit out of me when he chuckled.

He reached for my chair and pulled it out. "Take a seat, woman, and stop staring at me like you've just seen a unicorn," he muttered.

I did as he said. "Who would have known you had a sense of humour underneath all that?"

"Underneath all what?" he asked as he finished his lunch, and sat back in his chair.

I waved my hand at him. "All that armour you wear."

"You'd be surprised what shit I've got buried underneath all that." He raised a bottle of beer to his mouth and took a long drink, his eyes never leaving mine.

"No, I don't think I would." At his look of doubt, I continued. "I may not have a clue what it is, but you fascinate me enough to know you're not a simple man by any stretch of the imagination. I'm fairly sure you're the most complex man I've ever met."

"It may seem that way, but when it all boils down, I'm fairly simple."

I leant towards him. "Tell me about that. Like, in what way are you simple?" He was deluding himself

115

if he thought he was a simple man. I'd had simple men, and Griff was nowhere near any of them.

"I'm your average guy, Sophia. I like booze, women, and the occasional fight. Not sure how much more simpler you can get."

"I call bullshit. If you were an average guy, you'd have slept with me by now. You'd have sweet talked your way into making me think you were offering me more than a one-night-stand, and you may have even come back for seconds, not even caring that I thought it was headed somewhere. If you were an average guy, you wouldn't have turned up at my house last night to apologise for being a dick, and you sure as hell wouldn't have stuck around and shared parts of your life with me after working out there would be no sex on offer. If you were an average guy, you wouldn't have quietly dealt with the thieving bastard who tried to steal my neighbour's car, for nothing in return. Don't kid yourself, Griff, you're not a simple man. I think you've got a lot to offer a woman, and I hope one day you decide to put yourself back out there." I leant back into my chair and watched as he thought about everything I'd just said. The thing about Griff was that while he wore some of his emotions, he hid most of them, so I struggled to read him. That both frustrated me and excited me.

Finally, he said, "You saw that? The thing with the car?"

I nodded. "Yeah, I saw you beat the dude up and threaten him so he'd never come back. I also know that you made him pay the owner for the damage he'd done, and that when my neighbour put the call out in the neighbourhood to give a reward to whoever helped, you never stepped up."

"Don't give me too much credit. I may not have known about that reward."

"Something tells me you know everything. I bet Mrs. Jones down the road could sneeze and you'd know."

The corners of his lips twitched as if he was about to smile, but he didn't. Instead, he moved his face closer to mine, and murmured, "Something tells me you're very good at reading people."

I stared at him in silence for a moment. "Everyone but you."

His chest rose as he took a deep breath. "You wanna get out of here?"

My eyes widened. I hadn't seen that question coming. "Depends where you're going."

"I feel the need for a long ride today."

"I've never been on a bike and I suck at balance so maybe it's not the best idea." Even as the words came out, I felt disappointment move through me.

Spending time with Griff today would round out an amazing day.

He stood and reached for my hand. "You'll be fine. All you gotta do is hold on tight."

With slight hesitation, I placed my hand in his and let him pull me up. "Let the record show, I'm still not convinced. You can't get upset with me if I fall off."

"Sweetheart, the only person I'd get upset with if you fall off is myself. Trust me when I say, I'm not going to let you do that."

Josie appeared in front of us, her eyes betraying their excitement to see Griff and I talking. "Are you two leaving?"

Griff shook his head and swore under his breath. "Don't make something out of this that isn't there, Josie. We're simply going for a ride."

I grinned. It was kind of cute to see this big, tough man explaining himself to his aunt.

"I'm not making something out of it, Michael. I just needed to know if you were leaving so I could give you your present before you went."

He narrowed his eyes on her. "My present?"

"Yes," she said. "Now don't go getting annoyed at me, it's just a little something."

"I wouldn't dream of it," he muttered, and I swore I could imagine him rolling his eyes at her. I bet he did when he was a kid.

She left us for a minute and returned with a small gift. After giving it to him, she squeezed his hand and said softly, "Open it later."

He nodded, and then placed his hand on the small of my back. "Let's go," he said as he ushered me outside. "Just wait near my bike while I grab you a helmet from under the house."

"You keep a helmet here? What, for Josie to ride with you?"

"Smart ass," he murmured. "I store some of my stuff here because I don't have much storage at my place."

Grinning, I said, "I kinda liked the thought of Josie riding on a motorcycle."

His hand pressed against my back as he directed me in the direction of his bike. "Go. I'll be back in a minute."

It was only a few minutes at the most before he returned and handed me a helmet. "Things you need to know - you can get on once I'm on and have started the bike, keep your feet on the pegs at all times and watch out for the pipes – they get hot – if I lean, you need to lean. And you need to sit as close to me as you can and hold on tight."

119

"What if I need to tell you something? You won't be able to hear me."

"No, I won't, so if you want me to stop, you're gonna have to give me a signal." He contemplated that for a second. "Just point at the side of the road if you want me to pull over, okay?"

I nodded, but my brain had already moved onto the next dilemma I had. "These things," I gestured at the bike, "aren't meant for women wearing dresses, are they?"

His gaze dropped to take in the short dress I wore today. And then he looked back up at my face, and – *holy God* – he had a smile on his face, a sexy ass smile that did good things to me, and said, "They mightn't be made for dresses, but I'm sure as fuck not complaining."

Butterflies took over my stomach. I tried to force them away, because he might be flirting with me but he'd made it abundantly clear nothing would happen between us. But I couldn't force them away. Griff made me feel something I'd never felt from a man before – alive. And he made me feel good about myself in a way no man had before. If I couldn't have him in the way I wanted, I wasn't going to stop myself from having him as a friend.

I pointed at his bike, and said, "Get on before you say something that makes me reconsider everything I've ever said about one-night-stands before."

He smirked. "Bossy...I don't usually like bossy, but rolling off your tongue it sounds good."

"Oh my God, if you don't stop talking, I am going to lose my shit. There's only so much sexy a woman can handle, Griff, and I'm almost at my limit, because let me tell you, just standing next to you is hard work sometimes, so you can only imagine how hard it is to have flirting from your sexy mouth thrown in to the mix. What the heck was I thinking when I agreed to sit on the back of your bike, with my body pressed as close to yours as you're telling me I now have to do, and my arms wrapped around you? I'm going to need a medal for this." And the words just fell out of my mouth. Nervousness always made me ramble, and God how I was rambling now. He'd think I was a neurotic basket case by the end of today.

Full points to him – he processed everything I'd just said, hit me with a smile, and said, "I take it you're ready to get on the bike now."

I nodded and a moment later he was on the bike, ready for me. I put my helmet on, got on, and positioned myself close behind him. The dress hadn't been too much of an issue because it wasn't a tight one, but I did spend a little bit of time making

121

sure it was secured under my ass and legs. The last thing I wanted was for it to fly up and reveal everything during the ride.

I'd placed my hands on his waist to hold on, but he took hold of them and pulled them right around him so they met in the middle. I figured that when he joined them with a firm squeeze, it meant I should keep them there, so I did.

Then he took off, and an exhilaration I'd never experienced flowed through me. I'd often wondered what it would be like riding on a motorcycle, and the reality of it was a hundred times better than anything I ever imagined. And that was just while we were still amongst traffic in Brisbane. When we finally made it out of the traffic and onto the highway where Griff could go faster, it was even more amazing.

We headed out on the highway towards Toowoomba, and rode for about an hour and a half before he found a picnic area away from the road a little to pull into. I was confused as to why he was pulling over, but I figured he must have his reasons.

He cut the engine and pulled his helmet off, so I removed mine, too. Placing his hand on my leg, he said, "Hop off, sweetheart, and stretch your legs."

Now this was something I could get used to. Griff's hand on my leg, him calling me sweetheart, and the gentle tone of his voice. *Especially that tone of his voice.* It hit all my sweet spots.

I did as he said, and as soon as I was standing, I realised why he'd pulled over. Watching as his powerful body moved off the bike, I said, "You stopped to let me stretch."

His eyes found mine and he nodded. "Yeah, figured you might appreciate that."

"Thank you."

I took the opportunity to stretch and walk around for a few minutes before turning back to him. He was leaning against his bike, watching me in a way that clearly told me how much he wanted me. I loved that look on his face, but I didn't know what to do with it. I wanted him just as much – wanted the chance to get to know his deepest thoughts and feelings, his heartache, his biggest regrets, his happiest memories, and the way his body would feel moving against mine. But, damn it, our wants weren't on the table...only our denials.

Frustration overcame me, and I stalked to where he waited. "Don't do that," I said with a little more force than I'd meant to.

"Do what?" he asked, not moving from his spot.

God, he was so cool and calm. And that frustrated me even more. "Don't look at me like that. It's not fair, because I want you, and I can't have you, and when you look at me like that, it turns me on. And what the hell can I do with that if you're not interested enough to consider a relationship with me? Jesus, at this point, I'm gonna have to go home and take care of myself with BOB, and seriously, dude, that's nowhere near as fun as having a man take care of me." I took a moment to get my breathing under control. My frustration had worked itself out into my words and the breaths that were coming hard and fast now.

He moved fast and a second later stood so close to me that I could hear his breaths. His cool demeanour had vanished. A man clearly as affected as I was now stared down at me. "Just being in the same room as you turns me on, Sophia. I met you, what...four days ago, and you're not like any other woman I've known or been with, and as much as I try, I can't get you out of my mind. When you tell me you're gonna need a fucking sex toy to take care of you, it makes me want to throw caution to the wind and make sure you're taken care of, but I refuse to do that to you. You deserve so much more than a man like me."

"From what I know of you, I deserve a man just like you,' I said softly.

His nostrils flared and he shook his head. "No, you don't. If you knew what really lived in me, you would run the other way."

I'd never heard him speak this way. It was like disgust and regret had weaved their way into his voice. I couldn't understand why he would think I wouldn't want anything to do with him. "We've all got secrets and demons that take up residence in us. If we never show them to anyone, how will we know who would choose to accept us regardless of them?"

The vein in his neck pulsed as his eyes turned hard. "Don't push this because, trust me, you wouldn't like where it would go," he said, his voice as hard as his eyes. A shiver ran through me, and I wasn't sure if it was a good shiver or a bad one. It was like a switch had been flipped in him, and while I still felt safe with him, there was an edge I was unsure of now.

Stepping away from him, I nodded. "Okay, you win."

His chest rose and fell quite hard as his breathing picked up. "Good," he said with a nod in return.

I wrapped my arms around my body and rubbed my arms. It was far from cold, but a chill had fallen over me. "Can you please take me home?"

Without another word, he got on his bike and I joined him when he was ready for me. As we sped off in the direction of my house, I wondered what the hell had just happened. We'd been having a great time, and then it was as if the Griff I knew disappeared, and a harder version of him appeared. A version I wasn't sure of. And yet, this new version had my complete attention because he looked at me through eyes of pain, and pain was something I knew well. Pain was what I lived and breathed for years, and my life had only really begun when I finally freed myself from it. And more than anything, I now wanted to help Griff escape his pain.

Chapter Ten
Griff

"I'm no closer to figuring this riddle out, but I'm needed back home," King said the next afternoon when Scott and I met with him and Kick at the clubhouse bar to fill each other in on where we were at with investigating the club members, the fire, and everything else we had going on.

"You're leaving?" Scott asked.

King nodded. "Yeah, but I want you to keep looking. At least one of your boys has been talking and spreading lies, and that shit doesn't sit well with me. I want him identified and dealt with. Soon.

I'd stay but my club's got some trouble to deal with. Fuck, it's never-ending."

"I'll put Nash onto it," Scott promised.

"Good. Tell him not to drag it out. My members are calling for retaliation over this, and I'd like to avoid it. We've got too much other shit going on with the Silver Hell boys, and we don't need any distractions while dealing with that."

"Anything we can help with?" Scott asked.

"I think you've got your hands full, but if we need you, I'll let you know," King said as he started to make his way out. He and Kick said their goodbyes, and a few moments later, Scott and I were alone in the bar. Boxing Day at the clubhouse was quiet with most members spending the day with their families.

"Did you hear from Wilder?" I asked.

He scowled. "Yeah, he asked me for another twenty-four hours."

Frowning, I said, "This chick has to be someone he's close to, but I've never heard him talk about anyone for as long as I've known him. You?"

"No. I've given him until tomorrow morning to bring me the information so we'll know everything then."

"And if he doesn't?"

He rubbed the back of his neck. "It won't be pretty, Griff. Not with the mood I'm in."

"I'm behind you one hundred percent, brother. Whatever you need from me, you have."

He eyed me. "I always said the day you joined Storm was a good day. If there's one member whose loyalty has never been questioned, it's you."

I fought to hold his gaze as a sense of unease slid through me. All I could hope was that my loyalty never would be questioned. Storm was my chosen family now and I would fight till my death for family, regardless of what they might think if my past was exposed.

***

I arrived at my usual drinking spot around eight that night, and chose a quiet table in the corner instead of my seat at the bar. The waitress came to take my order and I ensured she would just keep the drinks coming. I'd need them tonight.

Leaning back in my seat, my thoughts drifted to Sophia. She'd been upset with me when I'd dropped her back at her house yesterday afternoon, and I didn't blame her, but it didn't mean my stance had changed. And I'd been more than okay with her being upset with me; it made it easier to keep my distance.

Who the hell are you kidding?

I took a long swallow of my drink. Fuck, I wanted her in a way I'd never wanted a woman. Not even Charlene. Sophia was the kind of woman who gave a man hope he could do better and be better. Her lightness shone all over my darkness, and sometimes, even if only for a sliver of time, she made me feel like a good man. And I hadn't felt like a good man in far too long.

My phone rang, distracting me from my thoughts.

Danny.

"Evening," I greeted him.

"Fuck, Michael, what the hell are you doing?"

Time to tread carefully – one never knew when someone was recording a conversation. "Sitting in a bar minding my own business."

"Don't give me that shit. You know what the hell I'm talking about."

"Get to the point, Danny."

"My point is that this changes nothing except for the fact it has stirred up the Bond family. They're calling for retribution and that's gonna cause me and my buddies more headaches that we don't have time for."

"I gave you an alternative suggestion the other night."

"There's no way Bond is walking out of prison. I've worked too damn hard for that to be an option. As far as I'm concerned, he'll rot in there for all the crimes he has committed."

"I'd say this conversation is done then."

"Yeah, it is," he agreed and hung up.

As I placed my phone on the table, I had a different thought to the one he'd just expressed. This might not have changed anything on his end, but it had proven to me that the Bond family wasn't as untouchable as they liked to think they were. If need be in the future, I had the knowledge and tools to stand my ground with them. And I was pretty fucking sure that if the trial went ahead, I'd need every available weapon I could find to go up against them.

I took another long swallow of my drink and assessed the bar tonight. Not too busy, but it was Boxing Day. As I looked around, a woman across the room smiled at me and raised her glass. She looked to be either my age or a little older, with blonde hair that was a shade just a little too white for my liking. Her clothing was all tight and skimpy in a way that did nothing for me. I shifted my attention from her and kept eyeing the room, however a minute or so later, she joined me.

Sliding into the seat across from me, she purred, "Hello, sexy. I couldn't not come and say hi after we just had that moment."

Raising my brows, I asked, "Is that what you call a moment?"

"Yeah, isn't it what you would call a moment?"

Fuck. I wasn't even sure what the hell a moment was. "I've never had a moment to know what I'd call one."

She couldn't hide her surprise. "Well, hell, I'd be more than happy to give you a few moments."

All this fucking talk of moments was making me irritable. "I'm right, thanks."

"How about I buy us a drink and we can get to know each other?"

"I'm not interested in getting to know anyone." I hated to be a prick like this, but some women didn't know how to take no for an answer so I'd learnt the best way was to piss them off.

She gave me a huge smile, and I knew this was going to be drawn out. This woman was the kind who never got the message. "Never met a man who I couldn't make mine for the night, and I'm not starting tonight. I'll get us a drink and you'll see how good I can make it for you."

I stood. "No need. I was just leaving," I announced and made a move to leave.

"Really? You're not even gonna give me a chance?"

"It's not you, babe. I've got a woman who I can't get off my mind, so I'm going to say no and let you find a man who is right for you. That man isn't me."

She smiled. "They don't make men like you very often anymore. Go and tell that woman how you feel. And I'll find me a man, don't you worry."

I had no doubt she would. Leaving her, I headed outside to hail a cab. Five minutes later, I was on my way to Sophia's house. It was the last place I wanted to go, but, fuck, it was the one place I was beginning to think I needed to be.

***

Her wary eyes narrowed on me. "What are you doing here, Griff? It's late and I thought we covered everything yesterday."

"I thought we'd covered everything, too. Turns out I'm not done. It seems you're the only thing I can think of at the moment, and at a time of year I usually reserve for other thoughts, it's confused the fuck out of me that you can so easily steal their place."

She didn't say anything straight away, and I began to think she was going to turn me away. But then she said softly, "How do you do that?"

"Do what?"

"Every now and then you bare a piece of your soul to me and it makes me want to know more about you. It makes me want to know everything."

I sucked in a breath. *Don't say that.* "Can I come in?" I placed one foot inside her house, willing her to say yes.

She made my fucking night when she took a step back and ushered me in. I didn't give her a chance to change her mind, and strode in towards her kitchen. When I reached my destination, I turned to look at her. Jesus, she was something else. Dressed in a pair of those denim shorts that killed me every-fucking-time and a white almost see-through t-shirt, with her hair pulled up in a ponytail and her face free of makeup, she was easily the most beautiful woman I had ever met.

Moving past me into the kitchen, she grabbed a glass out of a cupboard and poured herself a drink of water. Resting her back against the kitchen counter and one foot on the other, she sipped her drink and said, "So, you came to talk or to screw me?"

Fuck.

134

Straight to the point.

I rubbed the back of my neck and frowned. "I don't really know."

She stared at me for a long minute before placing her drink on the counter and moving to where I stood. Taking my face in her hands, she brushed her lips across mine, and fuck if my dick didn't react straight away. Her touch was like a lightning bolt through me, lighting every nerve ending on fire.

I groaned into her mouth. I knew I should stop her, but I couldn't. This woman had crawled under my skin and I was helpless to stop my need for her. I slid one hand around her neck and gripped her there while my other hand moved to hold the back of her head. Deepening the kiss, my tongue found hers and I kissed her in a way I hadn't kissed a woman in a long time.

Fuck knew how long we kissed for. It was both heaven and hell for me - a constant push and pull of needs. All I wanted to do was take her body and bend it to give me what I desired – *what I needed* – but I refused to break her, so I denied myself.

She ended the kiss, and stared into my eyes. "You wanna talk about the thoughts you usually reserve for this time of year?"

"No."

"Well, there's your answer, handsome. It seems you came here to screw me."

I still had hold of her, and I moved one of my hands to grip her ponytail. Yanking it back, I bent my mouth to her neck and sucked her hard enough that I was almost biting her. The moan that escaped her lips only encouraged me, and while I was fighting my urges as hard as I could, I lost my battle for a moment. My teeth sunk into her skin and I marked her neck.

When I was finished, I lifted my face and loosened my grip on her hair slightly. "You don't do one-night stands, sweetheart, so it seems we have a small problem there."

Her eyes watched me for a beat, and next minute, she had her hands on my jeans and had undone the button and was sliding the zip down.

Fuck.

"Careful," I warned. "Once you signal your move, there's no going back."

She took hold of my cock and gripped me firmly before moving her hand up and down my length. "I'm breaking my one-night-stand rule for one night, and I'm trusting you to make it worth my while."

"Jesus," I muttered, not convinced this was the right thing, but knowing there was no way I could stop now even if I wanted to.

Ah, fuck it. I moved my hands to her ass and lifted her into my arms. "Which way to your bedroom?"

As she placed her arms around my neck to hold on, she said, "Down the hall and to your left. It's the room at the end of the hallway."

Without wasting anymore time, I strode down the hall and found her bedroom. She had a room that matched her personality exactly. Classy with mostly white throughout, and a touch of black here and there. She also had one of those tables women sit at to apply their makeup, and I took in the jewellery and perfume that covered it. Hell, I already knew Sophia loved perfume – she always smelled fucking amazing.

I placed her on the floor next to the bed, and let my gaze travel over her body. "Have you got any idea what those shorts do to a man?" I asked as I reached out to undo them.

"They're comfortable," she said, as if she was justifying her choice.

I flicked the button undone and pulled the zip down before stripping them off her. "Much more comfortable now," I said as I took in the strip of lace covering her pussy.

My dick jerked and I restrained myself from tearing that piece of lace in half. Instead, I lifted her shirt over her head and dropped it on the floor before reaching around to undo her bra. As much as it would have been fun to drag this part out, she and I had been dancing around each other for too many days now, and I struggled to even go this slowly.

I did, however, leave her panties on.

My mouth had plans for those.

"Sit," I ordered her, pointing at the bed.

Her eyes widened a little, but she did as I'd said. In that moment, I knew my suspicions had been correct – Sophia had never been dominated in the bedroom.

I removed my clothes and stood naked in front of her. Taking hold of my cock, I stepped closer to her and reached for the back of her head. Pulling her mouth to me, I said, "I want you to suck me."

I caught the widening of her eyes again, and wondered if she'd back out, but she didn't. She took hold of my dick and sucked me into her mouth. Jesus, her warm mouth felt fucking amazing around me. And when she began sucking and licking with her tongue, I closed my eyes as the pleasure moved through me.

138

My grip on the back of her head tightened, and as she moved me closer to orgasm, I held her head to me, needing to feel my dick at the back of her throat. The gagging sounds she made got me even harder, and I wondered if she would make me come. It usually took a lot fucking longer for me, but Sophia worked me with her mouth, lips, tongue and hand so fucking well that I could well orgasm as fast as a horny teenager tonight.

She got me close and I almost came but I decided to prolong it. Pulling out of her mouth, I reached my hands under her arms and pulled her up. The way she stared at me told me she thought I was going to kiss her, and I was, just not where she imagined I would. I moved one of my legs so I could kick her feet apart before dropping to my knees. My hands gripped her ass as my mouth moved over her panties. Her scent invaded me, and *god-fucking-damn* if it wasn't the best thing I'd ever smelt. I used my teeth to remove her panties and when I finally had them off, I worshipped her pussy with my mouth. She was bare which I loved, and I ran my tongue the length of her, stopping every now and then to place kisses on her skin.

Her hands threaded through my hair and my mouth stilled for a moment. It wasn't something I'd experienced for a long time, but it felt good to have a woman's hands in my hair.

"Griff," she almost moaned, "I love what you're doing, but I need your mouth all over me, and I want you inside me."

Fuck.

I stood, and quickly picked her up and placed her on the bed. Positioning myself over her, I took hold of her wrists and pinned them to the mattress above her head. I then placed my other hand around her neck for a moment before moving it down her body to take hold of one of her breasts. My gaze followed my hand and lingered on her breasts before shifting back to meet her gaze. "We're going to make the most of this one night, Sophia. No fucking way am I having you fast. I'm going to taste every last inch of your skin before I give you my cock," I said as I moved my hand down to her pussy and pushed a finger inside, watching closely as her eyes flared with desire. Bending my face close to hers, I growled, "Never tasted a pussy as good as yours, so believe me when I say this is gonna be a long night. I need to get my fill."

She lifted her head off the bed to catch my lips in a kiss. Her mouth pressed gently to mine, and I let her have it her way for a moment before pushing for more. The way her body arched up into mine as I kissed her deeper and harder told me she loved the fuck out of this kiss, and that only made me try and drag more from her. I needed to take everything I could from her tonight.

Ending the kiss, I dipped my face to her neck and began to sample every inch of her skin as I'd promised her I would. And fuck, the hollows and curves of her body were as sinful as I'd thought the first time I'd laid eyes on her. The man Sophia chose to give herself to for life would be one lucky fucker. This woman was built for pleasure and I made the most of every second I had her.

As I moved down her body pressing kisses all over her, she tangled her fingers in my hair again and made the sexiest fucking sounds I'd ever heard. And when she moaned my name every now and then, my dick threatened to explode.

I fucking need to be inside her.

I tasted my way down to her thighs before lifting my head and finding her eyes. She stared at me for a beat before moving so fast I didn't have time to think. A moment later, I was kneeling on her bed, with her wrapped around me, and her lips to mine again. Gone was the gentle Sophia who'd kissed me before, and in her place was a fucking goddess who had abandoned herself to the pleasure.

She kissed me hard, and when she pulled away, breathless, she said, "God, I've never had a man like you before. Please don't ever stop." Her wild eyes searched mine, and, *fuck*, she was a sight with her messy hair, swollen pink lips and an expression that screamed out how much she loved this.

My arms tightened around her, and I growled, "We can go all night, but I need to fuck you now. There's not a chance in hell I can last another minute without being inside you."

Without giving her time to say anything, I shifted us so she was on her back, ready for me. "Stay there, and don't move," I ordered.

I then left her to find a condom in my jeans, and when I had it on, I came back to her. I gripped her thighs, and pushed her legs apart. Positioning myself at her entrance, I bent to take one of her nipples into my mouth. And then I lightly bit her, and she cried out, but the way her back arched up off the bed told me she loved that.

I reached down to run my finger through her pussy to make sure she was still ready for me, and when I found what I was looking for, I thrust my dick inside her as hard and as far as I could. My palms rested on the bed on either side of her, and her legs wrapped around me, and I thrust in and out, over and over. Her cunt was tight and wet, and fucking perfect.

We watched each other while I fucked her, and I loved seeing her lose herself in the pleasure. Loved watching her completely surrender to it. Fuck, I craved that from her.

I wanted her to give herself over to me completely.

I wanted to take power over her.

I fucking wanted to own her body, even if just for tonight.

"Fuck!" I roared as I orgasmed. My body tensed as it wound its way along my spine and through my body. I dug my palms into the bed as it consumed me. And I lost myself in it enough for Sophia to take the moment and kiss me through it. Her mouth on mine felt so goddamn good that I couldn't drag my lips from hers. I opened myself up to her and allowed her to wring every drop of whatever-the-fuck she was after from that kiss.

And when her pussy squeezed around my dick, and she came, I thought I might come all over again it felt that good. Instead, I waited for her to finish, and then I collapsed onto the bed next to her.

After I'd caught my breath, I left her to go and dispose of the condom, and then came straight back. I'd intended to have her again, but she curled into me and closed her eyes as she let out a long sigh. I lay next to her for a long time, listening to her sleep. Sophia was a quiet sleeper but every now and then a soft moan escaped her lips. Christ, this woman exuded a sexiness she wasn't even aware of, and that turned me on so damn much.

My intention hadn't been to stay the night, but tiredness crept over me and I closed my eyes. As sleep claimed me, I had a vague sense of arms and legs over my body, but I couldn't bring myself to open my eyes. I drifted off into a deep sleep, and for once, the nightmares didn't claim me.

Chapter Eleven
Sophia

I pulled my legs up onto the armchair and curled them under me. Resting the sketchpad on my lap, I finished off the drawing I'd started on Christmas night after the bike ride with Griff.

Another one of him.

The man inspired me. I hadn't picked up my sketchpad as much in the last six months as I had this week. I'd been so consumed with a huge workload, buying and renovating my first home, and spending time with Magan, that I'd lost the urge to draw. Making art had gone by the wayside, too, and this had all concerned me somewhat because as long as I could remember, doing those two things had been like breathing to me. Creating had always been my saviour - a solace in shitty times. Over the years, as I'd grown older and started putting my pieces back together, creating had become food for my soul more than anything.

"Morning."

Startled, I jumped and knocked the sketchpad onto the floor. Looking up, I found Griff leaning against the doorjamb with his arms folded across his chest while he watched me. He'd dressed in his jeans, but his chest was bare, and I couldn't help but stare at his muscles for a few moments. I'd expected to find ink on his skin, and while he did have a Storm logo on his back, the rest of him was free of ink. He also didn't have his boots on, and there was something about a man standing in front of me barefoot and shirtless – the vision made my tummy flutter.

"Shit," I muttered. "Way to give a woman a heart attack."

I scrambled off the chair to retrieve the sketch before he saw it. He didn't need to know I'd now drawn him twice this week. However, he pushed off from the door and bent to pick up the pad at the same time as me. Luckily, I got to it first and scooped it up before he could.

As we both stood, the corners of his lips curled into a smile. "Been drawing again, sweetheart?" he asked, and I wanted to take the pad and smack him with it.

I closed the pad and placed it on my desk. We were in my art room and while he spent a minute looking it over, I asked, "Did you sleep well?"

His gaze came back to me. "Yes." He seemed a little distant, as if he was thinking about something.

"Do you want some coffee?" I asked, ignoring the fact he was a little lost in his thought. At his nod, I led the way into the kitchen.

"You look like you've been awake for hours," he observed as I made the coffee.

It was still only early – six thirty – but I'd been awake since four. "I suffer from insomnia so I'm always awake from around three."

"So you draw?"

I eyed him as I poured hot water from the kettle into our mugs. "Not always. Some mornings I paint, others, I read. And there's always movies – they get me through hours of sleeplessness."

"Painting...as in art? Or do you paint walls at three am?"

I smiled. "Art. I really dislike painting walls. I mean, I'll do it, and I love the result, but damn, that job requires the kind of discipline and attention I don't have in me."

His eyes narrowed on me. "What does that mean?"

Passing him his coffee, I explained, "I'm more of a fly-by-the-seat-of-my-pants kinda girl. I make shit up as I go, and love spontaneity. Painting a wall requires doing a job in a particular way and not missing any steps, you know? Steps annoy me. I don't want steps."

Amusement flickered in his eyes and a faint smile touched his lips. He drank some coffee and then said, "Steps are a necessary evil a lot of the time."

I held my coffee in both hands and shook my head. "Yeah...no. I'd rather live in Sophia world – there's no steps there," I said with a wink.

He caught my wink and stilled. I almost expected him to shut down on me because it seemed to be his thing whenever he stilled like that, but he surprised me. "Tell me about Sophia world."

"What do you want to know?"

"What do you do for a living?"

"Graphic design. I design business logos and branding mostly, but I've been doing it for about five years now, and I think I'm getting to the point where I need a change. And the company I work for are a bunch of assholes who make us work overtime with no pay, and that sucks."

"What type of work would you prefer?"

"I would love to paint for a living, and no, I don't mean the wall variety of painting," I said with a smile. "God, can't you just imagine travelling the world painting all the amazing things you see? My dream has always been to get paid to make art, but realistically, I'd still do graphic design, just for a different company."

He watched me in a way that made me nervous – it was like his eyes were undressing my soul, trying to figure something out. I waited for him to say something but he didn't. He drank the rest of his coffee and moved to the sink to rinse his mug out. Turning back to me, he said, "I've gotta get to work."

My heart sunk a little. I didn't know what I'd expected; I mean, he'd made it clear he was only interested in one night, but a part of me had hoped if he had his night, he'd find something that made him come back for more. I'd hoped for more this morning, and when he'd asked me about my work, I'd gotten my hopes up.

I couldn't fault him, though. I knew the score.

"Okay," I said, and watched as he left me to go and get dressed.

God, he was such a complex man. Sex with him had been like no other sex I'd ever had. He'd been so bossy and intense in a way that turned me on more than I'd ever been turned on in my life, but there'd been something else there – something I wasn't sure of. He'd told me he was close to losing control, and I wondered what that actually meant. The look in his eyes had scared me a little, but at the same time, I felt completely safe with Griff, so it was like one big contradiction.

I want to know everything about him.

I headed into my bedroom where he'd gone and found him sitting on the side of the bed putting his boots on. "Do you want to have a shower?"

He glanced at me, a strange look in his eyes. "I'm good."

"How about breakfast? I can't let you go to work hungry. How about I cook you some bacon and eggs? Or an omelette, or pancakes... I've got the ingredients for all those so it wouldn't be a problem. You choose." I stared at him, waiting for his reply, my belly alight with butterflies under his gaze.

He didn't speak straight away, but rather finished putting his boots on and then stood. "You knew what this was," he said. "And it was never going to involve breakfast."

Disappointment speared my heart, but it was all my fault because he was right. I'd known it wouldn't be a sex-and-breakfast night.

Shit. Why had I broken my one-night stand rule?

Because you thought you could change him.

I'd deluded myself. Griff wasn't the kind of man a woman changed.

I took a step back. "Yeah, you're right," I finally said.

He watched me for a few moments and then nodded, as if he'd made up his mind about something.

And then he walked out of my house without a second glance.

And I crawled onto my bed and curled up into a ball, accepting that I'd brought this upon myself, but still letting the hurt wash through me.

***

Five hours later, I sat in the sun by the pool at my friend, Zara's, house. Today was her annual Christmas pool party and it was exactly what I needed.

Sun, warmth, friends and cocktails.

"It's a man, right?" Zara said as she passed me a margarita.

"Am I that obvious?" I took a long sip and smiled at the familiar taste. Tequila and me were old friends.

Tania, who lay on the sun lounger next to me, laughed. "Your heartbreak is bleeding all over you, babe. Spill."

"Ugh. It's not heartbreak – I hardly know the guy for it to be heartbreak. It's just my stupidity making me feel like an idiot."

Zara's eyes widened. "You broke your one-night-stand rule, didn't you?" She settled next to me and stared, waiting for my reply.

Nodding, I confessed, "Yeah, I did. And the stupid part of all this was that he made it crystal clear he only wanted one night, so it's my fault that I'm disappointed."

"You also broke rule number one in the women's handbook, didn't you?" Tania said.

"What rule is that?" I asked as I drank more of my drink. Besides my one-night-stand rule, I wasn't really a rules-following kind of girl.

She sighed. "I really need to teach you more stuff. Rule number one is that you can't change a man. He might come around, but you can't change

152

who he is at his core. Any change has to come from him. And remember, once a stubborn ass, always a stubborn ass. Same as, once a lying douche, always a lying douche."

I laughed. "What's the second rule in this handbook?"

"Men are a lot of hard fucking work. Only tread where you're willing to put the work in." She raised her glass at me and grinned. "You're welcome for that information, by the way. Us girls have gotta stick together and look out for each other." She took a huge gulp of her margarita and then added with a wink, "Let's get drunk today; I need to get drunk so I can forget your heartbreak."

Laughing again, I said, "You'd use any excuse for a drink, but I'm down. Let's drink!"

"Wait," said Zara. "At least tell us the sex was awesome. There's gotta be one good thing from all this, right?"

My core lit up just thinking about how good the sex had been. "Best sex I've ever had."

"Thank goodness for that! At least the man gave you some good memories you can call on in lonely times." Zara winked at me as she said this. She was right – I would definitely use Griff for inspiration when I had to rely on BOB.

One of the other party guests bomb dived into the pool at that moment, distracting us from our conversation, and completely covering us in water. As Tania and Zara grumbled about being wet, I jumped up and dived into the pool. If you couldn't beat them, join them.

"Come on!" I motioned to the girls. "It's beautiful in the water." The heat of the day was forgotten as I did a lap of the pool.

Zara and Tania eventually joined me, and we got a game of water volleyball going. One way or another, I would put Griff out of my mind today.

Chapter Twelve
Griff

As I stared out at the tree in my backyard where my family's ashes were buried, the brutal humidity clung to me, but I hardly noticed it as memories of my father filled my mind. These memories were the reason why I only allowed myself to think about him once a year. My father had been a hard man. A man with his own demons; a man who struggled with how to cope with those demons. And in the end, history repeated itself and the sins of the father became the sins of the son as he did to his children what had been done to him.

I took a deep breath.

Fuck.

I swallowed the rest of my drink and turned to go back inside and came face to face with my cousin who had been standing behind me.

"Michael."

I scowled. It had been two years since he'd cut me out of his life, and he was the last person I wanted to see today. "What are you doing here?"

He'd aged quite noticeably since I'd last seen him. Grey peppered his hair, lines etched his face and the weight had crept on. The life of a cop was not kind to the body. I knew that from my father, too.

"It's ten years today."

"Your point?" I fought to remain calm as the rage built in me. I wasn't sure if this current rage came from the ten years or the last two.

"I thought you might be one of those sentimental bastards who marked these kinds of things." His shoulders were tense as if he were ready for an argument.

"Sentimental and me don't go in the same sentence. You should know that by now."

"The Michael I knew is long gone; I'm not sure of anything about you anymore."

"You're the one who walked and chose not to know anything about me anymore so don't come here and give me that bullshit."

He shook his head. "No, you're the one who chose Storm and they're the ones who changed you."

Pain shot through my head as a headache began to take shape. The tightrope of control I walked threatened to snap, and I clenched and unclenched my fists in an attempt not to use them. "Storm were the only ones who accepted me for who the fuck I was, Danny. And as much as you never wanted to acknowledge it, the great and fucking almighty Rod McAllister made me into the man I am. Don't put that shit on my club."

He scowled. "Your father was a good man. So he believed in punishing his kids when they did something wrong...that didn't make him a bad man."

The ghosts of my past collided with the self-control I dedicated hours to daily. I stepped closer to him, and snarled. "Taking to a child with a belt over and over is not punishment for being naughty. Locking a child in a dark cupboard for hours isn't either. And tying them up and ridiculing them sure as fuck isn't written in the *Good Parenting* manual." My head felt like it would explode off my

157

shoulders as I got to the family history that fucked me up more than my own experiences. "Having to watch as your father did the same to your brother, but worse because he believed your brother was a little 'cock-loving shit' – as my father called him – was like a living hell. My father may have been respected by his cop buddies and adored by those higher, but in my house, there was no respect and no adoration for that man. And if you think Storm has made me into who I am today, you wouldn't be far off the mark. My brothers have shown me what it's like to have a family who give a shit about me and they're teaching me to give a shit again."

My cousin was an asshole. Growing up, we'd been close and he'd had my back, but I'd figured out a couple of years ago just how much the badge can change a man. I'd seen it at the academy in my time there, and my decision to leave was the best damn decision I'd ever made in my life. Danny stood in front of me now, listening to everything I'd said, but I knew the truth still wouldn't alter his perception of my father. And I was right. "Why did you avenge his death then? If you hated him so much, surely you would have been celebrating his murder."

"For a smart man, you can be dumb some times. I did that for my mother and brother." Images of

158

their tortured bodies flooded my mind, and I sucked in a deep breath as the rage swam behind my eyes. I could have cared less that my father had been tortured – he deserved every second of pain he went through. But my mother and brother should *never* have been subjected to any of it.

He cocked his head. "Why did you stay in Storm once you figured out they weren't the ones to blame? I never could wrap my head around that."

Trying to explain my reasoning for something *I* even struggled to understand at the time was like trying to explain the blind faith I used to put in God. Faith is trust in action. It's something believed in, not from proof, but from feel and a deeply held belief. I may have ended up in Storm for all the wrong reasons, but it was my faith in them that kept me there. "They cared about me." I may have given him only four words, but those four words packed a punch. Sometimes you didn't need a lot of words to explain yourself.

He scrunched his face. "What the fuck? I cared about you. My family cared about you. You can't fucking say we didn't."

"There are many ways to care, but needing the person you supposedly care about to change themselves *for* you...that's not the kind of care that's good for a person, Danny. I always had to

159

prove myself to you and your family; always had to tow a fucking line and fit in with who you thought I should be. Storm might have expectations, but they never once tried to change who I am."

He looked at me in disgust and I knew we were done here. Probably done for life. "I will never understand you or your choices. I've tried to help you over the years but you've made your decision and now you have to accept whatever consequences that decision brings you. Don't come crawling back to me when the shit hits the fan."

"I don't ever come crawling to anyone, asshole, and I'm not about to start now. I rely on one person, and one person only – me. Less chance of getting screwed over that way." I took a step away from him and said, "Now, if you've said all you came here to say, I suggest you fuck off and leave me to get on with my night."

He sneered at my words as he made a move to leave. "You always were a bastard, Michael. You've managed to take it to a whole new level."

"It works well in my life," I muttered and turned to walk inside.

I didn't glance back at him – I had no intention of looking back anymore.

Danny and I were done.

***

A couple of hours later, I was a few drinks in, watching mindless television in my lounge room, and trying unsuccessfully to shift thoughts of Sophia from my mind. It astounded me that on the day I usually couldn't delete shitty family memories, I was this year, instead, being bombarded by a woman.

I'd treated her exactly the way she'd told me she didn't want to be treated. Used and discarded. I hadn't intended for that to happen – fuck, I hadn't intended to have sex with her, but I couldn't have said no to her even if I'd wanted to. She had no idea how beautiful she was, and no idea how much I'd wanted her from that very first time we'd met in the car park at the bar. Hell, that was half her allure. The beauty of a woman who was unaffected by it was, by far, one of my biggest turn-ons. And, Christ, the way she lived in her vulnerability and let her mask fall – that sealed the deal for me.

Fuck.

I want her.

Again.

I couldn't do it, though. We'd had our night, and now I needed to move on and find a woman who could take what I needed to give. Sophia was not the woman for me.

My phone buzzed on the seat next to me.

Scott: Can you meet me and Wilder at the clubhouse now?

Thank fuck – a distraction.

Me: On my way.

***

I walked into Scott's office to find him and Wilder deep in conversation, and a woman in her early-twenties sitting on the chair in the corner. Her feet tapped in front of her like she was nervous about something and her hands fidgeted in her lap. When I got to her face, I realised why. She was craving a hit.

"Griff," Scott said, looking at me. "Wilder's got that info we were after."

I jerked my chin at the woman. "Who's she?"

Wilder faced me with a look I'd never seen on his face before. Fuck, she meant something to him. I hoped this situation wasn't about to fuck us in the ass more than it already had. "Carly is my ex. She was dating Slug."

"Shit," I said. "And she knows something about the fire?"

Wilder nodded. "Yeah, she said he started it."

"Why?"

Carly joined in the conversation. "Because he was threatened by Ricky Grecian that if he didn't do it, he'd be killed."

My eyes met Scott's and he nodded once at me. Ricky fucking Grecian.

I turned my attention back to Carly. "What's the connection between Ricky and Slug?"

She looked blankly at me. "Huh?"

I took the few strides to where she sat, and crouched in front of her. Placing my hands on the armrests of her chair, I got in her face. "What the fuck did Ricky have on Slug to even make him give that ultimatum to him? There had to be something between them." I needed to know if she was telling the truth. Junkies had a way of making shit up when it suited them.

She glared at me and leant forward. "Slug owed him a fortune for drugs, and Slug's never been good at paying his debts. I'd say Ricky got sick of his shit."

I watched her closely, and decided there was truth to what she was saying. Pushing up, I stood

163

and turned back to Scott. "Looks like Blade's prediction was spot on – Ricky's playing with us."

Anger sat on Scott's face. "Yeah, brother. So now we have to figure out a way to play back."

"Any news on that drug deal?" We'd never gotten to the bottom of that, and the fire had consumed our attention over the last few days. The fact Ricky had never come back to us on the deal was of concern.

Scott pulled out his phone. "Let me call Ricky and find out where he's at with that."

"I'll be back in a minute," I said and headed out of the office. It was just after nine pm and the club bar was busy with members blowing off steam. I was working on rebuilding relationships so I spent some time chatting with the boys. I was also trying to get a feel for who might be causing problems for Scott and King, but I had no luck on that front tonight.

When I entered Scott's office again, he'd finished his call with Ricky. "What gives?" I asked.

"Apparently it's going to take place in four days. He won't tell me where so we need to get some eyes on him. I wanna tail him and see who the fuck it is. He's still adamant his source is saying it's us, so someone is screwing with us, brother."

"Agreed."

"Can you round Nash and J up for that job?"

I nodded. "Consider it done."

"Tell them I wanna know everything Ricky does – who he sees and where he goes. I want confirmation that he was the one who gave the orders for the fire and once we have that, we're not holding back on him."

"I've increased security at all our premises, too. We can't afford to have any more businesses closed down."

"Good thinking, brother."

The last thing we needed was Storm to lose its sources of income.

Chapter Thirteen
Sophia

The sounds of the office reverberated around me, and the headache I'd had since I woke up this morning intensified. It was the first day back at work since Christmas and I wasn't feeling it. The pool party yesterday had worn me out – between the alcohol and the sun, I'd been exhausted last night. Sleep had actually been my friend for the first time in ages, and I'd slept right through until six this morning. But now, at eleven thirty, I was ready to call it quits. Pity I still had another five and a half hours to go.

"Sophia, have you finished that design for the Dawson job yet?"

I looked up from my computer to find my boss, Andrew, standing in front of my desk looking at me with demanding eyes. He was always demanding something, and I was almost at breaking point with him. There was something to say for manners and office etiquette, but sadly he'd skipped that lesson in his work life.

"Yes, I emailed you the info about ten minutes ago." *Take that, asshole.*

"I should have had it half an hour ago."

Oh my, God. Seriously?

My face burnt as the anger moved through me. Clenching my fists so that I didn't give him the finger, I said, "You're interrupting my time here, Andrew. I'm almost finished with the next job so if you want that on time, I'd recommend you leave me be for the afternoon."

His eyes widened. "There's no need for snarky comments."

"I beg to differ. You throw out nastiness like it's going out of fashion, and I've put up with it for years now. I need you to know that starting from today, I'm not putting up with it any longer." I maintained eye contact with him and stood my ground. He couldn't fire me, but he could make my

167

work life more of a misery than it already was. And I guessed, he could talk to his superior and she could fire me. So this was a risky move, but screw it, I'd had enough.

Anger rolled off him as he said, "We'll see about that." As he stalked to his office, I wondered what that meant, but I wasn't wondering for too long because my phone rang, diverting my attention.

Magan.

"Hey sis, what's up? It's not like you to call me in the middle of the day."

"Sophia..." Her voice cracked and my skin prickled with apprehension. Something wasn't right. "It's Mum."

I frowned. "Who? Your foster mum?"

She was silent for a beat. "No. Our mum."

My heart dropped to my stomach and my hand curled tighter around my phone. "What do you mean? I don't understand..." My thoughts ran through my mind uncontrollably and my throat turned dry.

What the hell does she mean, 'our mum'.

"I mean, our mother needs us. She's sick in the hospital and has asked for both of us to go to her," she snapped, anger clear in her voice. "Can you come pick me up so we can go and see her?"

168

I hadn't seen my mother since I was nine. Twenty years was a long time not to see or hear from the woman who was supposed to love you forever and teach you everything you needed to know to navigate life and love. The thought of seeing her today terrified the hell out of me and I wasn't sure why.

"Sophia, are you there?" Magan's voice had an urgency to it and I realised she was desperate to see our mother.

"What's wrong with her? And how do you know this?" I asked. My brain was scrambling to make sense of it all, but I was coming up short today.

"They think she's had a heart attack. Sophia, *she* asked for them to call us."

I ignored the part about Mum asking for us, grabbed my bag and said, "I'll come pick you up now."

"Thank you," she said and I could hear the relief in her voice.

I ended the call and left the office without informing Andrew. I didn't need one of his high and mighty lectures about putting work first...not today.

***

"You're not coming in?" Magan stared at me in confusion as I parked my car at the hospital.

God, even just sitting in the car park of the same hospital my mother was in caused nerves to shoot through me. I didn't understand my reaction, and I needed some quiet time to process it all. "I'm not ready to see her just yet," I said softly.

Frown lines marred her forehead. "But haven't you wanted to see her your entire life? I don't understand."

"I have,' I said carefully, "but I'd accepted I would never see her again. That took me a long time and a lot of work to get to, and to now be presented with this...I need some time to get my head around it, that's all."

"She might die! You might never get to see her again." Her eyes were wild with confusion and a desperation I knew well. I'd suffered from that same desperation while growing up – desperate to see my mother again and to know that she really *did* love me even if she'd never told me or shown me.

I nodded and took a deep breath. "I know. And that's something I'll have to deal with if it happens, but *for me*, right now, I need to not see her today. I know that won't make any sense to you, and I'm sorry, but I can't come in with you."

Frustration took over her features as she grabbed her bag. Opening the door, she got out of the car and then leant back in to say, "You're right, it makes no sense. I just hope you don't live to regret it."

"I hope so, too," I said, and then added, "Do you want me to wait or will you phone me when you're ready and I'll come pick you up?"

"Don't worry about it. I'll call Brody and get him to come pick me up after he finishes work."

I'd upset her, but that couldn't be helped. These days I had to put myself first, especially where my mother was concerned.

"Okay, but if you change your mind, let me know, okay?"

"Yeah. Thanks for dropping me off," she said and then walked away from me as my heart cracked a little. It felt like a divide had grown between us in the last five minutes, and I wanted more than anything to fix that. But the thing I'd learnt about life was that you couldn't force something that needed time to heal.

I started the car and drove home. It was only twelve thirty but I wasn't going back to work; I'd never get any work done when my mind was all over the place like it was now.

When I arrived home, I noticed Griff's bike parked across the street. It had been two days since I'd seen or heard from him, and I didn't expect he'd ever reach out to me again. God, why did I sleep with him? We could have just stayed friends.

I collected my mail and trudged up the path to my front door. My thoughts banged around inside my head and I figured my headache was going nowhere now. Between my mother and Griff, they had my pain covered. When I made it to the front door, my gaze narrowed on the welcome mat. There was a pair of boxing gloves on it.

What the hell?

I bent to retrieve them, and realisation dawned on me. Without entering my house, I turned and marched across the street to Josie's house. Her front door was open but neither she nor Griff were anywhere in sight, so I knocked and waited. A few moments later, he walked down the hallway towards me, and as much as I fought it, the sight of him caused butterflies in my tummy.

No, no, no!

To make matters worse, he only had on a towel.

Wrapped around his freaking waist.

His chest bare.

His sexy ass muscles on full display.

172

And his hair wet like he'd just stepped out of the shower.

God, help me, 'cause I'm not sure I can help myself.

And then he spoke, and I remembered why I was here. "Sophia." He said my name as if it was the last word he wanted to be saying, and it caused all the butterflies in my tummy to whoosh right on out. The hard look on his face did the same.

I held up the gloves. "Did you leave these at my front door?" Even as I was holding them up, I was confused. If he didn't want to be seeing me, why would he bring me gloves? This man made no sense.

He eyed them and nodded. "Yeah, I thought you could use them for boxing classes."

I shoved them at him. "Thank you, but I don't want them."

"I bought them for you. Keep them," he growled as he pushed them back at me.

Shaking my head in a crazed type way – *like the freaking crazy woman I was today* – I shoved them at him and said, "I can buy my own damn gloves, Griff. Screw needing a man in my life to do shit for me, because that clearly isn't working out for me." My eyes dropped to his chest before shifting back to his face. Gesturing at his body, I said, "And for the love of God, would you *please* put some clothes on?

173

When the hell did it become alright for men to answer doors dressed in towels?"

Without waiting for a reply, I turned and stalked down the stairs, across the street and into my house.

Goddamn, fucking men.

And then I collapsed onto my bed and let the tears stream down my face.

Today was one of those days where it felt like everything and everyone was out to get me. My boss, my sister, my mum, and the man I wanted so damn bad.

But mostly, it was my mum.

I cried the tears that my nine-year-old self had cried when I came home from school to find my mother gone, and in her place, an aunt who didn't want me.

I cried the tears that my thirteen-year-old self cried when I got my period and didn't know what the hell to do because my mother hadn't been there to teach me and hold my hand through the transition into puberty.

I cried the tears that my seventeen-year-old self cried when my heart had been broken by a boy for the very first time.

And I cried the tears that my twenty-eight year old self had cried last year when I'd made the decision to let my mother go – when I'd *finally* decided she was never coming back so I was best to move on and find love from other people.

My mother didn't love me enough to ever want to be in my life so why should I now love her enough to be there for her when she was sick and reaching out to me?

And – *oh, God* – did it make me a bad person that I *didn't* want to go to her?

***

I cried myself to sleep and slept for a few hours until someone banging on my front door woke me. Trudging to the door with a heart that felt as heavy as it had before I fell asleep, I hoped it would be someone who had good news for me. I was over the bad for today.

Magan stood on the other side of my door when I opened it. She gave me a small smile and simply said, "I'm sorry."

I burst into tears again.

She stepped inside and put her arms around me. "I'm such a bitch," she apologised as she hugged me.

Her touch was just what I needed, and I clung to her for a couple of minutes while the tears fell. When I let her go, I wiped my face and said, "No, you're not. It's just a shitty situation, and on top of that, I've had other crappy stuff happen today so I'm a blubbering mess. Just ignore me."

I led us to my kitchen and put the kettle on to make tea. While I made it, she sat at the kitchen counter on one of the stools and watched me.

"How's Mum?" I asked. God, it felt strange to call her that. In my opinion, the name 'Mum' was reserved for someone you knew almost as well as yourself, and I didn't know this woman at all.

"She did have a heart attack, so they're keeping her in for more tests. They're talking about an operation or something to help her. But she also has diabetes that she hasn't taken care of so they're helping her with that, too. I'm pretty sure she's going to be okay, though." She paused for a second and hesitantly said, "She asked about you. Said she wanted to see you if you were up for it."

Apprehension ran through me, and my hand moved to my chest as I took a deep breath. "I'm not sure, Magan. I need some more time to work it out in my mind. I've spent my life desperately wanting her in it, but last year I got to a place where I accepted she didn't love or want me. To rework that will take some time. Can you understand that?"

"Sort of, but mostly, I don't understand why you wouldn't want her in your life. I think about her

176

pretty much every day and am so glad she's come back."

I squeezed her hand. "I'm happy for you, but for me, I just don't trust she's back to stay, and I don't think I could take another rejection from her. I think it would break my heart completely." My voice caught and I swallowed back more tears.

I can't do it.

I can't take the chance.

She stared at me for a moment, like she was really processing what I'd said. When she spoke, her words broke my heart. "That, I *do* understand. I can't imagine how hard it's been for you...you never got to see her again after she left you...at least I have. I saw her twice in my life – once when I was nine, she came to see me on my birthday, and then when I was thirteen, she came to one of my sports days at school."

The thing that broke my heart the most about her words was that she was so happy to have seen her mother twice in her life – *twice.* In a world where most children take for granted that they'll see their mother's face every morning when they wake up, here was my sister, happy she'd been blessed with two visits. This made me want to visit the woman even less now. I felt my indecision begin to blur into anger and tried to shove it away. Anger never solved anything. In my experience, it only ever seemed to make it worse.

I finished making our tea, and as I passed her a mug, I said, "Can we change the subject for a bit? I'm feeling overwhelmed with this and need to think about something else or I might start crying again."

She gave me a sympathetic smile. "Sure."

I leant my elbows on the kitchen counter. "Tell me about your boyfriend."

A look crossed her face but she quickly pushed it aside and gave me a happy smile. I wondered at what that meant, but she threw me when she said, "I'd rather know about your man."

"My man? I don't have a man." I couldn't count Griff as a man in my life so there was no point talking about him.

"You must. You've got this glow or something to you. Like you've recently had sex, so fess up." She waited with a huge grin of expectation on her face.

"There is someone, but he's not my man and never will be my man. We slept together once, and I'm sad to report, it won't happen again. He's a stubborn hard-ass who will never let anyone in."

"Wait, didn't you tell me you don't believe in one-night stands?"

I threw my hands in the air and sighed loudly. "God, that rule is coming back to bite me in the ass.

I swear I'm never telling my friends about my sex rules anymore. I break them once, and everyone wants to give me grief for it!"

She frowned. "How many sex rules do you have?"

I laughed and took a sip of tea. "None, but if I ever make another one, I'm not telling you."

"So tell me about this dude. He must be hot for you to break that rule. Have you got a photo? I need to see what he looks like!" she exclaimed. I was sure red blushed across my entire face, and it must have because she pointed at me and asked, "Did you take a sneaky photo of a man?"

I covered my face with my hand and nodded. I'd never done something like it in my life, but I hadn't been able to resist a photo of Griff while he slept the other morning. "Yes."

She put her hand out. "Give me your phone. I need to see this photo."

I found the photo on my phone and passed it to her. "See why I broke my rule?"

Her eyes widened and she looked at me in disbelief. "Holy fuck, Sophia, this dude's way hot. Are you sure he's not interested in seeing you again? I'd be doing everything in my power to get him if I was you."

"Trust me, he's not interested in me. I've practically thrown myself at him, and made a fool of myself numerous times, but we won't talk about that... he's made it clear he only wanted one night." A thought hit me. "God, for all I know, he probably thought the sex was bad... I hadn't even thought of that until now."

She stared at me for a moment. Handing my phone back to me, she said, "Geez, this relationship stuff never gets easier, does it?"

Laughing, I said, "It probably does for women who have their 'man-shit' together, but I don't, so it's not getting any easier for me."

"What is 'man-shit'?"

I glared at her. "Are you making fun of me?"

She held her hands up defensively and shook her head. "No! You just say the funniest things sometimes, and I don't always know what you mean."

"When you've got your 'man-shit' together, you're good with men. You know those women who seem to effortlessly flirt with a man and always seem to know the exact right thing to say to them? They're the women with it all together. That is *not* me. I open my mouth and the crap that comes out of it makes men run...I'm sure of it. I kid you not, I've been in a bar before trying to flirt and after I've said something totally cringe-worthy, I've watched as the guy's eyes glaze over and then he excuses himself and I never see him again."

Her expression had turned soft, and she gave me a huge smile before saying, "I love having you as a sister. I couldn't think of anyone I'd rather have to teach me about 'man-shit' and how to take sneaky photos of men while they sleep."

I laughed and then she started, too.

And I realised that even on shitty days when nothing seemed to be going your way, it was the little moments with those you cared about that could help pick you up, dust off your hurt and get you ready to go back out into the world.

***

The next morning, I dressed to impress for work. I'd slept fairly badly, but I was determined that today was going to be a good day, and I'd always had good days when I dressed well and looked good. So that's how I decided to start this day. I wore a red pencil skirt that sat just below my knees, a white, fitted blouse that – if I did say so myself – made my boobs look freaking awesome, and red stilettos. I curled my long, blonde hair into soft curls that fell over my shoulders, and paid more attention to my makeup than I usually did for work

– almost the same level of attention I would pay to it if I were going out for the night.

I was running on time, I'd made my lunch, which meant I didn't have to spend money on it, and everything was going well as I headed out to my car. And then everything turned to shit.

As I backed the car out of the driveway, something didn't feel right, so I pulled up in the driveway, and got out to check my suspicions. I was right – one of my tyres was flat.

Argh!

I had been shown how to change a tyre once in my life, a very long time ago, and I was sure that if I attempted to do it now, I'd screw it up. I recalled something about chocks and jacking, and not much else. Knowing my luck, the car would roll down the freaking street.

I wanted to throw my hands in the air and scream out an obscenity, but instead, I pulled out my phone and googled how to change a tyre. *How To Change A Tyre – For Dummies* came up and I figured that was as good a place as any to start. I scrolled through the instructions and it actually didn't sound that hard. Surely, I could do this.

The first thing it said to do was block the wheels at the opposite end of the flat tyre so the car didn't roll. Bingo! I was on a winner here – my car would not roll while I changed this damn tyre. And luckily, I had some spare bricks in my back yard, so I headed out there to grab them. Everything was going great guns until my bloody stiletto wedged itself in the grass and as I tried to walk, the shoe didn't want to come with me, and I tripped. And I landed on the mound of dirt I'd recently had delivered. Landed, as in, face first, body flat against the tiny hill of dirt.

I hate my life!

Like seriously, could this week get any worse?

I pushed myself up and dusted off all the dirt I could, but I was going to have to change outfits now because this one looked like it was in the middle of a zombie apocalypse. *I bet I looked like I was fighting goddamn zombies.*

Grabbing the bricks, I carried them out to the front yard. I briefly considered calling the RACQ to come and change the tyre for me, but I figured I could do it much faster.

I placed the bricks where my instructions told me to and then checked what I had to do next. It involved a screwdriver so I quickly ran inside to find one. Five minutes later, I had the wheel cover off the flat tyre, and was secretly proud of myself for getting this far.

Next, I had to loosen the lug nuts and this was where it got tricky for me. The damn nuts had been put on so tight that I didn't have the strength to undo all of them. I managed to loosen two of them, but I struggled with the rest. And as I was putting all my weight behind it, I fell on my damn ass on the driveway.

"Oh my God, I fucking give up!" I yelled out.

As luck would have it, it was right at that very minute that Griff pulled up across the road and stared at me sitting on my driveway looking like a zombie fighter from some damn apocalypse movie, yelling swear words out at whoever would listen.

He removed his helmet and walked across the street to where I sat. Looking down at me with a smirk, he said, "Sitting down on the job there, sweetheart. Tyres don't change themselves...you kinda have to do some of the work."

I scrambled to stand, but the length and tightness of my dress did not help my cause, and the manner in which I finally made it to a standing position would have to be classified as the most unladylike manner known to exist. Griff *did* extend his hand to help me, but in my wisdom – or lack of it, if you chose to be honest about the situation – I declined his help. He shrugged, crossed his arms over his chest, stood back and watched as I made a fool of myself. All with that huge smirk of his that I wanted to wipe off his face with my zombie-dirty hand.

Glaring at him, I said, "Don't even get me started, handsome. Today was supposed to be a good day – unlike yesterday that was the shittiest day ever and shall never be spoken of again. I was having a good hair day, and my makeup was the bomb, and my clothes were awesome, and then the goddamn tyre decided to have a hissy fit on the one day that was going good for me. No problems, I said, I can handle this shit – *and I was* – but then my stiletto decided it liked the grass more than my foot, and it also decided that, hey, your hair and face would look so much better with some dirt – *dirt* – on it. Hell yes, let's make you look like a zombie fighter today, my shoe said. But, not to be outdone, my tyre decided to have the last laugh and knock me on my ass. Well, screw it all, I'm going to go inside, find another freaking amazing outfit to wear, fix my hair and face so that it still looks like I stepped out of Cosmopolitan and then I'm going to find a way to get to work that does not involve changing tyres, because there is no way I am letting a tyre dictate whether I have a good day or not." I finished what I was saying and took a long breath.

He stared at me as his smirk morphed into a grin, and then he said, "Go inside and do whatever you need to do. I'll change your tyre so you can drive to work."

I stared back at him. "Why do you do that? Why do you act like an ass and then do something really nice? It confuses the hell out of me. *You* confuse the hell out of me!"

"I confuse the fuck out of myself, sweetheart," he replied, and his sexy, gravelly voice was in full swing today. And it just made me even more confused. It was like he was flirting with me even though I knew there was no way he was.

I decided it was time to remove myself from his presence. "I'm going to go and get changed. I'd really appreciate you changing the tyre. Thank you."

"No worries," he said as he stepped closer to me. He reached a hand out and cupped my cheek, and then swiped his thumb over my chin. "You had a clump of dirt there," he said, his eyes never leaving mine. "I figured you would want it gone."

His touch shot through me, and – *good God* – I wanted him.

I wanted him like I needed air.

I'd never wanted a man who didn't want me back, and it caused all my insecurities and doubts about myself to flare up. And I hated that, because I'd put the time in to learning to love myself enough to be able to look past those doubts.

I took a step back, and said, "I won't be long." And then I hurried inside.

I had to find a way to forget Griff.

I had to move on to a man who wanted me as much as I wanted him.

Chapter Fourteen
Griff

I turned the television up as images of Jeffrey Bond flashed across the screen. The headline read – *Bond To Go To Trial* – and then they flashed to photos of his brother and discussed his murder. According to the news journalist, Bond's family had sworn revenge on the killer, and Bond himself had reportedly said that once he got off the charges and released from jail, he'd personally take care of his brother's killer.

Good luck, asshole.

Switching the television off, I grabbed my keys and headed out to my bike. It looked like it was time for me to put another plan into action in order to force Danny's hand on getting me off the trial as a witness. No fucking way was I going on that witness stand.

As I sped off towards the clubhouse, I began piecing the plan together that had been sitting there waiting for me to decide to act upon it. Problem was, my thoughts kept drifting off to Sophia and this morning. She'd looked so damn cute sitting on her driveway with dirt all over her. When she'd taken the time to tell me what had happened - in only the way Sophia could - my dick had hardened because, *fuck*, that woman was sexy when she dropped her mask and let the words fly out of her mouth.

Christ, I had to get her out of my head. She was occupying too much of my time.

The trouble with that was I liked her being in my head.

And that was a whole other problem in itself.

***

I spent a few hours going over the surveillance from our restaurants and Indigo, looking for anything that might give us a clue about the fire at Trilogy, but came up short. Leaning back in my chair, I rubbed my neck. The knots I had there were only getting worse, and my training sessions weren't doing much to take the edge off.

"Griff, you got a minute?"

I looked up to find J standing in the doorway and motioned for him to come in. "What's up?"

"Just wanted to give you an update on Ricky."

"You found much on him yet?"

"He likes Asian women and coke. Besides that, he's kept his nose clean the last couple of days so we've learnt nothing."

"Shit. This motherfucker is smart. Who would have figured?" I said, frustrated as hell that we were still no closer to getting confirmation he was behind the fire.

J grimaced. "We'll keep tailing him, and Nash is working on some other angles. He's gotta fuck up somewhere soon."

"I'm not so sure he will, J. He's been around for years, and you don't build a business like that by making stupid mistakes."

"We talking about Ricky?" Scott asked, joining us.

"Yeah, there's still no leads on the fire," I answered him.

He nodded his head slowly, his gaze fixed firmly on me, and my skin prickled – something was off with him. Keeping his eyes on me, he said, "J, can you give Griff and I a moment?"

Fuck.

I'd always trusted my instincts and right now, they were telling me something was very wrong.

"I'll keep you updated," J promised and left us alone.

Scott entered the office, closed the door behind him, and stared at me as if he was trying to figure something out. And in that instant, I knew that he knew.

Standing, I said, "You know."

His nostrils flared and his shoulders tensed. He clenched his jaw, and nodded. "Yeah, I know."

My gut clenched in a knot. I'd always wondered if this day would come. Had been unsure how I'd feel if it did, but I'd never figured I'd feel the way I currently was. Regret washed over me. Scott had become my family, and to see the look of disbelief, anger and pain on his face now...that shit cut deep. "How?"

"Jesus, Griff - *how?*" he thundered, his face a dark cloud of rage. "Ricky fucking told me. He showed up with a file on you. But I don't want to talk about how; I want to talk about why. Why the fuck did you do this? I trusted you like a brother. *Like fucking family!* If I hadn't seen that file, I wouldn't believe it to be true." He raked his fingers through his hair, and added, "You had me fooled, that's for sure."

I stood my ground. I had a lot to say, and needed to find a way for Scott to understand and believe that I spoke the truth. Because this would be the truth. Finally. "I'm gonna give you the truth, but it's gonna take a bit to get there. Can you give me that at least?"

His hard look didn't change, but he nodded. "Go on."

"I was raised to be a cop. My dad was one, my uncle was one, and my grandfather was one. My cousin and I went through the academy together, but it never felt right to me. I never wanted what everyone else wanted for me. I finished my training but I never pursued a career after that."

"So you just walked away?" he demanded. His face had contorted into ugliness at the mention of cops, and I didn't blame him. The police weren't high on Storm's list of trusted people.

"Yeah. I fucked around for a while doing random handyman type jobs until private investigation work fell into my lap. A friend hired me to work with him while I did my study, and I never looked back."

He crossed his arms and planted his feet wide. "Keep talking. You need to get to the point."

"My parents and brother were murdered ten years ago. Tortured for hours and then had their throats slit. The day after Boxing Day, I came home to find them. I'll never get the blood and horror out of my mind. I had no faith in the cops to find justice for their deaths. The idea of life behind bars for someone who killed my family didn't sit well with me – I wanted blood for blood. And I believed I knew who the killer was."

"Who?" Still that hard look on his face.

"Marcus." I paused, taking in the flicker of surprise on his face. "My father had been investigating Storm and their involvement in drugs. I'm fairly certain he was close to arresting Marcus at the time of his murder. The investigation into Storm never really went anywhere after his death, which only convinced me further of Marcus's involvement, but after eighteen months of my own investigations, I couldn't pin him for the murders."

"This isn't adding up, Griff. You didn't join Storm until three years ago, yet the murders were ten years ago."

I nodded. "Yeah, I walked away from it all after eighteen months...left town and tried to move on from it because, fuck, it was changing me. I was

193

doing shit I wasn't proud of so I got out before I lost what little of my soul I had left. But revenge has a way of running your life, and I came back four years later determined to get justice. When I couldn't do that outside of the club, I found a way in. I found a way to get close to the people I thought had killed my family."

His wild eyes were glued to mine and his body was tied up with tension. "Fuck," he swore. "So none of this means anything to you? What the fuck are you still here for? Marcus is dead so you've got no reason to still be here."

Scott's anger fueled my frustration. My chest tightened with the need to get everything out, and my head began to throb with a growing headache. "Storm means everything to me. Fuck!" I paced away from him towards the window. Balling my fists, I took some deep breaths, trying to get myself under control. Turning back to him, I said, "Marcus wasn't responsible for my family's deaths. I worked that out within a year of joining Storm. By then, I'd also worked out that Storm meant more to me than most of my own family had. There was no way I was walking away from that."

"Your *cop* family, who you're still fucking close to!" he spat.

I shook my head. "No, I don't have any ties to my family anymore, Scott. Except for an aunt who also has no ties to them."

"Don't fucking lie to me, Griff!" he roared. "I've seen photos of you meeting with your cop cousin – *this fucking week.*"

"Did Ricky tell you about the Bond case? I assume that's how he found out my past."

"No. He only filled me in on your true identity."

"Danny, my cousin, asked me to investigate the murders of Leon Bond and his girlfriend. With Bond being a high profile drug dealer, Danny wanted the real murderer exposed, but didn't have faith in his team to do that because he'd discovered his partner was dirty. I'd just come back to Brisbane to look into Marcus, and Danny decided I was the only person he could trust. Foolishly, I agreed to do it." I raked my fingers through my hair as I recalled the investigation. If I could go back and change anything in my life, taking on this case would be it. "In the course of my investigation, I witnessed another murder, and long story short, that's coming back to bite me in the ass because it's key evidence in the Bond case now and they want me to testify. That's why I met with Danny this week. To tell him to back the fuck off and that there's no way in hell I'm getting on that stand."

Scott stared at me in silence as he took all that in. Eventually, he said, "Jesus, Griff, what a shit fight." He appeared to have calmed down a little, almost as if he was reconsidering his anger at me, but wasn't sure whether that was the right move.

I nodded in agreement. "Yeah, it is. You've gotta believe that while I did mean to deceive you to get into Storm - and I don't regret that because I had to do what I did for my family - I wish it could have all happened under different circumstances. My loyalty lies completely with Storm now."

With wary eyes, he said, "I'm gonna need some time to work through this. To be honest, I'm knocked for fucking six and don't know what to make of it. I trusted you, one hundred fucking percent, and now that trust is gone, and I'm not sure where that leaves us. I can't have a VP I don't trust. And I'm not sure the boys would want a member they can't trust to remain part of the club."

His words gutted me.

Threatened to destroy me.

Without Storm, I had nothing.

I was nothing.

As the ghosts of the past circled, and the demons clawed at the soul I did have left, I swallowed back my fear and nodded. No words came, though. There were none left to say. Scott would make up his own mind, regardless of anything more I might say.

"I'll talk to you tomorrow," he said before turning on his heel and walking out of the room.

I stood staring at the nothingness in front of me.

Scott had been the one person I'd hoped would understand.

Instead, he'd walked out.

And my faith in family died the death it should have had years ago.

Chapter Fifteen
Sophia

I dumped my gym bag on my bed, stepped out of my gym clothes and hit the shower. It had been a long ass day and I needed an equally long shower to wash it all away. After my encounter with my flat tyre and Griff this morning, things had not improved. Andrew had been in a bad mood all day at work and had taken it out on me, especially after I ditched half the day yesterday without informing him. He'd been pissed off about that and I'd had to listen to a fifteen-minute talking-to from him about it. Then, after work, Magan had informed me how disappointed our mother was that I was yet to visit her. And to top it all off, I'd had a run-in with a bitch at the gym over using one of the machines. She didn't want to share and I refused to back down. Today was not a day I would let anyone walk all over me, and I'd stood my ground with her.

After fifteen minutes of standing in the shower and letting the hot water seep into my muscles, I stepped out and dried off. Then I dressed in shorts and a tank and padded into the kitchen to make dinner. It was late – just after eight – and I was starving. However, a knock at the front door interrupted me.

I opened the door, surprised to find Josie on the other side, smiling at me. "Hi, Josie," I said warmly.

"May I come in?" she asked, but I sensed that with Josie, the answer 'no' wasn't even an option.

I let her in and led her into my lounge room. We settled ourselves on my couch and I asked, "What's up?"

"I wanted to talk to you about Michael."

Griff.

"Okay," I said slowly, not sure where she would take this.

Her face softened but there was a seriousness to it I'd never seen from her before, as if what she was about to tell me was one of the most important

199

things she'd ever tell me. "Michael feels something for you. I've never seen him the way he is with you, and I wanted you to know that."

I frowned. "No, he doesn't. He's attracted to me, but he's not interested in pursuing a relationship with me." At the frown that appeared on her face, I added, "Trust me, Josie, he and I have discussed it. At length. There's no way anything will happen between him and me."

"But you want something to happen?"

"I'm interested. There's something about him that makes me want to see if we'd be any good together."

The frown left her face and was replaced with a smile. "You're going to have to be the one to make the first move, my dear. Michael's a stubborn man and doesn't know what's good for him most of the time."

I sighed. "You're not listening to me, Josie. He's really not interested. Let's just say that he and I have a difference of opinion on something fairly important."

She leaned forward in her chair and that serious look returned. "Michael used to visit me twice a week at the most. These days he's at my house every day. He asks me if I've seen you and whether you're okay. He doesn't ask me outright but he finds a way to get it into the conversation. I saw him change your tyre this morning, and I know he tried to give you those boxing gloves." She paused. "He cares about you, my girl, and I've only ever seen him care about a few people. You can't tell me that man is not interested in you."

I stilled and my heart skipped a beat. She'd surprised me and I was stunned into silence.

It's just sex he wants.

And yet, I knew that men didn't go to such extremes for sex, especially not for sex they weren't getting and knew they had no hope of getting. Griff could score whoever he wanted, whenever he wanted. He didn't need me for sex.

"Well, that may all be true, but I don't know what to do with it because, like I said, he's been very clear about what he wants."

She tsk'd. "You need to show a man like Michael what he's missing. And I'm not talking about sex here, Sophia. You're going to have to figure out why he's being so stubborn, and show him that he's wrong."

I had no idea on this, but I'd put some thought into it. "Okay," I said with a nod.

Standing, she said, "He's a good man. Just a little bit lost, but I know a woman like you can help guide him back."

And then she was gone, but as she left, she placed a piece of paper in my hand.

A piece of paper with an address on it.

***

I sat outside Griff's house for a good fifteen minutes, psyching myself up to go in. After Josie had left my house earlier, I'd tried to put this out of my mind, but when I was still thinking about it an hour later, I knew I had to come to his house tonight. I knew I wouldn't sleep if I didn't.

It was nearly ten pm but his lights were on, so I figured he was awake. After going back and forth in my mind, I finally said 'screw it' and headed for his front door. God knew how he would react to me being here, but Josie had given me the confidence to try.

He took his time answering the door, and the vision that greeted me when he did caused me to suck in my breath. Griff stood in front of me, dressed only in shorts, his body slick with sweat, his hair rumpled, and a ravaged look on his face.

"Sophia. What are you doing here?" he asked, and the pain in his voice blared like it had come out of a loudspeaker. Something was not right with him tonight.

"Can I come in?" I took one step forward to signal my intention of not leaving here without talking.

He glanced down at my foot. "It's not a good idea. Not tonight."

I wasn't taking no for an answer. I pushed past him and entered his home. "There's never a right time for things, Griff. Tonight's as good as any."

His home – if you could call it that because it seemed more like a place where he just crashed at night – was sparsely furnished. The only pieces of furniture in the lounge room were a couch, a television, and a TV cabinet. Cream paint coloured the walls, and not a painting or frame was in sight.

I turned to face him and found him watching me with an intense stare. My gaze travelled over his body, and I took in how rigid he held himself tonight. "Are you okay?" I asked, my eyes meeting his.

"I will be when you leave," he bit out, but I didn't buy it.

"No, I don't believe that. You look like something is deeply troubling you."

He forced his fingers through his hair, and muttered, "Fuck. Do we really have to do whatever this is tonight?"

I reconsidered. Perhaps he was right. Perhaps tonight was not a good time for him. It certainly didn't seem like it was. "No, we don't have to, but we do have to do it at some point, Griff."

His eyes narrowed on me. "You sure about that? I think we've both made our positions clear to the other."

I stepped closer, beginning to get frustrated as hell with him. "I've been thinking about it, and something isn't adding up with you."

"What?"

"You say you're not interested in a relationship with me, but I feel something between us, Griff. And you can deny it all you want, but I know it's there."

His eyes didn't leave mine, but he did close them for a moment while he drew a long, deep breath. When he opened them again, he spoke in a low tone that felt like a warning. "Sophia, I'm not the man for you. There are parts to me that aren't good, and if you got to know the real me, you would walk away. Starting something would only cause you more heartache in your life. So please believe me when I say that you need to forget about anything happening between you and me, and you need to go and find yourself a nice man who will be able to give you what you need. I will never be that man." He

204

took a step away from me as if he expected me to leave. He didn't know me very well.

I closed the distance between us and got in his face. "You think I'm a good girl who couldn't handle being with you, don't you?"

"That's not what I said."

"You didn't have to say the words, I can tell what you're thinking. I'm not asking you to marry me. All I'm asking for is for us to see what this could be. Why won't you take a chance on me?" I said, my voice rising as my frustration worked itself out.

I saw the moment he snapped. Saw the moment his carefully constructed control gave way, and he let himself go. His hand curled around my waist and he yanked me to him, his eyes wild, his breathing erratic. He dragged me up against his body, and rasped, "Because I don't want to hurt you, and make no mistake about it, I *will* hurt you. I won't be able to give you what you need."

His tone both frightened and excited me, and my heart began beating faster. Being this close to him while he was on edge like this was a huge turn on to me, and it only made me want him more. I pressed my body into his, enjoying the hiss that escaped his lips, and said, "You won't hurt me, Griff. I trust you."

His eyes flared – widened in an emotion I couldn't quite put my finger on. "Don't say that, Sophia. You should not trust me. I will fuck that up, and all you'll be left with is hate. And I don't want that for you." His chest thudded with every harsh breath he took, but the thing I noticed was that although he was telling me no, he wasn't letting me go. He still held me close.

His pain bled from him. I had no idea what it was, but I wanted to drag it from him and tell him this would be okay. I placed my hand on his cheek, and before he could pull away, I slid it around the back of his head and pulled his face to mine. Our lips met and it was like an explosion of chemistry. I'd expected him to yank his lips off mine, but he didn't. Instead, he growled into my mouth, slid his hands around my body and onto my ass, and gripped me hard there while his tongue desperately searched for mine.

Oh, God.

Yes.

He deepened the kiss and it gradually got rougher and harder, and at the same time, he lifted me. I wrapped my legs around him, and he walked me until we were up against the wall. While his body held me in place against the wall, his hands moved to the bottom of my tank and he ripped it off over my head. He then grabbed hold of my bra straps and yanked them down to free my breasts. Without a word, his head dipped to take one of my nipples into his mouth, and he sucked and licked me. And then he bit me lightly, and holy mother of God that felt good. The pain intersected with the pleasure, and caused my body to jerk as I let out a loud moan.

His head snapped up and he stared at me through his lust. "Did that feel good?" he demanded to know.

"Yes."

Holding my gaze, he took hold of my breast and kneaded it before squeezing my nipple. My back arched as the pain and pleasure shot through me. He narrowed his eyes on me, and suddenly let me go. His movements were swift, and a moment later, he had me on my feet with my back to him, face to the wall. He grasped my hands and placed them up against the wall. With a quick flick, he had my bra off, and then he reached around and undid my shorts and yanked them down. It all happened so fast, I struggled to keep up, but I loved every second of it.

"Have you ever fucked a man who likes control?" he asked as he ran his hand over my ass.

Excitement pulsed through me. "No."

"Fuck," he growled. "Does this turn you on?"

"Yes," I panted, wanting him to keep going, needing him to never stop. Whatever Griff had to give, I wanted to take.

He pressed his mouth against my ear as his arm circled my body and took hold of me. "You need to be careful what you beg for, Sophia," he ordered, and the dominance in his voice pushed me closer to the edge.

"I want you, Griff. Show me who you really are," I whispered.

He took a long breath, and I wasn't sure if it was to keep himself calm or to ready himself to do what I'd begged.

And then he stopped holding back.

He took a step back and I felt his hands on my ass as his fingers slid under the edge of my panties. And then he tore them off me. My pussy clenched at the sound of them ripping. And my body trembled, waiting for what was next. Hoping like hell he wouldn't stop anytime soon.

His finger trailed down my back, from the base of my neck to my ass. And then his hand ran lightly over my ass. "You sure you want to know who I am, Sophia?" His voice was all kinds of dark, dangerous and hot.

I nodded. "I'm sure."

Slap.

The sting of his palm against my ass caused my body to jolt. I dropped my head back and closed my eyes while my back arched my ass into his hand.

I need more.

"Fuck, you want me to do that again?"

"Yes."

I expected his palm on my ass again, but it never came. Instead, he spun me around and pulled me to him. His eyes bore into mine, and I saw the war he waged. "You don't know what you're asking," he ground out. His breaths were coming hard and fast now, and his features twisted in his own pain as his eyes begged me to say no, to push him away. But I couldn't. I wanted him too much to do that.

I took hold of his face with both hands. "Let me be who you need," I pleaded.

He stared at me for a long moment before briefly closing his eyes. When he opened them again, I saw the change in his stare. His resolve gone, he nodded once.

And then I met the real Griff.

Chapter Sixteen
Griff

Let me be who you need.

Those words out of Sophia's mouth were everything I wanted to hear in this moment, and everything I wanted her to take back and pretend like she'd never said. And, yet, here we were with them hanging in the air between us. They would either be our downfall or the beginning of something between us, because I sure as fuck knew that if she loved this and begged me to fuck her again, I'd never be able to say no.

Placing my hand against the small of her back, I ordered, "Start walking."

She did as I said, and I directed her to my bedroom.

"I want you to sit on the edge of the bed and wait for me," I said, and when she sat, I left her to go and find my rope.

When I returned, the sight of her naked, on my bed, waiting where I told her to wait, sent a new rush of need straight to my dick.

Standing in front of her, I dropped the rope on the bed and took my shorts and boxers off. Watching desire flare in her eyes at the sight of my dick being freed only intensified my desire. Sophia needing *me* made me need *her* even more.

Jesus, that need was dangerous.

"Stand," I commanded.

She stood, and I turned her around so her back was to me. Taking hold of her hands, I positioned them behind her. "Hold your hands together while I tie them," I said, still waiting for her to deny me, but she didn't.

I wrapped the rope around her wrists and bound her hands together tightly. The sight of rope against her skin nearly did me in. It looked ten times better than I'd imagined it would. With a flick of my wrist, I spun her around to face me

211

again. Her eyes found mine, and, *fuck*, I loved what I saw there.

Total fucking submission.

I took a step back and let my gaze travel the curves of her body. I loved the contrast of the muscles she was building in the gym with the softness of her body. When my gaze reached her pussy, my dick jerked as I remembered the feel of being inside her.

So sweet.

So fucking perfect.

When I'd taken my time admiring her body, I shifted my gaze back up to her eyes. "I have rules and if you don't follow them, this is over. Understood?"

"Yes." She spoke softly and waited for me to continue.

God fucking help me.

She's perfect.

"One – if you want me to stop, you say no. In my bedroom, no always means no, so use it whenever you need it, and don't say it unless you mean it." She nodded. *Good girl.* "Two – you do whatever I tell you to do. If you don't want to do it, we negotiate until we come up with something we're both happy with. I will never make you do something you're not comfortable with." Another nod. "Good girl."

I reached into my bedside table drawer and pulled out the blindfold I kept in there. "Turn around," I ordered her, and when she did, I secured the material in place. I then wrapped my arm around her, across her chest so that my hand held her arm firmly. Pulling her back into me, I tilted her head to the side and kissed her neck, softly at first and then a little more roughly. My teeth nipped her but I didn't bite her. At the same time, my free hand ran over her ass and when she relaxed into me while I kissed her neck, I spanked her again. She jumped at the unexpected touch, but her moan told me she loved it.

Fuck, I needed my hand on her ass more. I shifted her so I could sit on the edge of the bed. "You're going to lie across my lap, Sophia, face down," I said as I pulled her onto me.

I positioned her far enough down the bed so that her ass was right where I needed it. Laying one hand on her ass, I used my other hand to spread her legs so I could reach for her pussy. A moment later, I rubbed her clit and she moaned again. My eyes narrowed on her lips as she bit it, and fuck if that didn't drive me wild. I pushed my finger inside her and she writhed in pleasure as I fucked her with my finger, her breaths becoming more ragged as I built her bliss.

I took her to the edge before pulling out and spanking her again. Her body jolted and she moaned. My gaze shifted from her ass to her face and I took in the way her tongue ran over her lips.

Fuck.

I need more from her.

I lifted her off my lap to a standing position. Moving off the bed, I removed her blindfold, and then reached for her hair. Gripping it in a ponytail, I pulled her head back. Her eyes widened but she didn't utter a word or a moan. I held her head back, and murmured, "Good girl." I then took my other hand and ran it along her collarbone and down to her breast. My touch was feather light, and I loved the shiver it caused in her body. Bending, I took one of her nipples into my mouth, sucking and nipping lightly with my teeth. I kept hold of her hair, and every now and then, I glanced up at her, loving the sight of her exposed neck. I tended to both of her nipples before working my way up her body, kissing a trail along her skin all the way to her neck.

Letting her hair go, I watched as she brought her head forward, her eyes watching me intently. I traced a finger over her lips. "You okay?" I asked, and she nodded. I got lost in her lips as I traced them over and over. This woman held me hostage and she didn't even realise it. Hell, I hardly realised it. I had the power here, but for the first time in my life, a niggling thought at the back of my mind told me I was powerless.

Fuck.

I lifted her so that her legs wrapped around me, and backed her up against the wall. Her hands were still tied at her back so I had to hold her close to support her. She wiggled in my hold, and desire slammed through me again, and my instincts took over. I pressed my mouth to hers and kissed her with a passion I'd never felt before. It consumed me body and soul, and she returned it. Our lips and tongues tangled as we showed each other our need.

When I pulled away from the kiss, I growled, "Are you ready to come, baby?"

She nodded, and panted out her reply. "Yes." Her breaths were coming hard and fast, and her need was clear in her eyes.

I carried her to the bed and deposited her on the floor next to it. Turning her so her back was to me, I undid the rope, freeing her hands. Then I leant into her and spoke close to her ear, "On the bed, on your hands and knees. I need to see that perfect ass up in the air."

She did as I said, and a moment later, I was blessed with the vision of her ass. Fuck, a man could get used to that vision. I grabbed a condom from my side table, put it on, and then moved to position myself behind her on the bed.

I ran my hands over her back, down to grab her hips, and pulled her back to me. Taking hold of my dick, I slid it through her wetness, teasing her as I went. Pushing inside her a fraction and then back out. I repeated this a few times until I knew I had her panting for more.

Fuck, I need to be in her.

Taking hold of her ass, I thrust my cock into her pussy. She whimpered, and that sound lit me up with more need. I pulled out and thrust back in. God damn, so fucking beautiful. I thrust in and out, over and over, working us towards our release. The sounds of our bodies slapping together, my grunts and her moans filled the room, pushing me on.

Closer.

Almost there.

Fuck.

I lost focus of time and space.

Sophia cried out my name and her pussy squeezed around my dick.

I gripped her harder.

I slammed into her faster.

216

Rougher.

Jesus, so fucking close.

I grunted as I kept pushing, thrusting, forcing.

Reaching.

Fuck.

I roared as I came harder than I'd ever come.

And when I'd finished with it, and come to my senses, I pulled out of her, moved off the bed and left her so I could discard the condom in the bathroom. Taking a moment, I gripped the sides of the sink and stared into the mirror. I wasn't looking at a man in control. Hell no. The man staring back at me was as far from in control as he could be. And that shit messed with my mind more than it was already messed with today.

This woman had turned my world upside down. I'd gone from a man never wanting a relationship again to a man captivated by a woman to the point that the only word screaming through my head now was 'mine'.

Sophia is now mine.

Chapter Seventeen
Sophia

I blinked my eyes open and tried to move, but I couldn't. Strong arms held me so tightly that there would be no escape until they loosened. I looked up at Griff. He had me hard up against his body with my head on his chest. His arm was around my shoulders and his hand gripped me firmly to hold me in place. It was still dark, but I couldn't be sure of the time because he didn't have a clock in his bedroom. This room was another sparsely furnished room – a bed, bedside tables, a chest of drawers and a chair in the corner. From what I'd seen of his house so far, it spoke of a man who didn't put down roots. There were no family photos, no personal touches, and the tired feel to the carpet, paint and everything in between gave me a sense of someone who didn't get attached.

He shifted and even though he hadn't moved much, it was enough for me to wiggle out of his hold so I could go to the bathroom. However, the second I tried to move, his arm tightened around me again, and his eyes opened. Our gazes met, and he murmured, "You going somewhere, sweetheart?"

He doesn't want me to leave.

That knowledge made its way into my heart and settled there. It was the first time he'd given me something like that.

I smiled. "Just gotta go to the bathroom, handsome."

He didn't loosen his hold on me straight away. Rather, he continued to watch me in that intense way he often did, like he was working stuff out in his mind. Eventually, he nodded and let me go. He didn't say anything, though – still my man of few words.

I took my time in the bathroom, because, heck, I looked a sight. My hair sat on my head like a crazy bird's nest, my mascara sat clumped on my lashes and face where it had been wiped from my eyelashes during sleep, and my face looked all puffy and washed out. I had no tools to work with here, but I did my best to tidy up my hair and face. I also used Griff's toothpaste to freshen up my breath. No one needed morning breath after amazing sex.

When I finally made it back to his bedroom, I found him sitting in his bed waiting for me. His eyes tracked my movements as I went to him, and, good God, that made a woman feel good. When I crawled onto the bed, his arms reached for me and pulled me onto his lap so I sat straddling him with my face to his. My belly fluttered and my heart danced a little. This Griff was a man I could get used to.

"Morning," he said, his eyes firmly on mine. I loved that, because while a man's eyes on your body felt good, his eyes seeking yours – seeking your attention in the way Griff was now seeking mine – made you feel special. And I would take special over good any day of the week.

"Morning."

He raised his brows. "That's all you've got, baby? I thought for sure you'd have a lot more than that to say this morning."

"Smart-ass," I said with a smile. "I'm regrouping."

He chuckled. "How long does that usually take you?"

I tilted my head. "You know, just quietly, I'm liking this sense of humour thing you've got going on. I would so not have picked it from you, but that's one of the things I like about you the most – I never know what's coming next. And while we're talking, can I just say – I don't know where you keep your comb or your brush, but you seriously need to consider keeping it in the bathroom, because when a woman looks how I looked when I woke up this morning, she needs something to fix her hair with, and while my fingers did the trick this morning, they didn't really cut it, if you know what I mean. This hair would look so much better if I could have run a brush through it."

He glanced at my hair for a second and then his eyes found mine again. "I see the regrouping has taken place," he murmured, his voice deeper, more gravelly than before.

"Well, I'm not sure about that, but the thing about the brush needed to be said."

"I'll take it under advisement, sweetheart. I've never had an issue like this before...never had a woman wake up next to me in this bed."

Oh. My.

His words caused me to falter. More regrouping would need to take place now.

He watched me, waiting for me to reply, and when I didn't, he added, "And for the record, there was no need to run your fingers through your hair. Bedhead suits you."

God, he was killing me this morning. My heart almost swelled out of my chest with happiness.

His phone sounded with a text, and while he kept one hand firmly on my back, he reached for his phone with the other. I watched his beautiful face while he read the message, taking in the lines across his forehead that etched his thoughts onto his face, and the stubble he always wore, and those green eyes of his that held all his pain. Griff's was a face I could study for hours. I watched it now as he processed the message, and I knew that whatever that text contained, it hadn't been good news for him. Not if the way the lines and twitches on his face were anything to go by.

He placed his phone back on the bedside table and eyed me. "You working today?" And just like that, he seemed to compartmentalise the parts of his life. It was as if he'd swept aside whatever he'd just read so he could focus on me, not even allowing his emotions about the text message to touch his mind.

"Yes, unfortunately." I decided not to acknowledge the text or his feelings on it. I figured Griff was a man of so many layers, and it was going to take me awhile to peel each layer back. I also figured he wasn't the kind of man who would let a woman rush that process, so I was going to have to be patient.

"I'll take you to work and pick you up," he stated, and his tone told me there would be no arguing.

"That's a nice offer, but you seem to have forgotten that I don't have any clothes here. Not to mention, a brush, or makeup, or any of that stuff a girl kinda needs to get ready for work." I couldn't help tease him, but seriously, did he think women just got out of bed and were ready for work?

His eyes flashed a mixture of heat and frustration. And then he shifted so he could move me off his lap and deposit me on the bed next to him. He left the bed and eyed me. "I'm gonna get your clothes, you're gonna get dressed, and then I'm gonna follow you to your house." He raised his brows. "Where you can use your brush and makeup and all that stuff you think you need to make yourself beautiful. And then, I'm gonna put you on the back of my bike and take you to work. Where you can regroup and get that gorgeous mouth of

223

yours ready to give me more of the smart-ass I love from it." He paused for a moment before he asked, "You good with that?"

Oh, he had no idea how good I was with that.

I nodded. "I'm good with that."

"Thank fuck," he muttered. Then he turned and left the room to go in search of my clothes.

And I sat and waited while my heart did the jig in my chest.

This man.

Oh, my.

***

Griff followed me to my house, however as we were walking inside, he received another text message. This one caused him to swear and then he gave me a regretful look. "I'm sorry, sweetheart, I've gotta head out and take care of something for work."

"It's only just after six in the morning. Do you often get called out at that time of the day?"

"Some days, yes."

Disappointment filled me, but seeing his regret made it okay. It wasn't as if he wanted to leave. "Will I see you tonight?"

224

He put his hand out. "Pass me your phone. And yes, you'll see me tonight."

I gave him my phone and he keyed in his number and then sent himself a text. As he handed it back, he bossed me, "Use that number if you need it. I'm only a phone call away."

I smiled at him, loving his bossiness and what it told me about him – he wanted me. Pressing myself against him, I said, "You should go before I decide not to let you go."

His hands landed on my ass and his lips brushed mine. "I'll see you later," he promised, and I nodded, fully intending to make him keep that promise.

As he turned to leave, I was surprised to see Magan walking towards the front door. When she reached us, she looked Griff up and down. "Shit," she said before looking at me. "Dude's hotter in person than on your phone."

Mortified yet again, I widened my eyes at her, screaming 'shut up' through eye communication.

Griff smirked and raised his brows at me. "Didn't realise I was on your phone. I'm thinking I might need something similar on mine."

If I could have dug a hole and jumped in it at that moment, I would have. Magan and I would be having words. I pulled myself together and winked at him. "I'll be sure to send you something, handsome."

His smirk turned into a chuckle. "I see you're regrouping again."

I blinked as I stared at him, my cheeks burning what I figured to be a nice shade of red. The only thing a woman could do in a situation like this was hold her head high and brush it off. And give her man a little sass. "I may be spending the whole day regrouping at the rate we're going, so if you were hoping for some of that smart-ass you love so much, I'd advise you walk that sexy ass of yours right on out of here and go do whatever the heck a man does at six am in the morning. And as far as a photo appearing on your phone today...that's going to take a lot of regrouping which would only be helped along by either texts or photos, if you know what I mean. And I know you're a man who guards his words like he guards his secrets, so I'm more than good with photos, but, just sayin', words are so much sexier."

He bent to kiss me again, and murmured, "I'll be sure to take *that* under advisement, too."

And then he left us, and both Magan and I stared after him until he started his bike, at which point she looked at me, and said, "Holy shit, you scored big time."

I led her into my kitchen. "We'll see. He's a little shy about letting down his wall, if you know what I mean, so I feel there's a lot of work ahead of us." Eyeing her, I asked, "Why are you here so early?"

"I wanted to come over and see if you were thinking of visiting Mum today. I'm going to head to the hospital this morning if you want to come with me."

My stomach knotted with panic. "I can't...not today,' I said softly, willing her to leave it at that and not try to force me into going.

"Do you think you'll ever give her a chance?" Her words held no accusation; it was simply a question. One I didn't know the answer to.

"I'm honestly not sure."

She nodded. "Okay, I won't bug you about it again, but if you decide you do want to go, just let me know and I will go with you. She and I are getting close, and I can see how much she has changed."

Worry filled me. Her words revealed the truth of the matter – a truth a seventeen-year-old girl, desperate for the love of a mother, couldn't help but miss. How could she possibly see how much a woman had changed when she never knew her in the first place? I squeezed her hand and smiled. "I'll let you know if I change my mind," I promised, unable to burst her happy bubble. I hoped like hell our mother would not disappoint her again, but deep down, I doubted that would happen.

Chapter Eighteen
Griff

I walked the distance between my bike to the meeting point, surprised to see Blade waiting with Scott for me, but I should have realised this was the meeting point we set up when the three of us plotted to take down Marcus, so it was only natural for Scott to choose it if he was bringing Blade into something now. But what the fuck did Blade have to do with anything going on between Scott and me?

"Morning," I said as I approached.

The set of Scott's shoulders and the hard expression on his face led me to believe he was still angry with me. He jerked his chin, and said, "Morning." Although everything else about him seemed tense, his voice had lost the hard tone to it from yesterday.

Glancing at Blade, I asked, "What's going on?"

"Blade knows about your past. I needed to talk it out with someone and I didn't want that to be anyone from Storm," Scott filled me in, and I sucked in a breath. The more people who knew, the more chance of shit going south at some point. "Actually, I was just going to bring it up at Church, but Harlow picked up that there was something on my mind last night and suggested I talk to Blade."

Fuck, I had no clue where he would take this, so I nodded and waited for him to lay his cards on the table.

"What you told me yesterday, that shit stays between us...the three of us. I wasn't sure what to do with it, but Blade helped me to understand that life isn't all black and white, and that sometimes the deeds of the past shouldn't be a reflection on the person of today. I get why you did what you did. I mightn't like it or agree with it, but one thing I *do* get is loyalty to family with no questions asked and no stone left unturned." He took a breath before continuing. "You're my family, Griff, and the shit I said to you yesterday was in the heat of the moment.

230

You've proven yourself over and over to me...you don't have to prove yourself again."

His words hit me in the chest, and I took a minute to recover. "Fuck," was all I got out before Blade stepped forward and spoke.

"That being said, you've got a problem where Ricky is concerned. He knows your identity and I'm guessing he knows your involvement in the Bond case. That means he'll use that to his advantage, and fuck knows his agenda these days."

Scott nodded in agreement. "Yeah, so we need to move on him. And we need to move fast. Fuck waiting for the club to have its shit together to deal with the fallout...we need to do this today."

My mind was still trying to wrap itself around Scott's acceptance of my past, but I pushed that to the side to focus on our revised plan to deal with Ricky. "You got any ideas?" I asked.

"Yeah, we've come up with something," Scott said and we spent the next twenty minutes going over the plan.

Today was shaping up to be a good day – by the end of it, Storm would have one less headache.

***

As I sat back in position, watching Ricky's house from a few houses down and waiting for Blade's signal, my phone buzzed silently with a text from Nash.

Nash: We have the details for tomorrow's drug deal.

Me: Good. We'll go over it later.

Nash: How's our friend?

Me: Twenty minutes tops and he won't be our friend anymore.

I shoved my phone back in my pocket. Nash, Wilder and Scott weren't here for this part of the plan. They were out with the rest of our boys raising hell and giving Storm an alibi for this murder. Blade, J and I were taking care of Ricky with the help of Blade's boys.

My signal from Blade came – a flick of his wrist – and I started the Range Rover, and drove it down the street. It was Ricky's Range Rover that I'd 'borrowed' from his driver while said driver took a rest. Pulling up outside Ricky's house, I asked the woman in the back, "You ready?"

"All ready, Mr. Griff." She winked at me in the rearview mirror. "Maybe once we done for the day, you give me a go? I could show you good time."

I met her gaze in the mirror. She was a beautiful woman, especially if you were into Asian beauty. I, however, wasn't into any beauty other than the beauty that was spending today regrouping, so I shook my head. "I'll have to say no, babe."

"Ah, I see, you already got woman for tonight."

My dick jerked at the thought. I sure as fuck did.

The back door of the Range Rover opened, and Ricky got in. I held my breath waiting to see if our plan would be shot to shit before it even really began, but the woman in the back played her part well, and stole his attention completely off me. I'd dressed appropriately, and if he'd given the back of me a quick glance, he would have assumed I was his driver, but if he'd investigated closely, we would have needed to move to Plan B.

We knew from Nash & J's surveillance of Ricky that his driver collected women for him every day at two and then picked him up to take them both to a sex club. Today, we'd supplied the woman and Ricky wouldn't be making it as far as the club.

While she distracted him, I drove in the direction of the club. Blade and his boys followed at a distance, and just before we arrived at the club, I took the agreed upon detour.

"Why the fuck did you turn there?" Ricky demanded, and I pressed a little harder on the

233

pedal. We were nearly at our destination – an old warehouse that Blade owned.

I didn't answer him. Instead, J appeared from the very back of the Range Rover, hooked his arm tightly around Ricky's throat from behind and held his gun to Ricky's head. "It seems we have a slight detour to make, motherfucker," he snarled.

Ricky began kicking at the seat in front of him and clawing at J's arm. I concentrated on the road ahead, drowning out their yelling as best I could, even though my natural instinct was to take my gun and shoot him in the goddamn head. We'd agreed, though, not to shoot him in the Range Rover. We wanted nothing left in the car that could possibly lead back to Storm.

A few minutes later, I pulled into the warehouse and slammed on the brakes. Blade and his boys pulled in after us and then the doors to the warehouse were quickly pulled shut. I jumped out, rounded the car, opened Ricky's door and yanked him out. J followed close behind, and as I held him, J patted him down, removing weapons as he went.

Blade joined us, and Ricky scowled at his presence. "I see you boys needed Blade to tag along for this. Storm never did have any fucking balls."

Once J had removed all of Ricky's weapons, I shoved him away from me so he stood in the middle of all three of us. Blade's boys held back, ready for whatever went down.

"I'm merely here for fun, Ricky," Blade said. "And to see you get what you should have gotten years ago. I don't make many mistakes in life, but letting you live back then was one of my biggest ones."

"No, your biggest mistake will be what goes down today. If you think I don't have plans in place for what happens in the event of my death, you're all fucking stupid. But then again, I always knew that."

I punched him hard on the cheek. Something I'd wanted to do for a very long fucking time. I'd hit him with such force that he stumbled back quite a few steps. His hand moved to his cheek, and he scowled at me.

I held up my hands in a fighting position, and said, "Take a shot, motherfucker. I'm in the mood for some fun today."

He lunged at me, but I sidestepped his punch. Moving fast, I turned and punched him in the gut.

"Fuck!" he roared, clutching his gut. He then came at me again, and managed to clip me on the side of my face.

I was ready for him, though, and punched him so hard on his cheek that he fell to the ground.

Stepping forward, I pressed my boot into his gut to hold him down there. "You wanna know who made the mistake in all of this, Ricky? You, motherfucker. Storm is a force to be reckoned with now that Marcus is gone. We're not gonna just roll over and let people fuck us anymore," I snarled, my anger at him rolling through me, consuming me.

J eyed me, a look of pure dislike on his face. "Can we hurry this the fuck up? The shit coming out of his mouth is worse than the worst reality show on TV, and I should know how bad that stuff is 'cause my wife subjects me to it more than I care to admit."

"Tell you what, J...go for it, brother," I said, yanking Ricky up off the ground.

One of the things I knew about J was that he didn't screw around when given a job to do, and he only proved to me today how true that was. The moment I gave him the go ahead, he nodded, aimed his gun at Ricky and fired. Ricky barely had time to even process my words before he was dead on the ground before us.

I looked from Ricky to J, and said, "Fuck, you don't like to waste time, do you?"

"The only time I'm happy to do that is when I'm waiting for my wife's lips to move from one end of my cock to the other, brother. You give me an order, consider it done there and then," J replied as he walked to where Ricky lay.

Blade rounded up his guys. They would be taking care of Ricky's body to ensure it was never found, and dumping the Range Rover while Blade drove J and I back to the clubhouse.

"That almost felt too easy," J said.

"The thing I've learnt about easy is that it always comes back to haunt you," Blade shared. "I doubt Ricky's guys will rest until they figure this out, and my guess is they'll be looking at us first, so we have to stay alert. We've got the plan in place for our homes and businesses to be watched, but there's always that element of surprise – something we haven't thought of – so watch your backs at all times."

***

"Everything go down okay?" Scott asked when I entered his office an hour later.

"Yeah. J said it felt too easy and I have to agree with him," I replied as I sat opposite him.

"It helped that we knew his schedule so well; knew his area of weakness."

"True. How did your end go?"

He grinned, and it was the first time I'd seen a smile on his face for weeks. "It's been too long since Storm has had some fun, brother."

Brother.

Thank fuck.

"You think it worked?"

To give Storm an alibi for the time of the murder, for when Ricky's guys went digging, we'd set up a distraction. Scott, Nash and every other member we could round up had headed over to the busiest bar in The Valley where we'd arranged for about ten chicks to be at, including Velvet. She'd staged an impromptu wet t-shirt competition and when the boys had turned up, Nash had revved them up to get involved and cause a scene, dragging as many of the bar's customers into.

"Yeah, it worked. So many guys got into it that the bar owners called the cops who had to come and settle everyone down. The girls did a great job getting it all going, and it was fuckin' funny watching the cops try to do their job while all the drunks ignored them. And it must have been a slow news day because Channel Ten arrived and filmed it all."

"So now we wait and see where the dust settles," I said.

"Yeah. I figure we've got eyes everywhere, watching all members' families. We can't do much more than that."

I was silent for a moment, while I tried to get my thoughts in order so I could say what I needed to say. Eventually, I went with simple. "Thank you, brother."

He knew what I meant and nodded. "I'm sorry about your family."

"Yeah. My father was a prick, but my mother and brother didn't deserve what happened to them." It was odd to talk about the part of me I'd kept locked away from him for so long now.

"Fucking fathers," he muttered. "We wouldn't be here without the sons of bitches, but we're sure as hell better off without ours, Griff."

No truer words had been spoken about my father. And after all these years, it felt good to be able to talk about this with Scott.

Maybe my faith in family could be restored after all.

Chapter Nineteen
Sophia

I don't know what made me do it, but after work that day, I found myself at the hospital my mother was at. Perhaps it was the good day I'd had that began with Griff being amazing this morning and ended with my boss being fired for being inappropriate with a number of the female staff. Regardless of the reason, I stepped through the door of her room at around five thirty and my past collided with my present in a way I could never have predicted.

She knew who I was the instant she saw me. How could she not? I was her spitting image, minus nineteen years. "Sophia," she said softly, and I sucked in a breath at the sound of her voice. I'd recognise that voice anywhere.

With hesitation, I took the few steps to her bedside. I struggled with what to call her but in the end I went with the only name I knew her by. "Mum."

She motioned to the chair next to her bed. "Sit, baby."

I hated that word on her lips, but I silenced that thought. Sitting, I asked, "How are you feeling?"

She shrugged. "I'm okay. The docs are looking after me well."

"That's good." God, this conversation was so stilted.

"I want to know about you, baby. How are you?"

My eyes widened. Did she mean in general? Or how had I been for the last twenty years? Her question threw me and I was lost for words.

"Sophia?" she nudged me.

Without warning, my emotions surged forward and took over, and as the words fell from my mouth, I couldn't stop them even if I wanted to. Standing, I threw my words at her as if they were all the hurt she'd ever given me – the hurt I had desperately wanted to throw back at her my whole life. "If you're asking me how I am today – *now* – I'm good. Amazing even. But if you, by any chance, want to know how I've been for the last twenty years – *since you last saw me* – I've been up and down, to hell and back. All because of you." I stopped for a moment to catch my breath, and then continued. "I don't know why I came here today, but perhaps it was to ask you for one thing. Please tell me how a mother can walk away from her daughter and her husband when he's on life support, dying? Did you feel any guilt over that? Or did you just carry on with your life and build another family? Another family that you incidentally screwed over, too."

She sat staring at me, blinking – blinking away the tears that she didn't deserve to even have. "Baby – "

"No! Don't call me that. You don't get to call me that!" I yelled at her, my heart beating wildly, and my body pulsing with adrenalin.

"You don't understand...your father and I were over long before his accident."

I stared at her. "And what about me? Were we over, too? How does a parent even get to decide something like that? I was nine. Nine!"

"I wasn't mentally stable. It was better for you that I left. I did it for you." Her eyes were pleading with me to understand, but this was something I would *never* understand.

I shook my head. "No. You left for yourself, and even if you left for me, you should have come back. You should have gotten the help you needed, after you made sure I was okay, and then you should have come back. *That's* what a mother does. They don't just abandon their child when shit gets too hard...oh, my God, I can't even look at you right now." I turned away from her, my mind and body a mess of emotions and thoughts and hate. The hate was consuming me so much I felt like I would vomit. Clutching my stomach, I focused on my breathing and willed myself not to throw up.

And then my phone rang.

I ignored it.

I also ignored the pleas of my mother.

My phone rang again.

And again.

And all the while, my mother sobbed in her bed.

She had no right to sob.

No fucking right.

My phone rang again.

Shit.

I snatched it out of my bag and answered it without even checking who it was. "Hello," I snapped.

A pause. And then, "Sophia, are you okay?"

Griff.

A sense of calm washed over me at his voice.

"No, not really," I answered him honestly, still clutching my stomach and praying the nausea away.

"Where are you?"

"At the hospital." My thoughts scrambled to make sense. I couldn't make sense.

"Which hospital, sweetheart?"

"The Royal Brisbane."

"Which ward?"

"I can't remember. The one for heart attacks."

Don't make me answer any more questions.

I can't do it.

"I'll be there soon."

And then he hung up, and I doubled over in pain.

Emotional pain hurt so much more than physical pain sometimes.

"Sophia." My mother's voice shifted through my consciousness. "Please don't shut me out. I made a huge mistake all those years ago, and I want to try and make it right now."

I spun around and glared at her. "You can't make this right. Not now. Not ever. I spent the last twenty years waiting for you to come back. And all that time I thought that if my own mother didn't want me, how could anyone else want me? Do you know what that does to a child? To a person?" I glared at her harder. "It fucks them up," I spat. "And, I'm done being fucked up. I've moved on and so should you."

As I turned to leave, her last words floated through the air. "I won't give up, baby. I love you and I'll show you that I mean it."

Her words were worthless to me. I stalked down the hospital corridor to the lift, oblivious to everyone around me. The lift took forever to come – well, it felt like forever – and I travelled down to the ground floor in silence, alone with my thoughts. When the elevator doors opened, I stepped outside and into Griff's arms.

And I collapsed into him in a mess of tears and sobs and hurt.

He held me and let me cry it out, his hand running gently over my hair. When my tears dried up, I wrapped my arms around his waist, and clung to him.

His body and soul were my refuge.

Eventually, I lifted my face to look at him. His concerned eyes met mine, and he said, "I'm going to take you home now. Yeah?"

I nodded.

"We'll take your car and I'll come back and get my bike later."

I nodded again, and he led me towards the car park.

And then he took me home and continued to be the amazing man I was fast learning he was.

***

I tried to swallow, but my throat was so dry that as much as I swallowed, nothing helped. Blinking awake, I found myself secured in Griff's hold, up against his body again. This time on my bed.

I shifted and his hold loosened enough for me to move to a sitting position. Swinging my legs over the edge of the bed, I moved off it to go in search of water. I made it to the kitchen, filled a glass and drank every last drop. Turning, I found Griff standing behind me, worry on his face.

"Sorry," I apologised as I placed the glass on the counter.

"There's no need to apologise."

"God, what time is it?"

"Just after ten. You slept for hours which you must have needed."

"Thank you for coming to get me earlier...I don't think I could have gotten myself home."

He moved closer to me. "Do you want to talk about it, sweetheart?"

It was the last thing I wanted to talk about but the one thing I knew I had to talk about. I looked up into his face, and the care I saw there gave me the strength to bare my soul. "I haven't seen my mother for twenty years, and she turned up two days ago, sick in hospital and wanted to see me. God knows what I thought would happen, but I went to see her after work today and it was the worst thing I could have done."

He took hold of my hand and led me to the couch. Sitting, he positioned me on his lap, his arm around me. "Start at the beginning," he said.

"The beginning?"

"Why haven't you seen her for twenty years?"

Shit.

Thinking about this was hard work. I wasn't sure if it was good for a person's soul to dredge the past up like this or not. But I wanted him to know me, and this was a huge part of me. "When I was nine, my father had a horse riding accident and ended up on life support. He was in a coma for months and my mother walked away from us. I came home from school one day and she was gone. Her sister took me in for a few months, but she didn't want another kid to take responsibility for, and eventually I ended up in the foster care system. I think my aunt thought my mum would come back,

247

or my dad would wake up, but Mum didn't, and Dad passed away."

His jaw clenched. "You never saw her again?"

"No, not once. And I never knew she had another daughter until six months ago when Magan searched for me. Mum had walked away from her, too. When she was five. She's also now in the foster care system."

"Fuck," he swore, and I completely agreed.

I shifted so one arm was around him, and I tangled my fingers in his hair at the nape of his neck. "I don't think I can ever bring myself to understand her actions. Maybe I went to her today hoping it would help, but it didn't. It just dredged all the shitty feelings of not being worthy up. And hate...It brought up all the hate I feel towards her, and I don't want to feel hate, but I do." My voice cracked on that last sentence. I lived my life totally against the feeling of hate, but as much as I tried, I couldn't stop that feeling from bubbling up when I thought of my mother.

He was silent for a beat. When he spoke, I knew deep in my bones that he had first-hand experience with what he said. "Hate is a double-edged sword, baby. Sometimes it's all you've got and all you're capable of feeling. Sometimes it gets you through when nothing else can. When you think you'll go fucking crazy from what you're going through, you need something – *anything* – to grip onto and believe in...just to get you through to that next level of feeling. But it's not a good place to be for too long. It'll eat you up and rip your soul out if you hold onto it for any length of time. At some point you need to find a way to move past it, into an acceptance of sorts. You need to accept that the person will never be who you need them to be - and that's on them, not you. Acceptance doesn't mean you accept what they gave you...you never have to do that."

His words worked their way into my heart and I knew they would help me. Maybe not today, or tomorrow, or even next month, but at some point they would be like a switch lighting up my darkness and leading the way for me to move past the feelings that didn't serve me.

I pressed my lips to his and kissed him.

Slow and deep.

I loved that he gave the same back to me. He didn't push for anything else; he simply let me lead the way, and after last night, I knew that was out of character for him. And that meant so much to me.

I felt special.

He made me feel special.

Chapter Twenty
Griff

Sophia's bed was empty when I woke and goddamn if that didn't force me out of bed faster than I'd ever left one before. I found her sitting outside on her back patio in the morning sun, sipping coffee and staring into space.

She turned when she heard me. "Morning, handsome." Her smile lit her face, replacing the tears that had marred it yesterday. That smile could light a million dreams a man could ever dream.

I bent to place a kiss on the top of her head. 'Morning, beautiful."

Pointing towards the kitchen, she said, "There's coffee, help yourself."

"You want another one?" I asked as my gaze roamed over her. She wore the skimpy shorts and tee pyjamas that she wore to bed last night. Those pyjamas drove me wild all night as I slept next to her. Every time my hand made contact with them, I had to rein in the overwhelming desire to rip them off. Last night hadn't been about sex; it had been about Sophia trying to come to terms with the encounter she'd had with her mother. My need for her had to come second to that. If there was anything I understood in life, it was being fucked up by a parent.

"No, I'm already on my second," she answered and I left her to go and make coffee.

The day stretched ahead of me, half planned already. Nash had given me the information on the drug deal going down today that Ricky had assured us was a Storm deal. Scott, J, Nash and I would check it out and see if any Storm members were involved.

"I'm sorry about last night," Sophia said softly from behind me.

I turned and frowned. "I told you that you never need to apologise."

"No, not for that...for, you know...oh, God...well, when a man starts seeing a woman, it's all about the sex, right? And we had the most amazing sex the other night, and then the next day, I dump all that stuff on you about my mum, and you take it like a champion, and you stay the night, rather than running a mile like a lot of guys would. And you never even attempt to have sex with me, but I'm guessing it's on your mind – I mean, it's on *my* mind so it's gotta be on your mind – but, damn, you're not like any guy I've ever slept with, because all those guys would not have done what you did yesterday." She took a breath and her eyes widened. "Oh, my goodness, that makes me sound like I've slept with a lot of guys, but I haven't...well, I'm no prude, but I'm certainly no slut. I can count on two hands - "

I closed the distance between us and placed a finger to her lips. Fuck, she was cute when she rambled like this, but there was no way in hell I wanted to hear the number she was about to tell me. I didn't need to be thinking of another man with his hands on her skin. "Sweetheart, I don't want to ever hear an apology for not having sex with me fall out of your mouth again. And no, this isn't just about the sex for me. If you haven't worked that out yet, I need to do some serious work on my end of this

252

relationship. But I will admit that you, and your body, and the sin you're capable of leading a man into are always on my mind."

She gazed up at me with a look that took my breath away for a moment. I'd never had a woman look at me that way, as if all their suns could rise and set with me. And fuck if I didn't like that. She opened her mouth to say something, but then snapped it shut. After a moment of silence, she smiled and said, "You don't need to do any work on your end. I'm hearing you loud and clear; we're on the same page. And tonight, I've got some temptation to lead you into."

Fuck.

"Baby, you've already led me. I'm burning in the flames of hell because of the sins I want to commit with you."

Her smile grew and she brushed her lips across mine in a kiss. And then she deepened that kiss until my dick bulged in my jeans and I thought I would explode with need.

Pulling my lips from hers, I rested my forehead against hers, and said, "As much as I'd love to finish that, I have to get to work. And a quick fuck won't satisfy the need I have for you today. It would leave me just as frustrated as I feel now."

"Okay, handsome, you go to work and I'll be waiting for you here when you finish," she promised.

The last thought I had as I left her house was to question what I'd ever done to have Sophia come into my life. I may have only known her a short time, but there were some people you met in life who you just knew had the possibility of becoming someone very important to you.

Sophia was already one of those people.

***

"You really think someone's gonna show?" Nash asked as he fidgeted next to me in the back of the van.

We were waiting in position down the street from the rundown house in Redcliffe where his source had told him the drug deal would take place. The deal should have happened ten minutes ago, but so far, no one had turned up. Nash was all out of patience, but Scott and I had decided to give it some more time before we called it quits. We both felt in our guts that something was going on here, and we were committed to waiting it out.

"Yeah, I do," I answered him.

"I'm wondering if Ricky's fucking with us from the grave," J chipped in.

"Fuck me," Scott muttered and shifted in his seat as if he was trying to get a better look at something. "Motherfucking asshole."

"Who is it?" I asked.

"Fucking Keg," Scott replied. "I would never have picked him to be involved in this shit." Keg had been a loyal Storm member for eight years.

"I would assume none of our members would be involved in this shit, brother," I said.

"True," Scott agreed. "When there's bank involved, you just never fuckin' know. *Fuck*." He opened his door and exited the van, and we all followed suit.

A couple of minutes later, Scott kicked in the front door of the house and we entered. The plan had been to figure out the best course of entry once we got here, but it seemed Scott was running on anger now, so he didn't stop to discuss it before he entered.

The three guys standing at the kitchen table looked up in shock as we stormed the house. Fuck, this place stank, and the garbage littered over the table and on the kitchen counters reeked of deadbeats who didn't give a shit and had no pride. I recognised Keg, but not the other two, which was strange because we pretty much knew every asshole drug dealer in this town.

One of the guys pulled his gun and aimed it at us, but Scott was five steps ahead and shot at the dude's leg before he could pull the trigger. The bullet grazed his lower leg and he yelled out in pain, but Scott ignored him. "I'm not in the mood to be fucked with today, motherfucker," Scott thundered as he came to a standstill. Eyeing Keg, he said, "Wanna tell me what the fuck you're doing here, Keg?"

Guns were aimed all over the place as we all protected our own interests. Keg stared wildly at Scott. "How the fuck did you know about this?"

Scott seethed. "I asked you a fuckin' question, Keg, and I want that question answered so I can make a decision about what happens next. What the fuck are you doing here?"

While Keg contemplated that, the drug dealer who hadn't been shot spoke up. "I'm taking it that Storm had no idea this deal was going down?"

Scott's attention was focused completely on Keg, so I answered, "Not a fucking clue. We've made it clear we're not interested in dealing anymore so I'm not sure why you'd arrange this thinking it was us."

Keg's expression turned into a sneer. "Storm should be dealing. Hell, we used to be a force to be reckoned with, but now we're the laughing fucking joke of Brisbane. Scott and you have seen to that. Marcus was right when he said Scott didn't have the balls to run the club."

Scott's last ounce of control snapped and he wrapped his hand around Keg's throat. "It would seem we have a difference of opinion then, Keg," he snarled. "And I bet you're the one stirring up shit with Sydney, right?"

Keg scoffed. "The club's too easy to piss off; it was like a walk in the fucking park stirring them up. And King's a pussy; he'd never act on his threats."

One of the drug dealers piped up. "This is between you guys...we're gonna go."

Scott's hand flicked around so he could aim his gun at the guy. "Sit the fuck down, and shut the fuck up. No one's going anywhere until we've sorted this out."

The guy muttered something under his breath but he did what he was told, and Scott returned his gaze to Keg. "You seriously think King's a pussy? You don't know the man very well, but I'm thinking it's time you two got acquainted." He pulled his phone out and dialed a number. "King...I have a name for you...yeah, he's the one you're after...will do, brother. He'll be waiting for you when you arrive." He hung up and grinned like a mad man at Keg. There were days I was concerned Scott was heading down a path he didn't want to be on, and today was one of them. "King's on his way and I look forward to your play date with him."

"Fuck," Nash muttered behind me, and I couldn't help but agree. There was mad and then there was fucking insane, and I was fairly sure King fell into the latter category.

Scott turned to us. "J, can you bring the van up and we'll get Keg into it. We're not letting him out of our sight until King arrives." Looking back at the dealers, he said, "Storm's out of drugs. Make sure that knowledge gets spread far and wide, yeah?"

They nodded their understanding, and we left them to get Keg into the van.

What a way to end your year.

Chapter Twenty-One
Sophia

"So you guys are dating now?" Tania asked me over coffee. I'd scored an early mark off work and she had the day off so we'd arranged to catch up before she headed out to a New Year's Eve party tonight.

"I'm not sure what you'd call it, but it's gone from him keeping his distance to all of a sudden being there for me. It feels like it could be dating."

She laughed. "You need to clear that up with him, girlfriend, so you know where you stand. What do you want it to be?"

I smiled. "I want to get to know him, and spend time with him, and have lots of sex with him – and when I say lots, I mean *lots,* cause the man knows what he's doing in that department – so yeah, I want it to be dating."

"And you don't want to share him?"

My heart screeched to an almost halt at the thought of sharing Griff. "Hell no, I don't want to share him. Shit, do you think that's what he wants?"

She shrugged. "You know men...they often want different things to what we want."

The noise of the café swirled around me as I contemplated sharing Griff. I couldn't do it. If that was what he was into, I would walk. It would be hard to do, now that my heart was sold on him, but sharing men didn't work for me. Either the guy was all in or all out.

"I'm going to talk to him about this tonight. God, I hope it's not the end of what could be something amazing." And if it was, it would also be a crappy way to end the year.

My phone buzzed with a text.

Griff: What time will you be home?
Me: In about an hour.
Griff: I've gotta mow for Josie. I'll do yours, too.
Me: So long as I can have front row seats.

260

Griff: You can regroup while you watch.

Oh, my.
The man has an amazing sense of humour.

Me: I've already regrouped. I'm all about the porn now.

Griff: Fuck, baby. I'll see you later.

Tania watched me as I placed my phone on the table. "Going by the look on your face while you were texting with him – and I'm presuming it was him – you're one hundred percent in, so I hope he comes through for you." Her voice softened. "You deserve a good man after Tommy screwed you over. After you dedicated two years to that asshole, you deserve a fucking king."

I really did.

I just hoped I'd found one, rather than another lying, cheating asshole.

***

Griff arrived at my place an hour and a half later, carrying a bag from the hardware store. He placed it on my kitchen counter, snaked his hand around my waist, and pulled me to him. Placing a kiss to my

261

lips, he murmured, "Been a long fucking day and you're a sight for sore eyes."

I felt the same way, but at the same time, I was a little on edge after my conversation with Tania. Discussing my relationship with Griff was high on my priority list now, and while I wanted to think I was the only woman he said stuff like that to, I had to find a way to bring it up in conversation.

Eyeing the hardware bag, I asked, "What's in the bag, handsome?"

"I noticed the tap in your bathroom is leaking so I picked up some washers, as well as a light bulb for the light in your hallway that blew last night. Wasn't sure if you already had some, but I figured it wouldn't hurt to grab more just in case."

I stared at him.

Tears pricked my eyes and I felt so damn stupid for that, but I'd never – *not once* – dated a man who cared enough to do something like this. Blinking rapidly to try to get the tears under control made me feel even sillier, but it beat the alternative of turning into a blubbering mess in front of him.

He frowned as he watched me blinking. "Did I say something wrong, sweetheart?"

My emotions swelled and my breathing picked up as I fought the tears. And then, unable to keep the tears and the emotions in check, I lost my cool in front of Griff. *Again.*

"No, you didn't say anything wrong, or do anything wrong...in fact, you did everything right, and I'm not used to having a man around who does everything right. Oh, God, but you'll probably want me to share you, and I don't want to share you. I'm not the kind of woman who can do that, Griff, so if that's what you're looking for, we're going to have to call it quits now. And that would suck because for the first time in my life, I feel like I've met a man who has so much potential. I mean, you told me today you would do my mowing for goodness sake – *my mowing, in this heat* – no one has ever offered to do my mowing before. And now you're picking stuff up from the hardware that even I didn't know I needed." I gulped a breath, and he took that opportunity to interrupt me.

"Number one - sharing is off the table. In fact, it was never even on the table to begin with. No fucking way am I sharing you. Number two – I'm sensing some confusion about what this is between us, so we need to clear that up, before we go any further. You're mine now, Sophia. There will be no other men, and I will have no other women. I don't work that way, and I sure as shit don't date women who do." His eyes didn't let me go; it was as if they

263

were claiming me just like he had. And his voice was all kinds of commanding. It slid right through me, wrapping itself around me and making me feel both safe and desired.

I nodded. "I'm good with that," I said softly.

"Thank Christ. Now, I'm going to mow Josie's yard and then yours, and then after I take a shower, I'm going to taste that sweet pussy of yours again."

His eyes were fixed firmly on mine, and when I nodded in response – because I could hardly form a thought, let alone a word after that declaration - he dropped another kiss on my lips before leaving me to do the mowing. And I grasped the kitchen counter to steady myself. Griff's bossy ways caused a weakness in my legs that no other man ever had.

***

"Sophia."

Griff's voice held a dangerous edge to it; an edge that caused desire to pool in my belly. I waited in my bedroom for him to come and find me, and a few moments later, he stood in the doorway, his intense gaze on me. We watched each other, neither saying a word, neither moving to the other. And then he took control. And I escaped into a role where I felt more free than I'd ever felt in my life.

264

"Come here," he demanded, his powerful body strong and tall, and ready for me.

I left my dressing table where I'd been sitting brushing my hair and massaging body cream into my skin. Standing in front of him, I traced his body with my eyes. Griff's skin was free of ink and the artist in me imagined intricate designs of light and shade stretched across his hard muscles. He stood naked now, hard for me, and I shivered as I imagined what he would do.

"Take your clothes off."

I did what he said, removing my shorts, t-shirt and underwear, and a minute later, my body was revealed to him. My gaze shifted to his and I found him watching me – my face, not my body – and I watched him back. Our eyes communicated our desire, our need, and our stories.

He reached his hand out to run his finger lightly down my cheek. Bending his face, he kissed a trail of kisses along my collarbone and down to my breasts. At the same time, his hands massaged my breasts. Then one of his hands slid around my body and down over my ass. Gripping me there, he pulled my body to his.

Lifting his face to look at me, he said, "Have you got a scarf?"

I nodded. "Yes."

Heat flared in his eyes. "Go get it for me."

I stepped out of his hold and moved quickly to my wardrobe. Once I had the scarf, I went back to where he waited and handed it to him.

"Good girl," he murmured, his voice low and full of gravel. "Now, lie on the bed with your arms extended above your head."

My eyes held his for a moment longer, and then I moved to the bed, positioning myself how he had instructed. My skin pebbled with anticipation. I had no idea where this was going, but I didn't want to know. The unknown of sex with Griff was one of my biggest turn-ons.

He straddled me, resting on his knees, and tied my hands together above my head. Then he sat back and spent a few moments gazing at my hands before bringing his eyes to mine, and what I saw there made my core clench.

Raw need.

Griff's eyes had glazed over and his shoulders sat with a rigid stance as if he was only just holding himself back.

He wants me as much as I want him.

If my hands weren't tied, I'd reach out and touch him.

Oh, God, how I wanted to touch him.

I wiggled a little and his attention shifted to my body. He placed one hand on my stomach and one on my breast. His thumb circled my nipple while his hand on my stomach ran over my skin there slowly. It was almost as if he had no plan, but I figured differently. I believed Griff probably had a plan for everything he did.

With his eyes still on my body, he said, "Tonight you're going to show me how well you can obey me." He brought his eyes to mine. "I'm going to take you to the edge over and over, and you're not going to let go until I say you can."

I nodded my understanding.

He watched me nod as he continued to massage my body, and said, "Good girl."

The way he said those two words brought me to the edge almost. He had no idea how much his voice affected me.

He placed his hands around my waist and slowly lifted me off the bed in an arch so that my bottom and upper back were still touching the bed. Then he slid one hand under me and glided it up my back so he could hold me near the back of my neck. He rose back up onto his knees and slid his legs out either side which effectively brought him lower, closer to me. Griff's body might have been built, but he moved with an agility that was sexy as hell.

267

He moved the hand he still had at my waist so that it slid around and cupped my bottom. Then he lifted my ass and dragged me down the bed to bring my lower body to him.

He hooked my legs over his shoulders and brought my pussy to his mouth.

Oh, my.

When his tongue glided through me, I had to bite my lips hard to silence the moan wanting to escape. And in that instant, I knew this man was going to torture me with pleasure tonight.

With his hands holding me firmly in place, his mouth delivered a level of bliss I never knew existed. The sight of his head buried in my most intimate place, and the growls coming from him as he lost himself in what he was doing combined with the sensations taking over my entire body, and I had to concentrate hard on not falling over the edge.

After a few minutes, he lifted his head, and rasped, "Fuck, you taste good, baby. I could spend hours tasting you."

I wanted to tell him to keep going, and never stop – *oh, God, please don't ever stop.*

Dipping his face to me again, he circled my clit with his tongue over and over, building the pleasure again. It washed over me in waves – never-ending waves that crashed through me, wanting to take me with them over the edge, but I fought that all the way. And that only heightened every sensation and every feeling rushing at me. My mind was in overload as I focused on letting the pleasure come while trying desperately not to let it completely consume me to the point of orgasm.

"Sophia."

My eyes opened at the sound of his voice and I watched and waited for his next command.

"I'm going to stop holding you, and I want you to support yourself on the bed with your pussy in the air."

Did he have any idea what he was asking of me? To hold myself up like that would take a level of concentration I wasn't sure I had. Not while I was concentrating so hard on not coming.

"Okay," I agreed, though, because I would do anything he told me to do at this point. So long as he kept delivering pleasure.

He let me go, and I used my muscle and core strength to hold my stomach and bottom up off the bed for him. My feet were planted in front of where he sat on the bed, and when he tapped them to indicate he wanted them spread wider, I did as he'd asked, ignoring the burn beginning in my leg muscles.

The burn was all worth it when a moment later, his hands gripped my ass and he brought his tongue back to my pussy. And when he then pushed a finger inside me and began stroking, I wondered if every woman knew this type of heaven existed.

His strokes were slow and rhythmic, designed to work a woman to a crazed state. I should know because he was slowly taking me there. He didn't want me to come yet, but that was getting harder and harder with each new round of pleasure. Each time a wave crashed over me, my muscles threatened to let my body collapse onto the bed. I wasn't sure how much longer I could hold myself up.

And not to reach out and touch him? That was a whole other level of *how-the-fuck-will-I-make-it-through-this?*

He pushed another finger inside so I now had two delivering me heaven. I writhed under his touch, my muscles seriously beginning to tire. My eyes squeezed close and my fingers curled into a ball, wanting desperately to cling to something, but unable to latch onto anything the way they were tied. The orgasm that continually tried to shatter me, moved dangerously close until it reached the point where I thought I could no longer fight it.

"Griff, I can't...I can't do this anymore." I panted as my muscles gave way and my body dropped to the bed.

His fingers left me, and in what felt like a split second, he had me flipped onto my stomach, and he'd moved so his knees were on the bed, either side of my legs. One of his hands landed on the bed beside me while he placed the other one on my back. He growled into my ear, "Do you know what happens when you don't obey me, Sophia?"

My breathing had turned into pants and my muscles were screaming at me, all while my pussy pulsed with need. "No," I managed to get out, even though I struggled to form a thought while my mind tried to deal with all my senses at once.

"When you don't do as I say, I get to punish you, in any way I want."

He moved his face away from mine, and a second later, he placed his hand on my bottom and began massaging it in a circular motion. My ass cheeks tensed, knowing what was about to come.

"Fuck, baby, your ass is perfect."

He continued to massage me.

Teasing me.

Oh, God, how I waited for what he was about to do.

"You want this, don't you?" he asked.

"Yes." I whimpered.

"Tell me how much," he demanded, still massaging. Still teasing.

"So bad, baby..." My voice drifted off as my senses went into overdrive.

I need him.

Everything he has to give.

I will take all of it.

His hand kept moving over my ass, and then when I thought he was about to spank me, he said, "You need to learn that I'm in charge of your pleasure. And that I decide what you get." He pushed up off the bed and left me. A moment later, the sounds of my drawers being opened filled the room.

I focused on my breathing and preparing myself for what would come next.

"I want you on your back," he finally ordered after rummaging through my drawers for a minute or so.

I rolled onto my back and met his gaze as he stood next to the bed watching me, holding a couple of pairs of my panties in his hand. His breaths were slow and controlled as he let his gaze travel over my body. When he moved onto the bed, his movements were also controlled. I was slowly learning that Griff was the master at holding himself back.

He untied my hands, and then tied them to the bedposts using the panties he'd found. My heart beat faster. I'd never been tied to a bed before, and, holy hell, it was hot. And then he tied my feet to the bedposts at the bottom of the bed, and I thanked whatever force in the universe had led me to buy a bed with bedposts.

I lay spread-eagled on my bed as Griff moved off it to stand at the base. He stood in silence as he spent a few moments committing my body to his mind. His eyes didn't allow an inch of my skin to miss out.

"I am going to make you feel so damn good, and you are going to want to be involved in that, but you won't be able to touch me. And you are going to come over and over until you can't take it anymore." He paused to find my eyes. "And *that* will be your punishment."

I wanted to squeeze my legs together.

He is going to kill me with pleasure.

When he positioned himself on the bed in between my legs, and ran his hands over my thighs, I quivered at his touch. He was right – I wanted to touch him, and kiss him, and do so many things to him.

This will be unbearable.

But oh, God, it will be so damn good.

His hands glided up my sides, over my belly and breasts, and to my neck as he bent over me. Bringing his lips to mine, he kissed me with a hunger I matched, and we lost ourselves in it. Our lips and tongues devoured each other for so long I lost track of time. I never wanted the kiss to end, but eventually he broke it, and I lay there panting for whatever was next.

I tugged on my restraints and he placed a hand over one of mine. "Don't fight it, baby. You'll hurt yourself," he warned.

After I nodded my understanding he reached out to one of my bedside tables and grabbed a condom that he must have put there earlier. Once he had it on, he moved back down between my legs and buried his face in me again.

My back arched up off the bed slightly as his mouth and tongue worked me towards my release. His fingers expertly took me over the edge, and I finally – *finally* – let myself fall. I was helpless to stop it. He'd taken me to the edge so many times tonight and this time the orgasm shattered through me as my body jerked in its restraints and my pussy pulsed around his fingers. I bit my lip and squeezed my eyes shut as it took over.

"Fuck," he rasped, and I blinked my eyes open. He reached out to run a finger down my cheek.

"You are so fucking beautiful when you come, Sophia."

A moan passed by my lips as he slid his hands under my back and peppered kisses all over my stomach, breasts and throat. And then he moved his mouth along my neck, his teeth sinking in and marking me.

Exquisite.

I wanted his teeth all over me in that moment because it felt so damn good.

My legs fought their restraints, needing to be wrapped around his body, and my frustration grew at not being able to touch or hold him.

When he finished marking my neck, he pulled his face away from mine, and asked, "You want your legs around me?"

"Yes."

"And your hands on me?"

You've got no idea just how much. "Yes."

He was silent for a beat. "And your mouth on me?"

Worst form of punishment ever. "Yes."

He pressed a finger to my lips and then trailed it over my chin, down the centre of my neck, between my breasts, down my stomach and to my clit. "Not until I say so."

His finger circled my clit, and I writhed with the intense sensation that caused – a beautiful mix of pleasure and pain. My clit was so sensitive that I bit my lip and held my breath waiting for the painful sensation to pass, knowing it would soon and that it would take me to another exquisite orgasm.

When he pushed his cock against my entrance, I wanted to scream out my annoyance at not being able to wrap my legs around him.

I wanted to hold him.

And take his cock inside me.

And fuck him.

I wanted my body pressed hard to his, skin to skin, soul to soul.

"I want you." The words fell from my lips in a cry – a desperate cry of need.

His fingers kept circling...pushing inside...stroking...circling...pushing. "I want you, too," he said next to my ear, and my body sparked with excitement.

He didn't chastise me for not obeying, so I tested the boundaries. "Fuck me, Griff. I can't wait any longer," I begged.

He reared up onto his knees. "Fuck," he rasped, his eyes wild with desire. Taking hold of my hips, he positioned his cock and ran it through my wetness. "Jesus, Sophia, I want to draw this out, but, *fuck*, I need to be inside you, baby."

I couldn't move like I wanted to, but I tried to push myself closer to him, to encourage him to give in. It seemed to tip him over the edge, and he gripped my hips firmer and thrust inside me.

Oh, God, this is what heaven feels like.

I closed my eyes and let the pleasure envelope me as he pulled out and thrust back in, over and over. His grunts as he chased his release turned me on more than I already was. Griff expressing his need for me was something I loved hearing.

As my orgasm moved closer, I opened my eyes to look at him. His hands were on the bed on either side of me, and his face was above mine. His eyes were focused on my face, and he dipped his mouth to mine when our gazes met.

He kissed me hard.

Possessive almost.

And my orgasm hit while he took ownership.

I moaned into his mouth, and he caught my lip with his teeth as he dragged his mouth from mine. And then he came with a roar. He thrust hard one last time and then stilled as his orgasm took over. His eyes closed and his body tensed, and – *good God* – my powerful man came like I'd never seen a man come before. It was like he truly felt his orgasm, experienced it fully in not only his body but also his mind. He let himself go there completely, wherever 'there' was.

When he finally opened his eyes, he stared at me through eyes I couldn't read. We were silent for a few moments and then he pulled out of me, and moved to untie me. My arms were sore and my body was spent. Griff had exhausted me, body and soul, and sleep threatened to overtake me.

"I'll be back in a minute," he promised before he left me.

My eyes fluttered closed, and while I tried to fight sleep, to stay awake for when he returned, I failed.

As I drifted off, I wondered what it was about Griff I couldn't read after he came.

What was he thinking in that moment?

Chapter Twenty-Two
Griff

"Cheers!" King said as he raised his beer. "Here's to brothers and family and motherfucking loyalty." His eyes blazed with the level of crazy he was well known for. He'd arrived at the clubhouse this morning and had spent an hour grilling Keg about his involvement in stirring shit up between the Brisbane and Sydney clubs, and eventually dragged from Keg that he'd been responsible for it. Keg had also admitted he intended on dealing drugs regularly now that Marcus wasn't around to do it, and that Marcus had spread lies about Scott.

King had dealt with Keg in the only way King knew how – he'd ensured Keg never took another breath to cause Storm further problems. The most useful part of all this was the fact every Storm member now knew of Marcus's lies, and many had altered their view of Scott leading the club.

"Fuck, he's a wild bastard, but thank Christ he did what he did today," Nash said as he slapped me on the back.

"Yeah," I agreed. "Things should get back to some kind of order now."

"I fuckin' hope so, Griff."

As King and the boys partied, I went in search of Scott. Finding him in his office, I closed the door behind me and said, "You okay?"

He sat back in his chair and drank some of his beer before replying. "Yeah, it's just been a long day."

"Did you get hold of Blade?"

"He's on his way. Should be here any minute."

I rubbed the back of my neck trying to get rid of the knots that wouldn't shift. "Wilder's run into some problems with the insurance on the restaurant so I'm gonna go over that with him tomorrow. Everything else is good – no issues at any of the other restaurants or Indigo. I'm thinking we can

280

scale back the eyes we've got on everyone now that Ricky has been dealt with."

"You should be right to do that because from what I've heard, Ricky's second in charge isn't looking in your direction for his death." Blade's voice came from the doorway and we turned to him. He entered and added, "Your boys are having a good time out there. How's that all going?"

"We had a breakthrough today," Scott said. "One of our members admitted to everyone that Marcus had lied about shit."

"That should go a long way to you taking control," Blade said, and we both nodded our agreement. "As far as Bond goes, I've got a guy doing time with him, and he owes me. We can set the hit up for this week."

"Good," said Scott.

The uneasy feeling in my gut didn't ease at his words. It wouldn't until Bond was dealt with once and for all. "Thanks, man," I said to Blade, and he gave me a nod in return. I couldn't help but think how much Storm's relationship with him had changed in a year. He'd become one of our greatest allies.

Blade jerked his head in the direction of the bar. "You boys gonna have a drink?"

Scott nodded as he stood. "Yeah, I'm gonna hang around for awhile."

"I will, too," I said. "You should, too, Blade."

"Layla is working late tonight, so I've got a few hours to kill."

We headed out to join King and the boys. Most members had stayed for a drink when Scott and King put the call out this afternoon, so the bar was busy and loud. It had been too long since we'd let our hair down. This was just what we needed.

***

I woke up the next morning alone, in my own bed, and fuck if I didn't miss the fact Sophia wasn't pressed up to my body. Stumbling out of bed, I headed first to the bathroom, and then to the medicine cabinet. I'd drunk enough last night to give me one hell of a headache.

Swallowing some aspirin, I showered and dressed, and then headed over to Sophia's house.

"Morning, handsome," she greeted me at her front door. Her face had lit up when she'd opened it and that had warmed my cold heart. "I wasn't expecting you this morning."

I dropped a kiss onto her lips as my hand caught her around the waist and pulled her to me. "I know, but I have something I want to discuss with you before I head into work."

She took a good look at me, and said, "You look like you could do with some coffee first. I take it you stayed late last night."

As we headed into her kitchen, I said, "Got home at about three this morning."

"Do you boys do that often?"

I considered her question for a moment. "If you're asking me whether *I* do it often, the answer is no. The boys used to, but our club has been going through a rough patch the last year or so, and nights like that have been few and far between. Last night helped set us straight again, I think."

She smiled. "That's good to hear. And, just so you know, in case I came across as the kind of woman who keeps track of her man and tries to tell him what he can and can't do...I'm not that kind of woman. In fact, I feel sorry for those kinds of women, that they spend so much energy focused on that, and the men, too...having to put up with your partner dictating who you spend time with and for how long, that would suck. I only asked if that was a regular thing you do, so that I could make plans to have girls' nights when you have your boys' nights. I mean, perfect opportunity, right?" She took a deep breath and her eyes widened in the way they did whenever she rambled like this.

I pulled her close again. "Just so *you* know, I only answered your question because you're important to me, and I wanted you to know where I stood on this. Spending time with the boys is good. Spending time with you is better."

Her breathing slowed, and her face flushed with pleasure. "I'll make coffee now," she said softly.

I smiled and let her go with a nod. Pulling up a stool, I sat and watched as she busied herself in the kitchen. Sophia was in her element there, and I knew I could pass many hours watching her. There was something about a woman baking in the kitchen that turned me on.

"So, what's on your mind?" she asked as she placed a mug in front of me.

"I noticed the other day that your back patio needs a fair bit of work. I'm going to the hardware this afternoon and will order the supplies to rebuild it. The pavers are okay; I'll just need to redo the framework and roof."

She sat on the stool next to me, staring at me in silence. And then she placed her lips to mine and kissed me in the way any man would want their day to start. When she ended it, she said, "I would love you to do that, Griff. Thank you."

284

I didn't know what to do with her appreciation. It wasn't something I was used to from people. So I tucked it away and moved on. I drank what was left of my coffee and stood to leave. After placing my mug in the sink, I said, "I'll be over tonight after you get home from the gym."

She came to me and slid her arms around my waist. Looking up at me, she said, "We owe Josie a huge thank you. You do know it was her that pushed me to you that night, right?"

"Of course I know it was her. I knew from her eyes that day she faked her fall down the stairs that she had no intention of resting until she got what she wanted."

"Did you ever think she would get what she wanted?" The hesitation in her voice killed me. Sophia was the kind of woman any man would go to the ends of the Earth for and yet she doubted herself.

I tipped her chin up. "I'm a stubborn asshole and would never have admitted it to Josie, but I wanted you from the first moment I laid eyes on you."

The smile that lit her face was worth anything it cost me. "You might not say a lot, handsome, but the things you do say are priceless."

On the way to the clubhouse, I realised I'd give her a million words if it made her happy, and I couldn't say that about any other woman I'd ever met.

It was quiet when I arrived there. Most of the boys had left after me this morning and some had crashed right where they had their last drink. I ignored the sleeping bodies and headed into the kitchen to get more coffee. My head had almost stopped pounding and I figured one more coffee might do the trick.

As I waited for the kettle to boil, my phone buzzed with a text.

Danny: The trial has been delayed. Not sure how long, but giving you a heads up. Just so you know, though, there's no way out of this, Michael. You will be called as a witness and everyone will learn your identity.

I didn't send a text back. Slipping my phone back in my pocket, I thought about Bond. Everything seemed to be falling into place. The trial delay would work well for us with Blade's plan for Bond this week. No Bond would equal no trial. And my identity would be long buried.

Chapter Twenty-Three
Sophia

"What was it like for you growing up with Mum?" Magan asked me as we sat getting pedicures the next afternoon.

Her question surprised me coming out of the blue like that. We'd spoken a little about Mum over the last six months, but the topic almost felt out of bounds most days. Like neither of us wanted to confront our hurt. I guessed with Mum now back in our lives, the hurt was front and centre anyway, so there was nothing holding us back from talking about it.

"I was so young when I lived with her that I adored her. She could do no wrong in my eyes back then. But thinking about it now, as an adult looking back, she struggled as a mother. She didn't know how to deal with me when I was naughty. Instead of teaching me boundaries, she'd just send me to my bedroom and not talk to me. Her temper was so quick that she'd yell at me for the smallest thing, and I would then spend days trying to please her and make her happy with me again, because when she got mad at me, she held onto it for days, sometimes weeks."

Magan's eyes were wide. "I don't remember her being like that with me."

Telling the truth but at the same time not wanting to shatter my sister's rose-coloured memories was a hard thing to do. To top it off, I felt awful because I wanted her to see how badly our mother had treated us. I almost wanted to shake the God's honest truth into her, but I knew I could never be so cruel. Kids eventually grew up, and at some point their eyes would open and they would work the bad stuff out for themselves. That was one of the bitches of life. You couldn't hide from the truth forever.

"Maybe by the time she had you, she'd grown a little bit. She was so young when she had me. I don't know...no mother is perfect, and I don't ever expect perfection from a person, but I feel like she didn't try to do better," I said.

"She said she's going to try to be better now. And she still wants you to be part of her life. Do you think you ever will be?" The hope on Magan's face made me pause for a moment. She had an almost desperate need for me to want to be part of their lives, and I so wanted to be a part of Magan's life, but not our mother's.

I can't do it.

Not even for Magan.

I shook my head. "I'm sorry, Magan, but I can't. Too much has happened for me to be able to let her back in. I don't trust her...and without trust, I have nothing." My voice wobbled, and as much as I tried not to let this affect me – *because, goddamn it, she'd affected enough of my life already* – this stuff hurt.

She took all of that in, and finally nodded. "Okay." It was only one word, but I felt the emotion behind it, and I valued it for what it represented – her acceptance of my decision.

"Thank you," I whispered.

"So," she said, changing the conversation, "what's happening with lover boy?"

I grinned. "I'm sure he would love you calling him that. He's so far from a boy, babe."

"Good, I'll be sure to call him that when I see him next."

"He's the kind of man I've waited ages for. He did my mowing the other day, fixed my light bulb and washer, and now he's going to fix my patio." I all but sighed.

"So you're telling me that the way to your heart is by doing manly-type jobs?" she teased with a smile.

"Smart-ass," I muttered. "Seriously, though, men like this don't just hang around on street corners waiting for a woman to choose them. This is like gold. You have no idea."

"I can imagine, and I think I need to get to hang out with him for a bit so I can see his awesomeness in action. Do you think he'd also be down with doing assignments for your sister? 'Cause when school starts back up, I'm going to need help."

I laughed. "I'd love to see his face if you asked him for help."

We were busy laughing when my phone sounded with a text.

Griff: I'll be over at 7. Be ready.
Me: What do you have planned?

Griff: Trust me, sweetheart, you'll like what I have planned.

Me: I'll see you then.

"That was him, right?" Magan asked as she had her feet massaged.

"Yeah." My mind was already focusing on tonight and what he could possibly have planned.

"I guess I'm not getting an invite for dinner tonight."

I frowned. "Did you want an invite?"

"I'd never knock back dinner that you cook, because not only are you the best cook I know, but it gets me out of the house which means I don't have to eat the dinner Sue cooks me." Sue was her foster mother – a prime example of a person who should never have been accepted into the foster care system. She didn't abuse her foster kids, but she certainly didn't show them much love.

"I'll cook. What would you like?" I'd do anything for Magan to try and give her the family experience I'd never had.

Her smile made me happy. "Can you cook those sticky ribs you made that one time for me? They were so good."

"Sounds good. I'll let Griff know you're coming to meet him and have dinner with us." As I said this, the lady giving me the pedicure distracted me, and all thoughts of dinner were forgotten for now.

***

Griff: Get naked. I'll be there in ten minutes.

Me: Shit, I forgot to tell you my sister is coming for dinner with us.

He didn't reply for what felt like an hour but was probably more like a minute.

Griff: Your punishment for not telling me this is going to be exquisite.

I squeezed my legs together as I placed my phone down on the kitchen counter.

Oh, my.

He arrived eleven minutes later and I met him at the front door. His hand landed on my ass and he dragged my body up against his. "Just so you're aware, making me wait to have you is a form of fucking torture," he growled into my ear.

Lust somersaulted in my belly.

"I feel the same way, handsome," I murmured.

Letting me go, he entered my house. "Is your sister here yet?"

292

I nodded. "Yeah, she's out on the patio waiting for you. And Griff?"

He stopped and gave me his full attention. "Yeah?"

"Magan's really excited to spend time with you," I said softly.

His eyes held mine. "The feeling is mutual, sweetheart."

I followed him out to the patio and watched as my sister met my boyfriend.

She greeted him with a handshake – something I'd never seen her do before. And her voice was all formal at the beginning of the conversation. It was like she was making a huge effort with him. "Hi, Griff."

He shook her hand, and from the way she winced a little, I figured he'd forgotten to go easy. Grimacing, he apologised, "Sorry about that."

She pulled her hand back. "It's all good."

The atmosphere turned a little awkward with neither knowing what to say, so I intervened and offered drinks. Once we were all settled at the table with drinks, I asked Griff, "Did you have a good day?"

He took a sip of his drink, and answered, "Yeah, we got through a lot of stuff today that needed taking care of."

293

Magan tilted her head. "What do bikers do all day?"

Placing his drink on the table, he looked at her. "Storm has businesses that we run – restaurants and a club – so most of my days are spent working on that." His shoulders were tense, almost as if he didn't really want to be discussing this. I was impressed at how open he was being.

She seemed disappointed. "So it's not all shoot 'em up and hookers and drugs like they show on television, then? It kinda sounds boring the way you put it, dude. Why did you join Storm rather than one of those other clubs?"

His shoulders eased and a smile twitched at the corners of his lips. "Storm was the right fit for me."

She narrowed her eyes at him. "That's a very cryptic reason, but I won't push you. I know you bikers are the guarded type and all."

I stifled a laugh. Magan was trying so hard to be cool around him, and he was making an effort to let her get to know a little about him. It made my heart happy.

"You're still in school?" he asked her.

She rolled her eyes. "Yeah, I'll be in year twelve this year and then I get to escape this living hell at the end of the year."

"I take it you don't like school?"

"Did you, dude?" she threw out as if the answer was a no-brainer.

"I liked school," he said, stunning her.

"What the..? No way. You don't seem like the type who would have liked school."

He raised his brows. "There's a type who doesn't like school?"

She gestured at him. "You know...your type is like the people who give society the middle finger and tell them to eff off, you know? Like, you don't put up with bullshit, and I bet you didn't put up with the bullshit at school."

"I did well in school, Magan. And, yeah, I've always been the type to tell people to eff off, but the *type* you see sitting in front of you today? That's year's worth of work. You'll learn as you get older that you grow into yourself as you go. And part of that is taking all the steps through life that lead you to discover who you are."

"Ugh, I hate steps," she complained.

Griff chuckled. "Yeah, you and your sister, both."

My tummy fluttered that he'd remembered our conversation when I'd told him of my strong dislike of working through steps to get things done.

As I watched the two of them begin to get to know each other, I couldn't help think what a

295

strange world this was, bringing three people together like us.

Three people who truly needed what the others had to give – friendship and acceptance.

***

Griff dropped my car keys onto the kitchen counter and reached for my hand as I walked past him. Pulling me back to him, he said, "I like your sister."

We'd just dropped her at her house after dinner. She had planned on calling her boyfriend to come get her, but Griff had insisted on driving her in my car. I was pretty sure that made her feel special, and I loved that he'd given her that.

"I can tell that she likes you, too."

"How?"

"You're clueless on teens, aren't you?"

"Can't say I spend any time with them, sweetheart."

I laughed. "She spent the night talking to you, and asking you about yourself, and the conversation never felt stilted after the initial meeting. That's a sure sign a teen likes you."

He gave me the tiniest smile. If I'd blinked, I would have missed it. I felt for sure he was about to say something, but he didn't.

Frowning, I said, "What were you just about to say just now? It was like a thought ran through your mind and you let it go straight away."

He stared at me in silence until his chest rose and fell quite hard. Blowing out a long breath, he let me go, and ran his fingers through his hair. His eyes revealed a hurt or a pain that hadn't been there earlier, and I hated that I'd brought that on, but maybe he needed to talk about it.

"Griff?" I pushed him.

"This time four years ago, I thought I was gonna be a father..." his voice drifted off.

The pain was clear in his voice now. "What happened?" I asked softly.

"Turned out it wasn't mine after all. I was the fool who stuck around to see if it was mine, even after the bitch told me it probably wasn't." Hatred sliced through the pain in his voice as he spat his words out.

"Was this a woman you were dating?"

"We'd been together for two years. *I* thought it was more than just dating...I mean, *fuck*, when you share a house together, furniture together and a fucking bank account together, tell me you'd

297

classify that as more than just dating." He stopped talking and waited for me to give him my thoughts.

I nodded. "Yes, I would classify that as a relationship which is a lot more than just dating."

"Thank you. So, one day, I see her out to lunch with this other guy...kissing and flirting, and when I confront her, she admits that she's been seeing him, too, for over a year. *A fucking year.*" He paused, gathered himself and then continued. "Hedging her fucking bets, she told me. Said she'd been burnt before and wanted to make sure she chose the right guy this time, so she dated both of us."

My anger rose. I could hardly believe women like this existed. "Wait...was she living with him, too? And had a bank account with him, too?"

He shook his head. "No, I was the only motherfucking idiot who gave her that."

He's still mad, and not just at the woman.

He's so mad at himself.

"So, did you kick her out when you discovered all this?" I wasn't sure where the baby was going to fit into all this.

"No, before I had the chance to do that, she left and took all my stuff with her. I came home after work one Friday and the house was empty. Cleared out our joint bank account, too."

298

Oh. My. Goodness.

"People actually do that?" The words fell out of my mouth before I could stop them. Of course people did that...he'd just told me they did. But, damn, I struggled to comprehend how anyone could do that to another human being.

"Yeah, Sophia, people do that shit." His voice was hard and so full of hurt.

"Where does the baby fit in?"

He nodded, eyes glazed over, as if he was remembering his devastation. "I tracked her down the next day and she told me she'd chosen the other guy and was having a baby with him. I asked her how she knew it was his and not mine. She said she wasn't one hundred percent but believed it to be his. She refused to take a paternity test, and being the dickhead I was, I stuck around that shithole town until she gave birth and I could see for myself whose child it was."

My heart cracked a little for him. And for his loss – not only of the child, but also the loss of his belief in love thanks to that woman. I could wring her neck for what she had done to this man.

Staring at me, he said, "Clearly the child wasn't mine, and here I am four years later, childless and still pissed off." He shoved his fingers through his hair again. "Fuck!"

I moved closer to him and touched his cheek. "You obviously wanted the child to be yours?"

"I did, even though the relationship with the mother was fucked up. I had always wanted children."

"You don't want them anymore?"

"Fuck if I know. The thought of bringing children into this world and subjecting them to the hurt that people will inflict on them...that doesn't make me want to have children."

"I understand that...*God, do I understand that*, but, Griff, there's so much love to be had, too."

He didn't reply to that straight away. Rather, he let it settle for a moment. And then he shared another piece of himself with me, and it broke my heart. "My grandfather used to beat the shit out of my father when he was a kid. And then my father beat my brother and me when we were kids. He did take to my mother occasionally, too, but mostly he focused his anger on us. I grew up surrounded by violence, and violence lives in me, Sophia. I'm not sure I know how to love enough to have a child." Eyes full of anguish and torment stared at me as he bared that piece of his soul.

I wasn't sure what he needed to hear from me in this moment, so I just went with the words in my heart. "I've seen a little piece of your violent side, but I've seen far more of your caring side, too, and let me tell you, the care and kindness you've shown me so far is more than anyone in my life has ever shown me. You might have a gruff way of expressing yourself, and it's clear you hold yourself back from most people, but none of that means you're incapable of giving love. You have love to give...I mean, look at the way you love Josie. Love isn't grand gestures and fancy declarations; it's getting your hands dirty, and being there, and opening yourself up for the people you love...and letting them give all of that back to you. It's about being honest and handling their hearts with the amount of care you want yours handled with." I pressed my finger into his chest. "And you do all of that. I hardly know you, but even *I* can see that you do all of that and more."

He sucked in a breath. "How the fuck..." He didn't finish his sentence, seemingly lost in his thoughts.

"How the fuck, what?" I asked, dragging his attention back to me.

His hand cupped my cheek, and when he spoke, his voice was ragged. "How the fuck was I given you? Out of all the men available, you were led to me...you could do so much better, Sophia, and yet, I can't bring myself to give you up. I never wanted another woman after Charlene burnt me, but hell, I want you more than I want my next fucking breath."

I leaned closer to him. "You seriously underestimate yourself, handsome. And for the record, I don't want you to give me up so just get that thought out of your mind if it ever enters it."

His lips crashed down onto mine, and he stole my breath with a kiss that felt like he'd put all his emotions into. We were a tangle of arms, legs and bodies pressed hard against each other, hands all over each other, and mouths desperately seeking what we were both looking for in our lives – love.

When he pulled away from me, almost breathless, and eyes crazy with desire, he growled, "I need you in your bedroom, naked and kneeling beside your bed, waiting for me."

As he said the words, his hands moved to my t-shirt, and he pulled it over my head, and discarded it on the floor. His eyes shifted to my breasts as he undid my bra and removed it, too. And then his gaze moved lower as his fingers deftly undid my shorts and slid them down. He helped me step out of them before dropping them on the floor. I watched his face as his fingers slipped inside my panties and he removed them. I loved watching his eyes flare with desire for me, and tonight it was clear how turned on he was. My own desire sizzled through me like a heat that only he could cool.

He brought his eyes back to mine, and rasped, "Go."

I did as he said, and a few minutes later, I kneeled naked next to my bed, waiting with anticipation for what he would do to me. When he entered the room, my pulse quickened at the sight of his powerful body. He was in the middle of taking his t-shirt off as he walked through the door, and my eyes were drawn to his broad, muscular chest.

He dropped his shirt on the floor and flicked his jeans button to undo them. A moment later, the rest of his clothes fell to the floor, and he came to me, naked and ready. He held something in his hand, but I couldn't work out what it was. A ball, perhaps.

I faced the bed, and he stood behind me, and placed his hand on the top of my head. He ran his hand gently down my long hair, and then gathered it all into his hand in a ponytail. Pulling gently, he tilted my head back to look up at him and asked, "Do you know what this is, Sophia?" He held the ball up for me to look at.

I shook my head. "No."

Heat flashed in his eyes as if my answer had pleased him greatly. "I'm going to put this inside you. It has a bead in it that moves when you move."

He crouched and dipped his face to mine so he could speak close to my ear. "I am going to make you move so fucking much that this little ball is going to get you so goddamn wet that my dick will slide through you without even fucking trying."

My breath caught, and my core went into the kind of meltdown a girl has when she feels like all her Christmases have come at once and she can't believe her good fortune.

Thank you, God, for giving this man to me.

I remained silent, and he gripped my hair a little harder. "I want you to move to the end of the bed. When you get there, I want you to stand with your back to it and place your hands out so they are resting on the mattress."

The control in his voice, and the commanding tone he took, turned me on and called to a need I never knew I had before I met him - the need to hand control over to someone else.

I did as he said and waited silently at the end of the bed. He took his time, and when he finally stood in front of me, he held two pairs of my panties. Reaching for one of my hands, he tied it to one of the bedposts before repeating this with my other hand. Then he slid his hand around my neck and through my hair so he was holding my head. Dipping his face to mine, he bruised my lips with a demanding kiss. God, I loved the way he kissed me. It signaled his possessiveness over me, and while I knew a lot of women who weren't into feeling possessed by a man, I now realised I craved a man who needed me in that manner.

He ended the kiss, and brought his hands to my breasts. Massaging them, he said, "Fuck, your body is gorgeous, sweetheart. Why do you ever doubt that?" His eyes were focused completely on mine while he waited for me to answer his question.

I swallowed back my hesitation. This part of my soul was a part I chose to avoid as best I could. "I don't know," I said softly, not wanting to admit the truth to him.

His eyes narrowed on me. "I don't believe you. Tell me."

Shame washed over me, and I wished I could break free of his restraints and run far away from this question. "I don't want to."

He held his tongue for a beat, and then he kissed me again. When he pulled away from my face, his eyes were softer. Taking a step back, he let his gaze drop to my body and took it all in. Slowly.

Usually, I liked his eyes on me, but today, I felt so self-conscious in my own skin now that he'd put the focus on me that I dropped my face and refused to watch him looking at me. I couldn't do it. All my feelings of being inadequate and fat rushed at me – bad memories I wanted to bury deep and never think about again.

And, *oh God*, then he dropped to his knees in front of me, put his hands on my hips, and pressed his mouth to my stomach, and kissed me. He spent a few moments kissing my stomach before moving his lips all over my body, kissing every inch of skin. His hands ran all over me, too, and he kept murmuring over and over how fucking beautiful I was.

When he made his way to my mouth, he looked into my eyes and said, "Tell me why you believe what I see when I look at you isn't a beautiful body."

He's not going to let this go.

I closed my eyes as my heart beat faster, and my breaths quickened. When I opened them again, tears sat on my eyelashes. "I've always seen myself as fat, even when I was a nine-year-old kid who was far from fat. My mother was always on a diet when I lived with her, and everywhere I looked on television and in magazines, they talked about counting calories and not letting yourself get fat. So I began counting calories at the age of about twelve. And then, I did become a little overweight, but instead of counting calories, I just kept eating." My voice cracked as I admitted the sad truth of my hurt. "It made me feel good when nothing else in my life did. I don't know why, and I've never worked it out, but it is what it is. About five years ago, when the doctor told me I was obese, I finally took control and lost the weight. It was one of the hardest things I've ever done. And the really shitty thing? When you're fat, you think that if you could just get skinny, it would make your whole life better, and everything else would improve. Well, it doesn't. And you have to keep on top of it just as much as when you were trying to lose weight. It's fucking hard."

He listened to everything I said and didn't say a word.

I want to die.

I'd just laid my soul out for him, and he wasn't saying anything.

I'd never felt so vulnerable in my life – naked in front of a man with my heart bleeding all over the place.

And then he placed his hand to my stomach. His face grew fierce, and his eyes burned with fire. "I don't care what the fuck anyone ever tells you again, *you* are the most beautiful woman I have ever laid eyes on. Here," he gripped my stomach, before placing his hand to my chest over my heart, "and here. You have that rare thing a lot of women don't, sweetheart – an outer beauty that matches your

307

inner beauty. I never want to see you counting fucking calories again. I want you to eat the goddamn fucking chips every fucking time I take you to that diner, and I don't want you to put makeup on or do your hair when I take you there." He paused for a moment before speaking in a forceful manner. "Please believe every word I am saying because they are all the honest fucking truth."

If I wasn't tied to the bed, I was sure I would have collapsed onto the floor and sobbed. Instead, I sagged against him and he held me while I cried. He reached out and untied me before wrapping his arms around me and letting me get all my tears out.

He thought he didn't know how to love people. He was so wrong.

Griff's compassion and kindness blared from him.

When I'd finished crying, I looked up at him and smiled. "I'm sorry, I kinda ruined the sex, didn't I?"

With one arm firmly around my back, supporting me, he used his other hand to wipe my tears away. "Baby, no way am I not fucking you tonight, but I'll keep the balls for another time." His eyes darkened and he said, "I want you on the bed."

I quickly scrambled onto the bed, and lay back as I watched him put a condom on. When he moved over me, my body fluttered with excitement. And then, when he planted his hands either side of my body, and bent to kiss me, I couldn't hold myself back any longer. I wrapped my legs around him, and took hold of his face with both my hands.

He feels so good.

I want to explore every part of him.

A growl came from his chest, and he deepened our kiss, his tongue growing insistent, like he couldn't get enough of me.

I love that I do that to him.

He pushed his cock against me, sliding through me, but not pushing inside. My pussy clenched in anticipation.

Oh, God, I want him.

Now.

I have to have him.

I can't wait any longer.

"Griff - "

He growled again and pushed himself inside me.

Yes.

Hell, yes.

As he pulled back out, I moaned his name, and then he thrust inside again.

Hard.

I cried out again.

I couldn't stop myself.

He pulled out on a grunt, and slammed into me again.

Hot damn.

I clung to him, my fingers digging into his skin as he thrust in and out. His pace increased, and I held on tighter. My leg muscles would burn for days after this.

"Fuck, baby..." he ground out as he pushed for what we both wanted.

What we both needed.

"Don't stop," I yelled out, and he thrust harder.

And then I disconnected completely. I lost myself to the sex in a way I never had before. It was like every thought that sat in the back of my mind disappeared, and all I could focus on was the pleasure, and Griff, and reaching for that magical place he was taking us to.

When my orgasm hit, I felt it from head to toe. Every single nerve ending lit with pleasure as it rocked through me. I gripped him hard, and a moment later, he stilled as his release shattered through him.

We came together, and it was beautiful.

Unlike anything I'd ever experienced.

If this was heaven, I'd be a good girl for the rest of my life.

When he pulled me close to him afterwards, and held me tight, I knew I would do everything in my power to make Griff a permanent part of my life.

It was official.

I'd fallen, and I'd fallen hard.

STORM

Chapter Twenty-Four
Griff

Sophia's eyes widened. "You want me to wear this all day?"

"Yes."

"Goodness, where do people come up with these ideas?"

She stood in front of me in the bathroom, naked after our shower, and her naivety turned me on so damn much.

"Trust me when I say that you will love this," I said as I squeezed my hand around hers that held the ball. Smacking her lightly on the ass, I continued. "Now, go in the bedroom and let me watch as you put it in."

She shook her head as if she thought that was the worst idea. "I'll just do it - "

"No," I said, my voice firm. "I want you on the bed, on your back, legs wide. I want to see your face as you slide it in."

She stared at me for a moment, and I was sure as fuck she was going to argue with me over this. And it surprised me that I was turned on by that. Usually, I hated the women I slept with arguing with me. But if Sophia had proved one thing only to me, it was that I couldn't get enough of her, any way she came.

Finally, she snatched her hand from mine, and huffed. "Fine, but you're going to regret this, Griff."

I raised my brows. "How am I ever gonna regret knowing that your pussy is being turned on all damn day? And knowing I'm coming home to that? No fucking way am I gonna regret that, sweetheart."

She raised her brows back. "Trust me when I say that you are going to spend today wishing you'd never made me do this, handsome." And then she stalked past me and into her bedroom.

I followed her, my eyes glued to her ass, and the sexy sway of it as she walked. When she'd shared her heartache over her weight with me last night, I'd hated listening to every word come out of her mouth. I'd do everything in my power to make her believe in her own beauty. If she could read my mind, and realise how often thoughts of her passed through it each day, she'd never again doubt how fucking sexy she was.

She lay on the bed, spread her legs and inserted the ball just like I'd asked her to do. I watched from the end of the bed, taking in the absolute fucking beauty of her face as she did it. Her innocence was painted across her face like a magnificent piece of art. Sophia wasn't a virgin, or a prude, or inexperienced when it came to sex, but she had an innocence about aspects of it that was rare to come across these days. The kinds of women I'd previously fucked had tried everything before, so to have Sophia in my bed made me the luckiest bastard around. And the trust she put in me blew my mind.

I moved to the bed and sat next to her. Placing a kiss to her lips, I said, "I'll take you to work and pick you up today."

She narrowed her eyes on me. "You just want the movement and vibrations of the bike to move this damn ball, don't you?"

I chuckled. "I hadn't thought of that, but it'll be a bonus."

Pushing me off the bed, she stood, and said, "You're lucky I like you. I wouldn't do this for anyone else."

I smacked her on the ass again. "Get dressed, woman. I don't need you arguing with me while you're naked. We're already running late this morning; we don't need to run even later."

"I'll remind you that was your fault," she said with a mock scowl.

"Baby, you made us take the longest fucking shower known to mankind while you washed your hair and cleaned your face with all that skin care shit you have in there."

She placed her hands on her hips and glared at me. And fuck if her tits didn't jiggle when she did that, sending desire straight to my dick. "I was regrouping after you made me come three times, Griff. And you didn't have to stay in there with me."

"A man is hardly gonna leave his woman when she's naked in the shower with him."

I'd expected something smart to come out of her mouth, but she surprised me when her eyes softened and she didn't say a word.

"What?" I asked.

"What, what?" she asked as she took her hands off her hips.

"What was that look?"

She gave me one of her amazing smiles. "You called me your woman. I liked being called that," she said softly.

Fuck me.

The pure honesty she gave me never failed to amaze and surprised the fuck out of me.

"I'll be sure to call you that more often, sweetheart. Now go and get dressed. You've got a date with my bike."

She shook her head in mock irritation at me, but she did as I'd said.

And I began counting down the minutes till I got to see her again.

***

Later that day I headed to Josie's for lunch. I took her steps two at a time, and met her at the top of them. She sat in her chair and smiled at me. "Michael, what a nice surprise."

316

"I brought some lunch. You hungry?"

"Depends. What you got?"

I chuckled. Typical Josie – she never held back with me like she would have if it were anyone else who'd brought her food. "Oh, I don't know...just your favourite from Subway, but if you don't want it, I'll eat it."

She stood and swiped the bag from me. "I see that woman is bringing out your sarcasm again. It's been too long since I've seen that, and while I thought I missed it, I may have been mistaken." Turning to walk inside, she threw over her shoulder, "Be a good man and get an old lady a drink, will you?"

Laughing, I grabbed cold drinks from the fridge and joined her at the table.

We ate in silence for a few minutes, but Josie was never good with silence. "I'm glad you two got yourselves sorted out. It's good to see a smile in your eyes again."

"We never really stood a chance against you, did we?"

She didn't even blink, but just kept eating her lunch, and said, "I know a good thing when I see it, and as soon as that girl tripped through my front door, I knew she was made for you."

317

"Jesus, how long have you been planning this?" Nothing would surprise me with Josie.

She shrugged. "The day she moved in, she came over to ask me if I had any milk. I invited her in and she tripped, and when she got all embarrassed she began rambling – I'm sure you know what I mean by that – and with all the honesty that came out of her mouth, and the vulnerability that fell from her, I knew you would love her as much as I did."

I raised my brows. "How the hell did you know I would love that about her?"

She put her lunch down and stared at me. "I know a few things about you, Michael. Number one – you loved your mother more than most sons love their mothers. And your mother used to ramble like that. And, number two – some woman broke your heart so badly somewhere along the way that you don't trust women anymore. It was always going to take a woman who bared her heart easily and spoke with blatant honesty for you to even consider trusting her and letting her in. Sophia is that woman, and the minute I saw it, I had to make it happen, because if there's one thing I want to see before I take my last breath, it's my sister's child happy."

I sat back in my chair as if some unseen force had shoved me back into it.

Fuck.

I'd forgotten my mother rambled like Sophia. How the fuck could I have forgotten that? And everything else she'd said was so damn true. I'd just never realised it or put it all together. What I did know, though, was that Josie was a smart woman.

I leaned forward again, and placed my elbows on the table. "So the night you sent me over there for gravy powder was a set-up?"

She scoffed. "Do you think an old woman like me doesn't know how to make gravy from scratch? My boy, for a smart man, there are times you are easily manipulated. I only hope Sophia works that out."

I chuckled. "I have no doubt she will," I muttered.

She drank some of her drink. "Bring her to dinner soon. I'll cook you roast with gravy." The woman winked as she said gravy, and I shook my head as I laughed.

Jesus, I could see how this was going to go down, and I wasn't convinced it was safe to bring the two women in my life together.

But a man never said no to his aunt. "I'll bring her over on Sunday."

She smiled at me, and I couldn't be anything but grateful for her.

Without Josie, I wouldn't have Sophia.

319

***

As I was leaving Josie's, my phone sounded with a text.

Sophia: You have no idea how wet I am for you, handsome.

Fuck.

Not the kind of text I would have expected from her, but more than fucking welcome.

Me: I see you're enjoying the ball.

Sophia: Every time it vibrates, I imagine it's you in there.

Me: Jesus.

Sophia: Oh, is this getting you all hot and bothered?

Me: You're not even sorry, are you?

Sophia: Not in the slightest. Gotta run...like, literally, cause that shit is amazing.

I shoved my phone in my pocket and adjusted myself. My dick was hard now, just thinking about how wet she'd be for me tonight.

I was on my way to pick Sophia up from work when she rang to say she'd finished early and a work colleague had dropped her at home. However, she asked me to drop into the supermarket to collect a few items, and while there, I ran into Magan in the car park as I was leaving. She stood a few cars away from my bike with her head in her hands, sobbing. She didn't hear me approach until the very last minute when she abruptly lifted her head out of hands and stared at me, her mascara-stained face a mask of bewilderment.

Fuck.

Dealing with teenagers was not something I was equipped for, but she looked like she was in desperate need of help. "Do you want me to call Sophia for you or take you home?"

Her eyes flared for a moment in what seemed to be surprise. "No," she said, her voice catching on a sob. Her hand flew to cover her mouth as if that would stop her from falling apart again.

I watched as she gulped and tried like fuck to get herself under control but she failed and a moment later the sobs began again. Not being able to help myself, I took the few steps between us and pulled her into my arms. I was surprised as hell when her arms wrapped around me and she sobbed even harder against my chest. We stayed like that for a long time until finally her crying subsided and she pulled out of my embrace.

Looking up at me, she said, "Sophia's lucky to have you."

"Why?"

"Because even though you guys have just gotten together, you seem to be the kind of man who would always be there if she needs you."

"Yeah," I agreed because it was true. And then I pushed for more. "Are you gonna tell me why you were crying?" Fuck knew if this was the right course of action, but I was concerned for her.

She started crying again. Looking up at me through tears, she said, "My boyfriend..." A sob caught in her throat and she stopped talking.

I frowned. "What did he do?"

Her body was wracked with sobs as she tried to answer me. "He thinks I'm interested in other guys...and he just told me off..."

Fear was written all over her face, and I figured I knew the type of guy she was dating – the type who had no issues with pushing a female around. "Did he hurt you, Magan?" I demanded to know, my fist clenching.

Her eyes widened. "No...well, he did push me up against the wall, but he didn't mean to hurt me!" She rushed to defend a guy who had no right being defended.

"Jesus." I raked my fingers through my hair. "Has he done this kind of thing before?"

She shook her head. "No, Griff, he's always been amazing. Like, he's thoughtful, and caring, and he goes out of his way to always know where I am, and who I'm with so he knows I'm safe. He's always made me feel special, like I'm the only girl in the world."

"Have you got your phone?"

Frowning, she nodded. "Yes. Why?"

"Pass it here. I am gonna give you my number, and I want you to call me if he ever does this again."

She stood staring at me, not moving, so I held my hand out, indicating she should give me the phone. Eventually, she did, and I keyed my number in.

Passing it back to her, I said firmly, "Magan, tell me you're going to call me if shit goes bad. Guys like this don't usually just do this type of thing once. And you *never* deserve to be treated that way. Ever."

Nodding slowly, she said, "I will."

I was only half convinced, but I let it go for now. "You sure you don't want a lift home?"

"Yeah, I'm sure, but thank you," she said before giving me one last glance, and walking away.

I watched her for a moment, and then headed to my bike. I had no doubt that asshole boyfriend of hers would threaten her again, but I'd be watching to make sure he never got away with doing that shit again.

Just before I headed out of the car park, my phone buzzed with a text.

Blade: The Bond hit failed. He's still alive. I'm aiming to set up another.

Fuck.

But at least we had some time now that the trial had been delayed.

Another text came through.

Sophia: I'm ready for you, handsome.

Me: I'm on my way.

Sophia: If you're gonna be a little while, maybe I should get started without you.

Me: Don't you dare.

Sophia: But I'm so damn wet.

Me: Don't test me, woman. Do not touch yourself.

Sophia: I love it when you're bossy.

I'd just placed my phone away when it buzzed again.

Sophia: That being said, I also think you kinda like it when I defy you...

Jesus fuck.

I was beginning to think she didn't need any help from Josie to learn all about the fine art of male manipulation.

Chapter Twenty-Five
Sophia

Griff stalked into my house with a determined look on his face. I sucked in a breath at the level of bossy that was radiating from him today.

I stood in my kitchen as he came down the hall, and my core clenched when he hooked his arm around my waist, pulled me to him, and growled, "Those text messages of yours today have earned you a lot of punishments, Sophia. Punishments that I may spread across days."

Letting me go, he backed me up against the wall, and bent his lips to mine. His kiss was long and deep, and it had a sense of urgency to it. I moved my hands to the bottom of his t-shirt to take it off, but his hand stopped me. Lifting his face from mine, he said, "Not yet." His voice had that bossy tone to it that signalled he meant business so I moved my hand away from him.

His gaze dropped to my chest, and he began unbuttoning my blouse. He undid it effortlessly, and a moment later opened it to reveal my body to him. Sliding my blouse over my shoulders, he let it fall to the floor as he bent his face to my breast. He pushed the cups of my bra to the sides and took one of my nipples in his mouth.

I dropped my head back against the wall and closed my eyes as he ran his lips and tongue over my skin. My fingers threaded through his hair, and I let out a soft moan.

He reached around and undid my bra, letting it join my blouse on the floor. Then he moved his hands to my skirt and stripped me of that, too. Finally, I stood in front of him naked except for my panties.

Dropping to his knees, he spread my legs apart and ran his hands up the insides of my legs until he reached my pussy. One hand then slid around to cup my ass, while he slipped his other hand into my panties to run his fingers through my wetness.

"Fucking beautiful," he said before pulling my panties down.

When he had them off me, he stood and pulled his t-shirt over his head. He then stripped out of the rest of his clothes, never taking his eyes off me. Once he was naked, he scooped me up into his arms and carried me into my bedroom.

He placed me on the floor, sat on my bed, and pulled me across his knees, my head on my bed, and my ass in direct line of his hand. The rough movement caused the ball inside me to vibrate, sending sparks of pleasure through me. Then he rubbed my ass, and growled, "It's time for your punishment."

As I anticipated what was to come, I squeezed my legs together. And then he spanked me. The vibrations that shot through me from the ball inside were exquisite.

I truly am in heaven.

His hand rubbed my ass again for a little while before he spanked me again. Closing my eyes, I let the pleasure take over.

"Does that feel good?" he demanded to know.

"Yes," I moaned.

His hand ran up my back, and traced patterns over my skin before moving back down to rub my ass. Then he spanked me again, a little harder than before.

"I think you need more," he said. "Three spanks aren't enough punishment for those text messages." I could hear the need in his voice, mirroring my own.

He ran his finger through my wetness again and found my clit. Massaging me there, he brought me close to orgasm, but stopped just before I came. Then he moved his hand back to my ass, and without any warning, spanked me again.

I jumped, and the ball inside me vibrated, sending another wave of pleasure through me. Oh, God, he was going to drive me wild with need. I bit my lip to stop myself from crying out for him to fuck me.

"Stand up," he ordered, and I did what he said.

He remained seated and gripped my hips as I stood in front of him. Pressing his mouth to my stomach, he trailed kisses down until he reached my clit, and then he ran his tongue over me in circles, building my orgasm again. And *again*, he stopped just as I was nearing the edge.

Looking up at me, he said, "You won't ever send me messages like that again, will you?" The lust in his gaze hit me in my core and I was momentarily distracted, so I didn't reply to him as fast as he wanted. Standing, he grabbed my hair and pulled my head back. Licking his tongue along my collarbone, he demanded, "Will you, Sophia?"

"No, I won't," I moaned, my legs turning weak when he sank his teeth into my neck and began sucking and licking me.

My hands moved to his body and my arms wrapped around him as he continued marking my skin. When I moved closer to him, he hissed and let my neck go. His eyes held mine for awhile before he said, "Fuck, I can't wait any longer. My dick is so goddamn hard for you, and I need to be inside." He paused for a moment, and then continued, "I don't want to fuck you with a condom anymore."

"I'm clean," I assured him.

"Good. I am, too." As he said this, he took hold of my ass, lifted me, and backed me up against the wall. My legs and arms were wrapped around him, holding on tight, and my gaze was pinned to his. He reached down between us and pulled the ball out of me. "Next time you will wear both balls," he said, but I hardly heard him. My body was lit from head to toe with pleasure and I needed him to hurry this up or I was sure I would go crazy with lust.

When his lips found mine a moment later, I kissed him with a hunger that caused a growl to come from him. And as he kissed me back with that same hunger, I dug my fingers into his back, and squeezed my legs around him tighter. He growled again, and thrust inside me.

Oh, God, yes.

I squeezed my pussy around him each time he thrust inside, and I knew he loved that from the noises he made as he kept kissing me while fucking me.

As I inched closer and closer to the edge, my mind began to switch off to all thoughts except for the building release. Griff had stopped kissing me, and was saying words, but I had no idea what they were. It was like a hazy cloud surrounded me, and the only thing of any importance was my pleasure.

And then he slammed into me hard, one last time before stilling and roaring out, "Fuck!"

We came at the same time, and my orgasm took over me completely. Thankfully, Griff held me up because I'm not sure my body could have managed to support me. I wasn't even sure how long we stayed there, but eventually he moved us to the bed.

I was exhausted, and fought through the fog to gather my thoughts again, but I couldn't. The last thoughts I had were that sex with Griff was amazing and that dinner could wait. And when I heard Griff say, "Go to sleep, baby," I finally succumbed and let sleep claim me.

***

"Hey, Sophia," Magan answered her phone when I rang her first thing the next morning after Griff had told me about his encounter with her in the shopping centre car park, and what her boyfriend, Brody, had done.

"Magan, Griff told me about what Brody did. Are you okay? Because I'm worried about you, honey...in fact, I think I should just get in my car and come straight over to your house. Blow work, and if they want to say anything about me being late today, that's their problem." My words all rushed out in my anxious state.

"No, I'm not okay," she confessed, and I heard all her fears in her voice.

She needs me.

"I'm coming over now. Hold tight." I grabbed my keys and began walking out of the house while we kept talking.

"Thank you," she said quietly, and I knew I was doing the right thing. And it was just another reason to be mad at our mother.

It should be her holding Magan's hand through this.

It should be her ready to catch her if she falls.

I hung up and drove to her house. She lived about twenty minutes from me, and when I arrived there, she greeted me at the front door with tears in her eyes. I pulled her into my arms and comforted her while the tears fell.

"Have you heard from him?" I asked.

She shook her head. "No, he hasn't called," she said through her tears, and I wanted to kill the asshole for breaking her heart.

I frowned. "Magan, this guy treated you badly. Why do you want him to call? Wouldn't you rather move on and find someone worthy of your love?"

She swallowed hard and looked at me through eyes that gave her fear away. "I was lucky to find Brody, Sophia. I've never had a boyfriend who cared about me the way he does."

My heart hurt for her. I knew where this kind of thinking stemmed from because I'd been there, done that in my life. The vicious cycle of not wanting those we loved to leave us, so we let them walk all over us in order to keep them.

Our mother really has a lot to answer for.

"You're scared to lose him, I get that, but you're better off without a person like that in your life. It's not really him you're scared of losing...it's the love you think he gives you that you desperately want. Trust me, I know, because I've had asshole boyfriends, too, and I put up with a lot of shit before I realised I was worth more than that. He's not giving you love, honey. He's trying to control you by taking advantage of your insecurities."

She stared at me as if she was trying to wrap her head around what I'd just said. I figured she wouldn't come to fully understand the truth in what I'd said until she'd lived her life some more. Unfortunately in life, we usually had to make our own mistakes and learn from them before making better choices.

Eventually, she said, "I'm going to go and clean my face, and then I'll be back."

I let her go. She probably needed a little time to herself to have a think.

Looking around her foster home, I remembered how much I disliked her foster mother. Sure, the woman worked a full-time job, but she hardly cleaned the house, and she pretty much never cooked. She took on older foster kids and made them do all the chores, and that pissed me off. I was counting down the days until Magan could leave, and as far as I was concerned, she could come and live with me then if she wanted.

Magan came back and sat with me at the kitchen table. She fidgeted, and I reached out, and stilled her hands. "Whatever happens, we will figure it out, okay? You and me – I'll be there for you every step."

Tears pricked her eyes again, and she reached out, and put her arms around me. She hugged me for a long time, and when she pulled away, she said, "I'm so glad I found that photo of you and your address in Mum's stuff that day I found out about you."

I frowned. "Wait, you never told me that. I thought you got my information from her sister."

"No, she sent me a box of photos from when I was a kid, and on the top when I opened it, she had a photo of you and a post-it note with your address on it. That's how I found you."

My heart skidded to a stop.

She kept track of me.

"Did I say something wrong?" she asked.

"No, I just didn't realise she'd kept track of me," I said softly.

She smiled. "See, she does love you, Sophia."

I still didn't want to burst her bubble, so I changed the subject. "Do you want to come to dinner tonight? I'm going to get Griff to fire up my barbeque."

"Steak! I'm in."

"I knew I could totally bribe you with steak," I said with a wink. Standing, I said, "Okay, I gotta get to work, but I'll see you later. Do you want me to pick you up?"

"Nah, I'll catch a bus. See you then." She paused for a second before adding, "I love you, sis."

She didn't tell me that very often, so my heart swelled hearing it. "I love you, too."

***

I took a sip of wine and laughed at Magan's joke. She'd met me at home after I finished work, and wanting to take her mind off the fact her boyfriend was an ass, we'd turned the music up and baked some cupcakes. She loved baking as much as I did, and we often made cakes. They were our downfall, as both of us had a sweet tooth.

We'd moved into the lounge room and were almost rolling around on the floor in stitches of laughter when Griff arrived. I'd left the front door open for him, so he'd entered and now stood shaking his head at us, a grin fixed firmly on his face.

I jumped up and threw my arms around him. "Hey, handsome," I greeted him and then planted my lips on his in a long kiss.

When I pulled away from him, he raised his brows, and said, "I see you started without me, sweetheart."

I indicated with my fingers that I'd only had a small amount. "Just a little bit, I promise."

"'Just a little bit' she says as she slurs her words. Lucky I'm cooking dinner tonight."

"We made cupcakes!" I said a little too enthusiastically. "Oh, shit, maybe I did have more than a little bit...I kinda am slurring my words, aren't I? But, I had a good day at work...no, scratch that, I had a great day at work, and then I had you to look forward to seeing tonight. Oh, God, I'll just shut up now...I'm rambling, aren't I?" I slapped my hand over my mouth in an effort to stop the flow of words.

His arm slid around my waist, and he pulled me close. Brushing his lips over mine, he murmured, "I fucking love it when you ramble, in case you hadn't clued onto that, baby, so feel free to do it whenever you want."

Oh my.

A smile spread across my lips. "I'll take that under advisement," I said softly.

He let me go and left us to head into the kitchen. Once we were alone, her eyes widened, and with very expressive hand motions in the direction he'd

337

gone, she mouthed, "Dude! He's amazing! Where do you find men like that?"

While also making expressive hand motions, I mouthed back, "I have no clue! I got lucky for once in my life."

Griff cleared his throat and we both snapped our heads to face him. He smirked as he said, "Sorry to interrupt what I presume is a female kind of communication that I never need to be enlightened on, but I need to know what you want cooked."

Magan burst out laughing and I did my best to keep a straight face. Swallowing back my laughter, I said, "Sure, I'll come and show you."

As he followed me, I said, "You're never gonna ask me about Magan's and my female communication style, are you?"

"Nope," he said.

I grinned. My tummy somersaulted just from having him near, but also because I loved the way he'd grown from being so standoffish to now just going along with whatever I threw at him. "Good, 'cause it would confuse the hell out of you. You don't need to know girl stuff."

His arm hooked around me from behind, and he spun me around to face him. "Just to be clear, I'm interested in knowing about anything you think is important." His voice had changed from fun to serious, and my alcohol-riddled mind hurried to catch up to the conversation.

When I finally realised what he'd said, happiness whooshed through me.

Treasured.

That's how I feel with him.

Nodding, I said softly, "Okay."

His eyes searched mine for a moment, before he said, "Good. Now show me this food, woman. I'm hungry."

***

The next morning, I stumbled out of bed to find him sitting quietly at the kitchen counter, drinking coffee. "Why didn't you wake me?" I asked.

"Baby, you drank a fair bit of wine last night, and I had to put you to bed without even getting my hands on you. I figured that seems as though you've got the day off today, you might enjoy a sleep in."

"Thank you," I murmured as I made myself a coffee. "What have you got on today?"

"I thought I'd spend some time at my place. The yard needs some work which will probably take me most of the day."

"And then do I get to see you tonight?"

He eyed me with an *are-you-fucking-kidding* look, and said, "Try and keep me away."

I grinned. "I'll make you dessert. It'll be good, I promise."

He leant across the counter and gave me another look like the one he'd just given me. "Sophia, you *are* my fucking dessert. And tonight, we're skipping the main course," he said, his voice all gravelly, just the way I loved it.

Before I could say anything else, he stood and rinsed his mug. Then he gave me a long, deep kiss before placing something in my hand. "I'm gonna need one for your place," he said, and when I looked down, I found a key in my palm.

My head snapped up and I stared at him. "You want a key to my house?"

"Yes." His eyes held mine, and the certainty I saw in them hit me fair in the chest.

"This is serious to you, isn't it?" I held my breath, hoping he would say yes.

He didn't blink, and he didn't think about it. Instead, he said firmly, "Yes."

I smiled, and moved to where my handbag sat on the kitchen counter. Removing my spare house key, I handed it to him. "This is serious to me, too," I said softly.

340

He slipped the key onto his key ring, and then paused for a moment, watching me. There was so much unsaid between us, and yet so much of that had no need to be said out loud. Our souls spoke, and understood every ounce of pain and hope stitched onto our hearts. Bending to place another kiss to my lips, he said, "I'll see you tonight."

After I'd watched him go, I sat on the stool to regroup. His belief in us meant so much to me. It had been unexpected, but I was the happiest girl in the world today.

***

My day after he left consisted of more sleep and then domestic goddess work. As much as I disliked housework, I had a good day, and was sitting on my patio with a glass of wine in my hand later that afternoon when Magan called.

"Hey, honey," I answered as I took a sip of wine.

Silence.

And then a sob tore through the phone, and she managed to say, "Sophia..." and I knew something very terrible had happened.

I shot up out of the chair. "Where are you? I'm coming." My heart raced in my chest, not knowing what had happened, but fearing something bad.

"At home," she said in an almost whisper, her sobs coming harder now.

I was already in my kitchen with my car keys in my hand. "I'll be there soon. Will you be okay until I get there, or should I phone an ambulance or..." Having no idea what she needed, I was at a loss. All I knew was I had to get there fast.

"I don't need anyone. Except you." The way she said those last two words slayed me.

I will hunt down whoever did this to her.

We ended the call and I headed out to my car. And I drove as fast as I could to get to my sister. We may not have grown up together or even known about each other until six months ago, but I would do anything for her. She was my only family, and family doesn't let family down.

***

I found her curled up into a ball, sobbing on her bed. I wasn't sure I'd ever seen anyone sob the way she was. Tears pricked my eyes as I realised how devastated she was over whatever had happened.

Sitting on the bed, I dragged her into my arms and held her. Running my hand over her hair, I remained silent while she let her hurt out. We must have sat like that for about half an hour, and when she finally told me what had happened, I knew the hurt and pain she was in would never leave her. This level of heartbreak would sit deep in her soul and cause wounds that would never heal.

I should know because I had those same wounds.

She lifted her head and looked at me. The tears still tracked down her face, and she just let them fall. It would have been pointless to even try to wipe them away because fresh tears would only replace them straight away. "Mum's gone."

Those two words pierced my heart, and I was sure it stopped beating for a moment. A shiver ran over my body as the cold chill of disappointment and abandonment filled me. *Again.*

"From the hospital?" I asked as I tried to swallow the dryness from my throat.

She nodded. "Yes. I went there today and she wasn't there. When I asked the nurse where she went, they gave me an envelope from her..." A sob escaped from her lips, stealing her words.

"What was in the envelope?" I knew. Deep in my heart, I knew what was in that envelope, but I needed to hear it from her lips. Even after all these years, and all this hurt my mother had caused, I still clung to a tiny sliver of hope that she would change. *That she would want me again.* And asking silly

343

questions like the one I'd just asked Magan proved how much I clutched that hope.

Agony crumpled her face. "A letter...she's not coming back, and she told me that you and I should stick together because she can't be what we need."

She will never be what we need.

We stared at each other, sharing our pain for a minute or so, and then I pulled her to me, and said, "I'm so sorry, Magan." I fought the tears rushing at me and swallowed my own sobs sitting in my throat.

I need to be strong for her.

Don't break down.

Don't you dare cry.

She cried for another long stretch of time while I held mine back. When she stopped, she lifted her head. "I thought this time was going to be different."

Her words sat between us in a painful ache. How many times do you let someone trash your trust and abuse the love you've given them before you say enough is enough?

I took a deep breath and attempted to give Magan the honesty she deserved. "Honey, our mother doesn't know how to love. After all these years, I am convinced of that fact. I had hoped that perhaps it would be different for you than it was for me, because it seemed like she may have changed a

344

little in the years between having us. She never visited me after she left, but she visited you, so I thought maybe that meant she would try harder with you. I never wanted to have to say these words to you, but although she gave birth to us, she isn't a mother. A mother doesn't abandon her children in the way ours did. And I know you think she was amazing to have visited you twice in your life, but that isn't enough. A mother should be there to catch her child when she falls, not be the one who causes them to fall." I took another deep breath, mainly to pull my tears in before they fell. And then I continued. "I will always be here for you. You have my word on that. Anything you need – *anything at all* – you will have from me."

She took all of that in while watching me with wide eyes. I wasn't sure how she would react because I'd never been that forceful with her about my feelings. I'd always kept my thoughts to myself, not wanting to take any hope from her, but this was the last straw with our mother. And for her own sanity and self-esteem, Magan needed to hear those words today. I didn't want her to spend years questioning her own worth in the same way I had.

Eventually, she blinked and nodded. "I know you're right, but I think there might be a part of me that will always hope she'll come back," she said softly, and I couldn't fault her for having hope. It was something everyone should live with.

"I know, honey...boy, do I know. I don't ever want to take that away from you, but I want you to live with the truth of the situation and be realistic. False hope has more potential of hurting you than not having any hope at all."

This was a lot for a seventeen-year-old to deal with. She was at an age where her greatest worry should have been whether the boy she crushed on liked her back, and yet here she was dealing with pain that should never have been inflicted in the first place.

She listened to what I said, and then she placed her head back on my shoulder. We stayed like that for a long time, holding each other while dealing with our own thoughts. She cried, but I stayed strong for her. After not having a mother to care for her all these years, I wanted to be there for her in that capacity. And mothers stayed strong for their children. They gave them whatever they needed before they even thought about themselves, and in this moment, I didn't want to think about myself, and what I needed. If I did, I knew I would fall apart completely. My mother had torn the last shred of hope from my soul.

***

I stayed with Magan long into the night. When I finally got home at around ten, I had a long, warm shower and let my tears fall.

Each tear sliced down my cheek with the pain of rejection, abandonment and love that had never been returned.

Tomorrow I would be okay, but tonight I would let it all consume me.

Tonight I would finally say goodbye to my mother.

Chapter Twenty-Six
Griff

Fuck.

I re-read Sophia's text.

Sophia: I'm home now.
Me: Is Magan okay?

She hadn't replied and when I'd called, she hadn't answered. Since she'd let me know earlier that she wouldn't be home tonight because Magan had phoned her in distress, I'd been concerned. The worry in Sophia's voice had been enough to worry me. I'd made her promise she'd let me know when she was home so I knew she was safe. To not hear back from her now caused me even greater concern.

I grabbed my keys and headed out to my bike.

When I pulled up outside Sophia's house a little while later, I was surprised to find it in complete darkness. Even if she'd gone to bed straight away, she liked to keep one light on in the house. It was one of her quirky things she did – she'd told me it was something that had carried over from her childhood, and she hadn't been able to let it go.

I used my key and let myself in, heading straight for her bedroom. When I found her naked and sobbing on her bathroom floor, my heart crashed into my chest. She lay in the dark and wailed, and I felt every ounce of her pain. Her hurt engulfed her to the point she didn't hear me come in. When I crouched next to her, and placed my hand on her shoulder, her head snapped up, and she stared at me through eyes I wasn't sure even saw me.

Grief.

Devastation.

Heartbreak.

I saw it all in her eyes, and if I could have taken it all away for her, I would. Instead, I scooped her into my arms and carried her to her bed. She wrapped her arms around me, buried her face in my

349

neck and sobbed. Her body shuddered with her cries, and I wondered what the fuck had happened to bring on this level of pain.

Placing her on the bed, I found one of her t-shirts and put it on her. I then sat on the bed with my head against the headboard, and pulled her into my arms. She curled into me, almost sitting in my lap, and continued to cry. Long, deep, agony-filled wails of hurt filled the room. I sensed this must be to do with her mother, because these were not cries from a fresh cut, but rather from a long-held pain.

Eventually, she lifted her head to look at me. "She's gone." She gulped a breath and continued, "I'd given up on her, but then Magan told me she had a photo of me and knew my address, and I thought maybe – *just maybe* – she'd been keeping track of me for a reason. I thought maybe this time really would be different." A sob escaped her mouth, and I watched as her face crumpled with more tears. "None of it was true. She didn't mean a word she said to me at the hospital, and now she's gone. And I have to find a way to pick my pieces back up and put myself together again."

Fuck.

Why do people hurt each other, over and fucking over?

I wiped her tears and then tried to kiss them away. Trouble was, there were a lifetime of tears flowing down Sophia's cheeks, and no amount of effort from me could stop them. One person held the key to those tears, and she'd proven her lack of interest in stopping them.

"You're not alone anymore, Sophia," I said.

She didn't reply straight away, but, eventually, she whispered, "Thank you."

She placed her head against my body again, and stayed there for a long time as her tears slowly dried up. I would have held her there all night if she'd needed it. When she'd finished crying, she sat up and pulled her t-shirt off. "I need your skin tonight, Griff. Nothing else, just your skin next to mine. Can I have that?" Her words came out almost as if she was begging me.

I nodded and lifted my t-shirt over my head. "Whatever you need, sweetheart, you've got." I stood so I could remove the rest of my clothes and then settled into the bed next to her.

She placed her head on my chest, and wrapped her arms and legs around me. "I don't know what I did to deserve you," she murmured.

I knew exactly what she meant because I had the same thought about her.

And I would make damn sure those tears were replaced with a smile.

***

The next morning, I woke to find her in the kitchen, cooking breakfast, a smile on her face. I moved into her and slid my arms around her waist. After I'd kissed her, I said, "It's good to see a smile on your face, but I'm not convinced. You don't need to put on a happy face around me, sweetheart."

She was silent for a minute. "I'm not trying to fake it, but if I spend my days wallowing in my unhappiness, I'll feel like shit. I'm working through my feelings but I'm not going to do that with constant tears. Does that make sense?"

"Yes, but when you're feeling overwhelmed, you come to me. I'll work through whatever shit you need to work through with you," I said firmly.

She clasped her hands around my neck and pulled my face down towards her so she could kiss me. When she'd finished, she said, "I'm not used to having someone to count on like you, Griff. My natural reaction is to deal with stuff on my own, but I'll try not to do that. I just need you to know it might take some time for me to get used to it, okay?"

As usual, her raw honesty hit me in the chest.

This is a woman I can trust.

The thought flashed through my mind, unexpectedly, but clear as day.

Fuck.

I'd never expected to believe in a woman again, but I found myself unable to discount this truth. Sophia was a woman I could put my faith in. It would take me time, and I would do it slowly, but I knew without an ounce of doubt that she was a woman I could build a life with.

"We've got all the time in the world, baby," I finally said.

The smile she gave me in return was the kind of smile I would do anything to earn.

She pointed at me. "I'm going to finish making breakfast for you so you need to sit at the table and wait."

I shook my head. "No, Sophia, you need to get your ass into the bedroom and get naked for me. Breakfast can wait," I growled.

Her eyes widened, and I watched as heat flared in them. A moment later, she did as I'd said, and as I took in the sight of her discarding her t-shirt while she walked, I decided that lunch could also wait. Sophia would be busy for the rest of the fucking day.

***

My phone rang at six the next morning. It was the call I'd been waiting for, but hoping would never come.

"Danny," I said, noting his name on my screen.

"Today's the day, Michael. There will be a media conference and the case will be announced. Your name won't be revealed yet, but it won't take long before it's out there."

Goddamn.

We'd just needed a few extra days for Bond to be taken care of. Maybe Blade could still pull it off, but with each passing day, I felt a level of concern I'd never felt before.

You've got something to lose now.

Sophia.

"Thanks for the head's up," I said and ended the call.

Sophia rolled to curl up next to me. She reached her arm across my chest and laid it there. "Everything okay?" she mumbled.

"Yeah, baby. Go back to sleep."

I have to take care of this.

I'd worked out a worst-case scenario plan in my head, and I now knew I was going to have to put it into action. I only hoped it didn't backfire on me, because if it did, I would find myself not in control for the first time in many years, and that was not a place I wanted to be.

***

"Are you out of your fucking mind?" Scott asked, disbelief written across his face.

I nodded. "Probably, but I don't see many other options."

We were in his office, a few hours after my phone call from Danny, and I had just shared my plan with him.

"When do you want to do this?"

"Today. Call Church for one hour's time. We need to get the ball rolling."

He stared at me for a while and then scrubbed his hand over his face. "This is your call, brother. I hope you know what you're doing."

"You and me both," I said as he sent the text out calling the boys in.

An hour later, he announced to our members, "Griff's got something to discuss with you all, and before he does, I need to say that I've known about this for a little while now, and I have his back fully.

355

Before you make any snap decisions regarding what he tells you, take a minute to remember everything we've all been through. This club isn't just about family and loyalty, it's also about sticking together through the shit, and accepting that none of us are fucking perfect."

The mood in the room turned sombre and all eyes turned to me. I made a point to look everyone in the eye as I spoke. "Ten years ago, my family were tortured and murdered. My father was a cop and had been investigating Storm, and in particular, Marcus. I was working in private investigations so I used my skills and contacts to investigate my family's deaths, and everything led me to believe Marcus was behind them." I paused for a moment, mentally preparing myself to share the secret I thought I'd take to my grave with me – the secret that could change my life completely. "When I couldn't pin it on him, I walked away. Years passed, but I had to come back and avenge their deaths, and to do that, I had to get close to Marcus...I had to join the club."

I stopped talking as many of the boys swore, their faces revealing their shock.

"Fuck!" J roared as he shoved his chair back and stood. "You've been fucking deceiving us all this time?"

"Let him finish," Scott said, his hard eyes on J, warning him to let it go for now.

"You better have something good to say, Griff, 'cause at the moment, I'm struggling to grasp this," J said as he sat back down.

"A year or so after I joined the club, I discovered Marcus hadn't killed my family, and I could have walked then, but I didn't want to. Storm was my family by then, and my loyalty was and still is one hundred percent with the club."

J narrowed his eyes on me. "Why are you telling us this now, Griff? There's gotta be a reason to explain why, after three years, you suddenly come clean."

I nodded. "Yeah. Years ago, my cousin who is a cop asked me to help him investigate the double murder of Leon Bond and his girlfriend. I was close to my cousin back then and helped him - "

Nash cut me off. "Fuck, that is one fucked-up family to get involved with, brother."

Brother.

I nodded. "It was, but I didn't realise it at the time. I mean, no one assumed his crazy brother, Jeffrey, would turn out to be the killer. In the course of my investigation, I witnessed Jeffrey kill another guy who knew he was the murderer. And

357

that was one of the key parts of the case, which means they want to call me as a witness in the trial."

"Hasn't that trial been put on hold?" Nash asked.

"It's about to be announced that it's going ahead soon," I replied.

"And that's why you're telling us all this now," J muttered. "And on top of all this, you're from a family of cops?"

My frustration grew. "Yes, but I walked away from that, J. I have no ties to any of them, and I haven't for years."

"Once a fucking cop, always a fucking cop," J spat, his eyes full of anger.

My tightly controlled anger snapped. "I was never a fucking cop, J. And after the things I've seen cops do, I have very little respect for the badge, if any. You have a right to be angry with me for not being honest about who I really am, but don't lump me with them," I roared.

J pushed his chair back, and stood again. "I'll fucking do whatever the fuck I want, Griff. It seems that's what you do. What the fuck else have you lied to us about?"

I stood also. "My life's an open book now, J. Ask me whatever the fuck you want to know."

Scott's chair scraped as he shoved it back and stood. "We all need to settle down and figure out where we go from here." His jaw clenched, and his eyes flashed his anger.

J glared at me, and took a step backwards. It looked like he was about to walk out, however his phone rang at that moment, distracting him. He jabbed at it to end the call, but a moment later, it rang again. Scowling, he answered it. "Madison, I'm kinda in the middle of something." He listened to what she said, and his free hand raked through his hair as he roared out, "Fuck! Close the fucking shop and wait there. I'll be there soon."

Before he'd ended the call, Nash's and Scott's phones rang, and I watched as they appeared to have similar conversations as J just had.

When they ended their calls, I said, "We've got a problem, haven't we?" My gut knotted with worry. This wasn't going to be good.

Scott nodded. "Yeah, brother, we do." He turned his gaze to J and Nash, and said, "I take it Bond's family just paid a visit to Velvet and Madison."

J's anger rolled off him now, and he threw me a glare before answering Scott. "Yes. They threatened that if Griff testified, they would come after her."

Fuck.

"Same," Nash said, his eyes blazing with anger.

Scott's phone rang again, and he had a heated discussion with someone who I presumed wasn't Harlow from the way he was speaking. When he ended the call, he eyed me. "That was one of Bond's men. He told me they don't want a problem with Storm; they just want you. They want me to deliver you to them today."

Everyone began throwing in their two cent's, and I took the opportunity to call Sophia. I had to make sure she was okay.

"Hey, handsome," she greeted me, and I let go of the breath I'd been holding.

"You okay?" I asked, not wanting to worry her, but needing to make sure.

"Yes. Why?"

"Are you at work, Sophia?"

"Griff, you're worrying me. You sound tense. And yes, I'm at work."

I blew out a breath. "Good. Nothing to worry about, sweetheart. I was just checking in on you."

"Mmmm...I'm not convinced. You would tell me if I needed to worry about you, wouldn't you?"

"Yeah, I would. I'll call you later, but I've gotta go now," I said as I ended the call.

The noise in the room was deafening as everyone's voice grew louder the more they talked. "Enough!" I yelled.

All eyes came to me again, the noise quieting.

Looking around the room, at the men I'd called family for three years, I said, "There's nothing else I can say about the way in which I joined the club – it can't be changed now – but I will tell you this...I would lay my life down for Storm, for each and every one of you. I would do anything it took to protect all of you. If you look back over the years, my loyalty can't be questioned. Assuming you still want me in the club, I have a plan to deal with Bond's family. I've spent hours researching them and doing surveillance on them, and my plan is good to go – today, if need be. I just need to know whether you stand with me on this."

"First, we need to make sure the girls are all safe," J said, his angry glare at me softening a little.

"I agree," Scott said. "How many of us do you need for your plan?" he asked me.

"We'll need two teams of at least six in each, more would be better."

Scott nodded, and began barking orders as to who was to go where. Once he had everyone separated into teams, he sent one team out to keep an eye on the girls. He had directed two men to each – he wasn't taking any chances here.

I proceeded to share my plan with the rest of the men, and an hour and a half later, we put it into effect. Scott hadn't asked for a vote on my club membership, and no one had brought it up again. Not even J. But fuck knew where I would stand after the shit had settled and everyone was safe again.

Chapter Twenty-Seven
Griff

Bond ran his organisation from prison. He had one guy in charge on the outside who controlled their drug shipments, and who ran the operation from Bond's mansion. Ten other men backed up this guy. I'd kept the operation under constant surveillance since killing Bond's brother, in preparation for this day, should it come. Due to this fact, I knew they had a drug shipment arriving today that most of their team would be taking care of at one o'clock. That would be our best opportunity to strike – while the men were split between two locations.

Scott called Blade, who lined up some of his men to help us. I was confident that with ten guys in each team, we'd accomplish our goal without problems. Scott led the team that would ambush Bond's drug shipment, while I led the team at the mansion.

We took two vans to the mansion and parked them in two different streets close to our destination. I'd hacked into their surveillance again, and set it so we wouldn't show on their cameras, the same as I'd done the last time I came here. The same guy was stationed at the back gate when I approached. He turned just as we arrived where he stood, and he reached for his gun, but I already had mine out.

Aiming at him, I said, "Now, now, Justin, remember how much I know about your family. All we want are the keys and the code for the gate, and then we'll leave you like I did last time."

"There's no one inside, asshole," he sneered.

I raised my brows. "Now you're just lying." I moved closer to him, and held my gun to his head. "Give me what I want, and I'll let you live to kiss your wife and daughter again."

He didn't hand them over straight away. It seemed he was hedging his bets in his mind, until finally, he muttered, "Fuck," and he handed the keys over, rattling off the code.

I gave the keys to Nash, who also keyed in the code and once we had the gate open, I turned to Justin. "Unfortunately, this time, I can't keep my promise. Your boys threatened our women today, and no one does that and gets away with it."

His eyes widened with fear, and I pulled the trigger. He dropped to the ground, and we dragged his body inside the gate and closed it behind us. Then we moved quickly to the back entrance of the mansion and slipped inside without being seen. I motioned to the boys as to who should go where, and we split up in teams of two to tackle the house.

Nash and I made our way through two rooms and down a hallway before coming across anyone. A guy walked out of the kitchen with a sandwich as we approached. He eyed us, and dropped his plate in an effort to grab for his gun. The plate smashed to the floor, shattering into pieces, while Nash and I aimed our guns at him. He was dead on the floor before he even had a chance to aim his at us.

"Fuck," Nash swore, grinning at me. "That was too easy. I want a little fight from someone." He bounced a little, as if he was heading into a boxing match, and I grinned back.

"Let's see if we can find someone for you," I said.

As we continued on, Nash said, "For the record, I have no issues with you being a member of Storm. I don't fuckin' care how you came to us, Griff, you've always had my back, and that counts for everything."

"Thanks, brother." His words meant everything to me, but I still had no idea how other members would vote.

Nash momentarily distracted my concentration, so I didn't see the guy coming. The first I knew he was there was when he punched me in the face, knocking me back into Nash. We fell, and before either of us could get our bearings, the guy kicked me hard in the gut before attempting to also kick Nash in the gut. However, Nash had recovered enough to block him, and a moment later was on his feet, fighting the guy.

I pushed myself up off the ground, and attempted to get a punch in, but an arm hooked around my neck, and yanked me back.

Fuck.

You lose your concentration for one moment, and everything turns to shit.

"I see you used your common sense and came to us," the guy behind me said.

I shoved my elbow back into his stomach, but he laughed it off.

"If only it were that easy to escape," he said with a chuckle as he spun me around in his arms. Shoving a gun at me, he jerked his head toward the chair in the room, and barked, "Sit."

I had no idea why he hadn't just shot me, but wasn't arguing. I did as he said and sat. My gaze shifted to Nash who the other guy now had in his hold. Jesus, we were potentially fucked here. My mind quickly scrambled to come up with a plan to escape.

Nash stumbled towards me after being shoved, and the two guys followed after him. I eyed the two men, and realised the one who had ordered me into the seat was the guy who ran Bond's operation.

He approached me now and said, "Before I kill you, Michael, I'm gonna need some information out of you."

"Like what?" I doubted I had anything of use to him, but keeping him talking kept me alive longer.

"Who ordered the hit on Bond in prison?"

"Do you really think we're gonna tell you that?" Nash snarled.

The guy who stood over him threw a punch that landed hard on Nash's cheek. "Shut the fuck up, motherfucker. We didn't ask you."

Nash spat at the guy's feet, which only riled him up more. For that, Nash copped another punch.

The guy who had me restrained pressed his gun to my head. "Tell me who the fuck ordered that hit." His dark eyes revealed the darkness that I knew lived inside him. I'd investigated this guy, and he was responsible for a lot of death and destruction.

"What do I get in return?" I asked. I still hadn't figured out how the fuck to get out of this mess, and I desperately needed to keep him talking.

He scowled, and anger flashed in his eyes. Pressing the gun harder against my head, he spat, "If I don't get that name, the women we paid a visit to today will not be so lucky next time."

Motherfucker.

The guy had said the right thing to flip Nash's switch, and he lunged at the guy who stood over him, punching him hard in the balls. I caught it out of the corner of my eye, and knew I had to also make a move because the guy with the gun to my head turned the gun and aimed it at Nash. If I didn't do something, Nash would die.

As I lunged forward in the seat and wrapped my arms around his waist to try and push him over, a gun sounded, and blood sprayed everywhere.

Jesus.

Who the fuck had been hit?

It all happened so quickly that I struggled to get my bearings, until I heard J's voice boom, "Fuck you, motherfucker." And then another gun shot before J's hand reached out to mine, and he pulled me up. "You okay, brother?" he asked, looking me over.

He'd taken out both guys for us, and I surveyed the bloody mess on the floor. Looking up at him, I said, "Thanks, man. I was beginning to wonder how the fuck we were gonna get out of that."

His eyes held mine, and he said gruffly, "You would have done the same for me."

I nodded. "Yeah."

He nodded back at me, and then slapped me on the back. "I think we've got everyone now. The boys are just doing a final sweep to make sure."

"How many were there?" Nash asked as he stood.

"We took out two other guys."

We walked back the way we'd come in, meeting the others along the way. "The house is clear. We got everyone," one of Blade's guys informed us.

"Okay, let's get the hell out of here," J said, and we all moved as fast as we could back to the vans.

As we drove towards the clubhouse, I hoped like fuck that Scott and his team were successful. Who knew where it would all lead if they weren't.

***

"Fuck, where's Scott?" Nash asked as he paced the clubhouse bar.

We'd been back for an hour with no word from Scott or Blade who was with him. Nash had been pacing for the last fifteen minutes, and I was beginning to get worried. I would have thought they'd be back by now.

"Nash, can you give it a rest?" J snapped, clearly agitated by Nash's pacing.

They glared at each other, but Nash eventually sat.

My phone rang, and we all zeroed in on it. I checked the caller ID and frowned when I saw who it was.

"Harlow. What's up?" I said as I answered it.

"Are you with Scott, Griff? I've sent him some texts and tried to call him a few times today, and he hasn't answered any of them. It's unlike him, and I'm getting worried."

Fuck.

That *was* unlike Scott. Even when he was busy with shit, he always made a point to at least reply to a text from Harlow.

"I'm not with him, but as soon as I see him, I'll let him know you're looking for him. You good for now?"

"Yeah, I'm okay. Thanks, Griff," she said as she hung up.

I turned to J and Nash. "We need to head over to where the delivery was taking place. I've got a bad feeling about this."

They both nodded, and we rounded everyone up to come with us.

As we were about ready to pull out of the car park, a van screeched in, and pulled up at the front door to the clubhouse. Scott jumped out of the driver's seat, and quickly slid the back door open. Blade exited from the back and the two of them then pulled Wilder out. His shirt was soaked in blood.

"Shit," I muttered, and we left the van to follow them inside.

As we walked in, Scott's eyes came to mine. He shoved his fingers through his hair, and said, "Doc's on his way, but Wilder's in a bad way, brother.

371

Other than that, everything went to plan, and those assholes won't bother us again."

"How many were there?"

"Five."

"Fuck," I muttered, doing the maths.

He frowned. "What?"

"We've missed one."

Scott took that in, and said, "It's not what we would have preferred, but one guy on his own can't do a great deal. We'll deal with Wilder, and make sure he's going to be okay, and then we'll focus on finding that other guy. Yeah?"

He was right. "Yeah."

Our doctor arrived and took care of Wilder while Blade pulled Scott and me aside. "I just had word. Bond is dead."

"Thank fuck something is going our way today," Scott muttered.

Blade eyed him. "I've seen men worse off than Wilder pull through. He'll make it."

"I hope so, because if he doesn't, it's on me," Scott said, clearly angry with himself.

"Why?" I asked.

"It wasn't your fault," Blade said before Scott could answer.

"Yeah, it was. I lost concentration for a second, and that was all they needed to shoot him," Scott said.

"I'm not with you on that, brother," Blade said.

"I agree. You can never predict how this shit will go down," I said.

Scott scowled and began pacing while we waited.

"Harlow rang. She's been trying to reach you," I told him, and he nodded.

Pulling out his phone, he headed outside to call her back.

Eyeing Blade, I said, "He won't let go of the blame if Wilder doesn't pull through."

Blade nodded. "Yeah, I know," he said quietly.

We sat in silence in the bar as we waited for the doctor. Scott joined us at some point, but I hardly noticed. A tense cloud hung over the clubhouse, and I felt responsible for it.

If it hadn't been for me, none of this would be happening.

Chapter Twenty-Eight
Griff

The doctor was with Wilder for a long time. When he finally stepped out to talk with us, I couldn't read his face.

"He was in a bad way," he said, his voice holding no trace of positive news, and my gut twisted with fear.

"Fuck," Scott muttered, his face holding the same fear I felt.

"I've removed the bullet, and I'm hopeful he'll make a full recovery," the doctor said, and I realised that even when he gave good news, his voice still held no trace of positivity.

Relief washed over Scott's face. "Jesus, Doc, you had us worried there for a moment."

"He's not out of the woods yet, Scott. You're going to have to keep an eye on him, and call me if he deteriorates."

"We will," Scott promised, and he walked the Doc out.

When he returned, he sorted out a roster for who was going to look after Wilder while he recovered, and I took the opportunity to call Sophia.

"Hey, you," she answered the phone, and I could hear the smile in her voice.

"You having a good day?" I asked.

"Yeah, but I'm ready to go home. I've had enough of work today."

"Meet me at my house, sweetheart," I said, feeling the need to be there tonight. I had security on my place that she didn't have on hers, and with this one guy still on the loose, I needed to know she was safe.

"Okay, handsome, you're on, but I get to watch my show tonight." Christ, she had an unnatural interest in reality fucking television.

"The TV stays off tonight," I said firmly. "I've got other plans for you."

"Oh...well, that's good, too," she said, and I caught the desire in her voice.

"I've gotta go. I'll see you later," I said, and hung up.

Scott walked back in at that moment and jerked his head at me to follow him into the office. When we were inside with the door shut, he said, "We need to call Church again, Griff. Some of the guys aren't happy that I didn't call a vote on your membership today. I'm going to wait a day or so because I want Wilder to be able to vote, but I wanted to give you a head's up. I don't think there's enough numbers to vote you out from what I've heard, but fuck, you just never know. Obviously, it's not what I want to happen." The hard expression he normally wore had been replaced with torment. It was clear to me he was torn by this – torn by loyalty to his club versus loyalty to me.

"I appreciate the head's up, brother," I said, and he nodded.

When I'd joined Storm, I was made well aware of the only way a member left the club, and it didn't involve walking away drawing breath. That had never bothered me before because I had nothing in my life worth living for. Now, I did. And fuck, to even think about leaving her behind - that sliced pain through me.

***

I found Sophia waiting for me on my couch. She looked up and smiled as I came through the front door. And then she frowned. Moving off the couch, she came to me and asked, "What's wrong?"

"Nothing," I lied, not wanting to get into this with her tonight.

Her hand came to my cheek and she pulled my face down so we were close. "Griff, I can tell there is something wrong. I don't need for you to tell me, but I want you to know I am here for you if you *do* need to talk about it."

I held her gaze for a beat, nodded, and kept on walking. "I'll be back in a minute," I said as I headed into my bedroom to get changed. I'd already changed out of my bloodied clothes at the clubhouse, but the grime of the day felt glued to me.

Fuck it. I decided to have a shower and headed in there, stripping as I walked. A moment later, the hot water ran over my body, helping to ease some of the tension in me.

I was lost in thought when Sophia startled me. My gaze shot to her when she placed her hand on my shoulder. Dropping my eyes, I took in her naked body, and my dick jerked.

Fuck, she's beautiful.

"What are you doing, Sophia?" I demanded, not sure if I wanted to be interrupted. I had thoughts running around in my head that I needed to work through. Alone.

She stepped into the shower with me and closed the shower door after her. Having her this close to me made it hard to say no to her.

I curled my hand around her neck, and moved her back up against the tiled wall in my shower. My eyes searched hers. "Do you want me to fuck you?" I growled as I ground my dick against her.

"Yes," she replied, her eyes meeting mine and not letting go.

"How wet are you?" I demanded to know as I reached down and ran my finger through her pussy while keeping one hand firmly around her neck.

"I'm ready," she said.

"No. I want you wetter. I want you fucking dripping for me."

Her eyes flashed with desire and I began finger fucking her while circling her clit with my thumb.

She closed her eyes, and I ordered, "Keep your eyes open. I want to see what my fingers do to you."

While I kept fucking her with my finger, I let go of her neck and dipped my head so I could lick the skin along her collarbone. I just needed a taste and I had to force myself not to spend longer there, because I wanted to watch her eyes as she moved closer to her orgasm.

"Wrap your hand around my cock," I commanded, and a moment later she began stroking me.

Fuck.

Her hand around me felt so fucking good.

"I'm not going to fuck you with my dick, Sophia. I'm going to make you come with my fingers, and then you're going to get on your knees and suck my cock."

I need to see her on her knees tonight.

My fingers worked harder and got her so fucking wet that it took every ounce of my self-control not to turn her around, bend her over, and fuck her. The need to have her every way I could overwhelmed me, and I knew we were in for a long night of sex. But first, I wanted my dick sucked.

Her eyes fluttered closed but she snapped them open straight away, and I knew she wasn't far off coming. She looked so goddamn beautiful when she came – it was a sight I would never grow tired of. I watched her now as her mouth formed that perfect 'O', and her pussy contracted around my fingers, and I applied a little more pressure because I wanted her to scream out her release tonight.

Her hand around my dick squeezed me hard as she came, and a moment later, she screamed out my name, "Griff!"

Once her orgasm had worked through her, she knelt in front of me and took me into her mouth. Jesus Christ, her mouth was one of the best places to be. She took hold of the base of my cock and worked me with both her hand and her mouth. Her tongue slid over me, too, and fuck that felt amazing. I placed a hand on the back of her head and closed my eyes, letting go of all thoughts and letting the pleasure take over.

I was so far gone by the time she got my dick into her mouth that it didn't take long for me to blow. Sophia swallowed everything I gave her, and then looked up at me as she licked her lips. She always licked her lips afterwards, as if she loved my cum and couldn't get enough of it, and that turned me way the fuck on.

Reaching my hands under her arms, I pulled her up. "Fuck, baby, I think we need to start every day with a fucking blow job. Screw waiting until the end of the day for that."

She grinned as she curled her arms around my neck. "Sounds good to me. You know how much I love having you in my mouth."

I bent my mouth to her ear. "We'll begin tomorrow." Moving my face away from hers, I said, "Now, I'm going to clean you, and then you're going to go and wait for me in my bed."

She nodded as I reached for the soap and began lathering her body. I dedicated time to every inch of her and got her ready for me to fuck her when I'd finished in the shower.

As I watched her dry off and then walk out of the bathroom, my thoughts drifted back to today. And to the vote that was coming.

Fuck.

***

Sophia lay on my bed for me, naked, waiting. She turned to look at me as I entered, and I saw something in her eyes that I hadn't seen in anyone's eyes for a long time. Josie probably came close, but not to this degree.

Compassion.

Care.

Kindness.

It slammed into me and caused a wave of emotion I didn't even realise I was feeling.

I raked my fingers through my hair as my emotions assaulted me. Thoughts I'd tried to bury long ago rushed forward and smacked me in the face. There was no escape, and I realised that for once, there was no way around, but rather only a way through.

I sat on the edge of the bed, facing away from her, and said, "I do shit you probably wouldn't agree with, Sophia."

She placed a hand on my back. "Like what? Can you give me an example?"

Turning to face her, I clenched my jaw before saying, "I killed the man who murdered my family ten years ago."

Her eyes widened, and she looked like she'd been slapped. And then she gave me hope she could accept me for who I was. "Your family was murdered?" Not even a mention of the fact I had killed someone.

I nodded. "Yeah."

I told her the story and she listened intently. When I'd finished, she scrambled into my lap and put her arms around me. "I'm so sorry, Griff," she said, and I heard every drop of compassion in her voice. It was the kind of compassion that had been missing from my life for a long time – the kind of compassion I hadn't even realised I needed.

"I do work for Storm that involves violence," I admitted, needing her to know exactly who I was. If we were going to make this work, I needed to know she accepted everything about me.

She processed that, remaining silent for a few minutes. "Do you do it to help your club?"

"Yes. The only time I get violent is when I'm doing it to help either my club or someone I care about, but I do it, and I need you to know that."

Nodding, she said, "I have no problem with that. Ever since I saw you beat that guy up who tried to steal a car, I've known you had that streak. It didn't bother me then and it doesn't bother me now."

I watched her closely and knew she was telling the truth.

Thank fuck.

Before I could say anything else, she took hold of my face with both her hands. "Griff, I accept you for who you are and always will. You *never* need to change yourself for me. I'm still getting to know stuff about you, but I know who you are at your core – you've already shown me that. I've spent my entire life trying to fit in, and make people like me, and the thing I've learnt is that it never works. The trick is to find your tribe where you don't have to *work* to fit in, but where you effortlessly slide right in. And to find your person – that one person who just gets you and doesn't try to change you; that one person who only needs to take a glance at you to know if there's something wrong; that one person who would drop everything to be there for you when you need them...you're my person, Griff, and I'd do anything for you."

Fuck me.

She'd just given me the fucking world.

I claimed her lips in a kiss that went on for so long I lost track of time. And although she sat naked on my lap, my hands didn't roam over her body. I just needed her lips for now. When I'd had my fill, I ended the kiss, and said, "You're mine, Sophia. Forever."

Chapter Twenty-Nine
Griff

Two days later, when Wilder was in the clear from being shot, I walked into Church with a sense of apprehension. It had been quiet around the club over the last two days, and I couldn't read some of the boys. They avoided eye contact with me, as well as conversation with me, and I figured they were the ones who would vote me out. The fact there seemed to be a lot of them avoiding me was of concern.

I took my seat next to Scott who opened with club business. Looking around the room, I took in my family. These men had been there for me through good times and bad over the last three years. We'd packed a lot into a few short years, and I'd learnt what loyalty and acceptance meant. I guessed after today, I'd learn who believed in unconditional love.

Scott finished going through the business he had to discuss regarding the fire at Trilogy and a few other matters, and he asked if anyone else had anything to go over. Wilder spoke up, his voice full of nerves as he stumbled over his words. "You remember you asked me to find out a little while ago who those guys were outside The Eclipse Bar who none of us knew?" He waited for Scott to acknowledge that, and when he nodded, Wilder continued. "I was given the wrong information. We were also given the wrong information about who was behind the fire at Trilogy."

Fuck.

I sat forward in my chair, every muscle in my body tense. This was not going to be good news.

"Keep going, and don't stop until you get everything out," Scott ordered, his shoulders tense.

Wilder took a deep breath. It was clear he didn't want to tell us whatever it was he had to say. "One of the guys is Julio Rivera and he arrived in Brisbane about four months ago. He's been building his network, with an end goal of running this town. His fingers are already in a lot of pies, Scott, and he's achieved one of his goals thanks to us – getting rid of Ricky. Seems he was setting Ricky up to take the fall for the Trilogy fire because he hoped we would buy it and do exactly what we did. From what I've been told, he's slowly working his way to bringing down the big guys so he can take over from them. The Bond Family were another one on his list, and we helped him out there, too. That guy who was missing yesterday in your count of dead bodies, Griff? He had just shifted allegiance to Julio; that's why he was missing."

Scott's breathing had slowed, and anger clouded his face. "How the fuck do you know all this?"

Wilder hesitated, as if he knew this wasn't going to go down well. "It was something Carly said one night when she was high – it didn't add up so I've been doing some digging."

Scott slammed his hand down on the table as his eyes flashed a level of anger at Wilder that I'd never seen from him. Standing, he bellowed, "Next fuckin' time you have a gut feeling about something, Wilder, you need to bring it to the table. We're a club and sticking together is what makes us work. Running off and doing shit on your own doesn't fuckin' work."

"Okay," Wilder said.

"Have I made myself clear?" Scott's voice was still raised as he demanded an answer.

"Yes, loud and clear, Prez," Wilder said, almost tripping over the words to get them out.

Scott raked his fingers through his hair. Looking around the room, he said, "Right, we need to deal with that, but first we need a vote on Griff. I think I made myself pretty clear the other day as to where I stand, but so there is no misunderstanding – I accept Griff's reasons and support his membership in Storm. He always has our backs, and it would do you well to remember that when you cast your vote. I vote yea in support of his membership."

I nodded at him, and watched as the vote went around the room. After quite a few nay's, I swallowed back my concern this wasn't going to go my way. And then came some more yea's, but I wasn't convinced there would be enough. At some point, I actually lost count, so when Scott had the final vote in, and looked at me, I wasn't sure where I stood.

Scott's hard stare told me nothing, and my stomach knotted with stress.

Fuck.

Was I about to be kicked out of Storm?

Scott watched me for a few moments before turning back to the room. "Good, I believe we've made the correct decision. Griff stays."

The room spun a little as his words worked their way through my consciousness.

Griff stays.

I balled my fists as nervous energy flowed through me, and in that moment I realised just what this family truly meant to me. I thought I'd always known, but now that knowledge was lodged in my brain, never to be forgotten.

Storm meant everything to me.

And for them to accept me, knowing the real me now...that meant even more.

As I processed that, I lost concentration and had no idea what Scott was now saying, but loud voices pierced my thoughts, jolting me back to awareness.

"I'm not fuckin' staying if he stays!" Jones shoved his chair back and glared at me.

"Me either," said Truck.

I watched as five more guys joined them, threatening to leave Storm if I stayed. Jesus, if Storm lost seven men, at a time when a new threat had just arrived in town, shit would not be easy.

We can't afford to lose them.

Just as I was about to try reasoning with them, Scott thundered, "If you want out, there's the

389

fuckin' door." He pointed at the door while he glared at them.

"Fuck," I muttered. "Can we back this up and discuss it some more?"

Scott's head snapped around to look at me. "I refuse to run a club with divided loyalties, Griff. If anyone can't fully support an official club ruling, they can leave as far as I am concerned. The vote to keep you was fair and square, and I won't have a few members try to throw their weight around, issuing threats that fuck with that."

I agreed with him, but *fuck.*

"I'm out!" Truck spat and dumped his cut on the table before storming out of the room. And then we watched as every other member who'd threatened to leave followed him.

Once they'd left, and Scott had regained control of the room, he spoke loud and clear. "Everyone who is still sitting here must fully support me, Griff, and the club. That means when a vote is taken, you follow it because you believe in this club and what it stands for. That means when we decide on a course of action to protect our club and our families, you follow it, no questions asked. That means you would lay your life down for the club." He paused and looked at each member. "If anyone here wants out, now is the time to leave. With what

Wilder has just told us, it looks like we've got tough times ahead, so we're gonna need every member fully on board. This isn't a time for fucking around, this is a time for taking command and getting shit done the way Storm knows how to get shit done."

He waited a few minutes, giving everyone time to make their decision, and then he nodded, took his seat at the head of the table, and said, "Right, let's make a plan. Nobody fucks with Storm and lives to talk about it."

Chapter Thirty
Sophia

I watched Griff from my kitchen as he worked on my patio. He'd been out in the sun labouring for three hours this afternoon so I'd grabbed him a beer out of the fridge and was about to take it out to him. His muscles had distracted me, though. He wore no shirt, and each nail he hammered, and each piece of wood he cut, caused his muscles to flex in a hypnotising way.

Everything about him hypnotised me – his good looks, his bossiness, his hidden sense of humour that he only seemed to share with those closest to him, his protective nature, his fierce way of caring, and so much more.

He stopped what he was doing and looked at me. Goosebumps flooded my skin from the way he looked at me – like he wanted to devour me. I held up the beer, and he jerked his chin in that way of his – the way that said 'woman, come here'." I loved that chin jerk.

As I stepped foot outside, a noise at my front door caught my attention. Turning to see what it was, I smiled at the sight of Magan traipsing down the hallway towards us. "Hey, honey," I called out.

"I'm just going to use your printer, okay?" she said, and I nodded.

Turning back to Griff, I walked to where he stood and passed him his beer. "It's looking good," I said, looking at the work he'd done so far.

He took a long drink of his beer and nodded. "Yeah, much better. When I move in, we can use my barbeque. It's one of the only decent things I own and it's better than this one the previous owner built in. In fact, I'll pull this one out completely."

I blinked, and at the same time, butterflies whooshed through my stomach. "You're moving in? When is that happening? I mean, we haven't even discussed it...but I don't mind...what I mean to say is I'm down with it, but I hadn't realised we were at that stage in our relationship where we'd move in together, and I also am surprised you want to move into my house rather than me move into yours. And, wow, this seems so fast...are you sure?" I took a long breath and stared wide-eyed at him. I hadn't even seen that coming.

His gaze was glued to mine, and I saw a determination in it that I loved. He was sure about this. "A man could search his whole life looking for a woman like you, Sophia. I know what I've got, and trust me when I tell you this, I'm not letting go. As far as me moving in here...it makes sense because Josie lives across the road. And as far as moving too fast...I'm not good with waiting for something I know is going to happen. I've already started packing my stuff."

I smiled. "Sounds good to me, handsome."

He drank the rest of his beer and passed me the empty bottle. "Okay, you need to move your ass inside, woman, so I can finish this job in peace. Not a man alive who could do it with you sashaying around in those shorts you like to wear."

Grinning, I left him in peace, and headed inside to find Magan.

She met me in the kitchen, and said, "I got that job."

My brows furrowed. "Which one? You applied for two, didn't you?"

"Oh, yeah...I got the one at the dress shop. I start in a few days and have to take my birth certificate in for them so I thought I'd make a copy in case they want one."

I smiled at her excitement. "They shouldn't need a copy of that, but I'm so proud of you for being organised."

She stilled and gave me a strange smile. Almost a sad smile. "Thank you, Sophia," she murmured, and I had no idea what she was thanking me for. On top of that, I hated the sadness in her voice.

"What for, honey?" I asked as I reached for her hand, needing to hold her.

"For loving me like you do. I've gone my whole life pretty much without a mother figure, well, at least, one who cared for me like a mother. You might be my sister, but in a lot of ways, I kinda think of you like my mother."

The heartbreak our mother had caused both of us was still fresh, and we were still coming to terms with it in our own ways. It meant the world to me to hear these words from her. I put my arms around her and hugged her. We held onto each other for a long time, and when we finally let each other go, she said, "I love you."

"I love you, too, honey."

She moved to the table and stashed her documents in her bag before turning back to me, and said, "We have to cook cake. Josie will be here soon."

My heart felt like it could explode from happiness.

My new family.

***

"Oh, my dear girl, you did the right thing getting rid of him," Josie said to Magan later that afternoon when we were discussing the fact Magan had ditched her boyfriend.

Magan nodded. "I know."

"I know it's a cliché, but there really are plenty of other fish in the sea. Sometimes you just need to fish for longer or you need to change your fishing locations." She eyed Griff, and added, "Or you need to let someone else do the fishing for you."

I laughed while he shook his head and muttered something under his breath.

Holding up the plate with scones on it, I asked, "Josie, would you like another scone?"

Her face lit up and she nodded with a smile. "Your scones are the bomb, Sophia. I would love another one, thank you."

Magan burst out laughing and slapped her hand over her mouth. "Did you just say her scones are the bomb, Josie?"

"Yes, because they are," Josie said, looking confused.

"Oh, my God, I've never heard anyone over the age of, like, thirty say that word," Magan said, clearly finding this funny.

"Josie's been spending too much time with Sophia," Griff threw in, and although he said it like he rued the day, I knew he loved how close we were becoming.

Josie raised her brows. "Magan, you don't reach an age in life where you stop living and stop learning new things. I might be old to you, but in my mind, I'm still somewhere between thirty and forty."

Griff suddenly stood and headed inside without a word. When Josie and Magan gave me a querying look, I shrugged and said, "I don't know where he's going."

Josie ate her scone while Magan and I finished off our cake, and then she said, "I'm going to go home before it gets dark. Thank you for a wonderful afternoon, Sophia."

We all stood, but before we could go inside, Griff came back out, holding something in his hand. As he got closer, I could see it was something small wrapped in Christmas paper.

Josie eyed it and her face lit up with a smile, but she didn't say anything.

He moved to where she stood, and pulled a necklace from the wrapping. Looking at her, he said, "I found this the other day...had forgotten you'd given me a Christmas present until then."

Josie nodded, and I realised this was a significant moment for them because the mood had turned serious. "It was your mother's, and her mother's before that, Michael."

"I remember her wearing it."

Josie reached out, and placed her hand over his, squeezing it gently. "She wanted you to have that. Her first-born son was always to have that necklace to give to the woman he loved."

Griff nodded. "She told me that," he said gruffly.

Josie's eyes were full of so much love for her nephew. "I am glad you found it," she said as she moved towards me. Putting her arms around me, she whispered, "Thank you, beautiful girl. I'm going to die a happy woman one day."

I wasn't sure what she meant, but I smiled and hugged her back. "Thank you for coming. We'll do this again soon."

As Josie said her goodbyes to Magan, she also said, "Help an old lady home, will you, dear girl?"

Magan hooked her arm through Josie's and said, "Sure."

I watched them go until Griff's arms came around my waist, and he spun me to face him. I sucked in a breath at what I found there. He stared at me with an intense gaze that shot straight to my core. His lips landed on mine and he kissed me, and it had to be said, that kiss was one of the most intense, passionate kisses I'd ever experienced. It was as if he put all the want and need he had for me into that one kiss. When he ended it, he said, "I love you, Sophia."

He was full of surprises today. First the moving in, now this declaration.

I loved every single second of today.

And I loved everything about this man standing in front of me.

Smiling, I said, "I love you, too, Griff."

He took his mother's necklace and placed it around my neck. It was a beautiful antique gold necklace with a diamond pendant.

My hand moved to hold it in place for a moment as I fought back tears. He would never know just what this gesture meant to me.

Not only did it show me his love, but it was a symbol of family to me.

My first tear fell, and I gave up trying to hold them back. They needed to be shed.

They also symbolised something for me – a new beginning, and a new chance at building a family for myself.

He brushed my tears from my cheek and asked, "Are they good tears or bad tears?"

I smiled up at him through them. "A bit of both, handsome, but mostly, I'm just regrouping."

Watching his face was like watching a switch being flipped. Something I'd said caused him to switch to bossy Griff. He bent his face to mine, and growled, "You've got till Magan goes home to regroup and then I'm going to have you naked and under me for the rest of the night, doing whatever I tell you to do."

My heart beat faster at the thought of what was to come. "That's why you love me, isn't it?" I teased. "Because I let you boss me around."

He stared at me for a long moment before giving me something I would cherish forever. "I love you for your smart-ass mouth, and your purity, and your kindness, and your rambling, and your love of family, and for the way you care about those you love. But most of all, I love you because you're you, and you accept me for who I am."

I would always accept him for who he was, just as he had accepted me.

Griff had shown me that some of the beliefs we have about ourselves are illusive, and that we need to leave the pain and hurt behind, and step into our new skin. The past is part of us, part of our story, but it doesn't have to be who we are today, and it doesn't mean our story won't get better.

Together, Griff and I would write a new story – a better story.

THE END

ILLUSIVE PLAYLIST

I listen to music while writing and have a playlist
for each book.

Illusive was heavily influenced by Kid Rock's song.
"Johnny Cash". One line in particular spoke deeply
to me for this book, and always made me think of
Griff.

I walk that line because you love me

Other songs on the Illusive Playlist are:

Pleasure and Pain by the Divinyls
Come As You Are by Nirvana
Take It Out On Me by Florida Georgia Line
She Will Be Loved by Maroon 5
Shame by Keith Urban
No Lies by Jason Reeves
Rolling In The Deep by Adele

Piece by Piece by Kelly Clarkson

See You Again by Wiz Khalifa

Beneath Your Beautiful by Labrinth & Emeli Sande

Smoke by A Thousand Horses

Collide by Kid Rock & Sheryl Crow

Free Fallin' by Tom Petty

Alone by Heart

I Want To Know What Love Is by Foreigner

Photograph by Ed Sheeran

If Ever I Could Love by Keith Urban

Gold by Jessie J

Whatever She's Got by David Nail

Invincible by Kelly Clarkson

Run, Run, Run by Kelly Clarkson & John Legend

I'm A Fire by David Nail

Dark Side by Kelly Clarkson

ACKNOWLEDGMENTS

To Jodie – Thank you for beta reading this book; for loving my characters enough and for believing in my story and my writing enough to offer me honest feedback even when I know this is so very hard for you to do. You do it with such kindness and wisdom, and it means the world to me that I have you in my corner. Your ideas make my stories so much better.

To Karen – Again, you put up with me while editing my book, and I will always be grateful to you for working with me the way you do. You always make my words and sentences better while allowing me the space to be me. Thank you so much for all your hard work on Illusive.

To Letitia – Jodie and I thought you would quit on me... we truly did. Thank you so much for all your hard work on my Storm MC covers. Thank you for putting up with my constant back and forth asking for so many changes. I am in love with all my new covers in a way I have never loved any of my covers. Authors keep asking me who my new designer is and while I do tell them, I don't want to, but that's just because I want to keep you all to myself.

To E – Thank you for putting up with my crazy. I love you, baby.

To Team Levine – Thank you for your tireless sharing and promoting of my books and me. Thank you for believing in me like you do, and *thank you for your friendships.* You girls are amazing and I love you to the moon and back.

To My Bloggers – Thank you for all your hard work promoting books every day. I know the hours you put in, and I know it's all for love, and I adore you for that. I try to say it often, but in case you've missed it, if there is ever anything I can do to help you, please send me an email to authorninalevine@gmail.com

To My Stormchasers – Thank you for your amazing support and friendships. I love our group. I've said it before, but I'll say it again – it's my favourite place on the internet. And the really special thing? I've had the honour of meeting some of you ladies, and am looking forward to meeting more of you soon. I love that!!

To My Readers – Thank you for buying my books and loving my characters as much as I do. Actually, some days, I think many of you may love my characters more than I do! Without you, I wouldn't get to do what I love to do day in and day out. Thank you from the bottom of my heart.

To My Girls – Jodie, Jani, Nat, Chelle, River, Max, Lyra, Nadine, Melanie, Becca, Christina, Rachel – I love you ladies. Thank you for being my friends.

ABOUT THE AUTHOR

Dreamer.
Coffee Lover.
Gypsy at heart.
Bad boy addict.

USA Today Bestselling Aussie author who writes about alpha men & the women they love.

When I'm not creating with words you will find me either creating with paper or curled up with a good book and chocolate.

I love Keith Urban, Maroon 5, Pink, Florida Georgia Line, Bon Jovi, Matchbox 20, Lady Antebellum and pretty much any singer/band that is country or rock.

I'm addicted to Nashville, The Good Wife & wish that they would create a never-ending season of Sons of Anarchy.

Signup for my newsletter: http://eepurl.com/OvJzX

Keep up to date with my books at my website
www.ninalevinebooks.com

Join my fan group on Facebook:
https://www.facebook.com/groups/LevinesLadies/

Facebook:
https://www.facebook.com/AuthorNinaLevine
Twitter: https://twitter.com/NinaLWriter
Pinterest: http://www.pinterest.com/ninalevine92/

Also by Nina Levine

USA Today & International Bestselling Author

Storm MC Series
Storm (Storm MC #1)
Fierce (Storm MC #2)
Blaze (Storm MC #3)
Revive (Storm MC #4)
Slay (Storm MC #5)
Sassy Christmas (Storm MC #5.5)
Illusive (Storm MC #6)
Command (Storm MC #7) – COMING 2015

Sydney Storm MC Series
Relent (Sydney Storm MC #1)

Havoc Series
Destined Havoc (Havoc #1)
Inevitable Havoc (Havoc #2) – COMING SOON

Crave Series
All Your Reasons (Crave #1)
Be The One (Crave #2)